ALIAS FOR DEATH

ALIAS FOR DEATH

BARBARA LEONARD REYNOLDS

COACHWHIP PUBLICATIONS
Greenville, Ohio

Alias for Death, by Barbara Leonard Reynolds
© 2018 Coachwhip Publications

Published 1950
No claims made on public domain material.

CoachwhipBooks.com

ISBN 1-61646-438-0
ISBN-13 978-1-61646-438-7

PRELUDE
JANUARY 13, 1945

In the ordinary way, Abigail Potter did not mind the inconveniences of travel during the war years. She was able bodied in spite of her white hair and well-worn features. Her age was sufficient to insure her against having to stand on even the most crowded bus or train, yet she rarely had to sit by herself. This suited Mrs. Potter admirably, for she liked people and found that conversation, however trivial, helped to speed a trip.

When she transferred to the Lebanon bus, however, that winter morning in 1945, she did not long for companionship. On the contrary, she accepted a seat next to a most unsocial-looking gentleman and was careful to do nothing to encourage him. For Abigail had something on her mind.

You're being absurd, Abigail Potter! she chided herself. Certainly no young man who really intended to commit a murder would have outlined his plot to a perfect stranger! And in any case, there is absolutely nothing you can do about it!

All of which was true, yet Abigail could not still her uneasiness. The fact that the young corporal beside whom she had traveled all of the preceding night had failed at first to respond to her friendly interest had been less disturbing than his complete about-face later on. And then, there was the letter he had surreptitiously destroyed—and the strange plot he had outlined.

Above all, there was the matter of the false name. One who used an alias, Abigail was sure, could be up to no good.

She determined to jot down as much as she could remember of the incident while it was still fresh in her mind. From her

5

capacious handbag she produced a notebook and two pencils, a red and a black. Writing was no easy matter as the bus rolled and pitched along the rough Ohio roads, but Abigail achieved a scrawl that would at least be legible to herself.

She headed the joggled notes: "THE PERFECT CRIME (?): An Account of the Meeting of Abigail Farringdon Potter with a Suspicious Character, en route from Chicago to Dayton, Ohio; Night of January 12, 1945."

After a brief pause during which she made a mental outline of her presentation, she began:

"Corporal George Rascinski (?). Description: About twenty-four or twenty-five. Tall (about 6'1"); dark eyes; dark curly hair; square jaw; rather handsome; long legs (curled uncomfortably on barracks bag at feet). Pacific Area campaign ribbon. Expression: moody, almost sullen.

"First stage (11:25 P.M. to about 1 A.M.): Unsociable, uncommunicative, apparently troubled. Brooding over thoughts of an unpleasant nature. (Hatred? Fear? Guilt? Anger?)"

Abigail was more than a little put out by the young soldier's failure to welcome her kindly overtures. She rarely failed to win the confidence of shy, reserved, or homesick young servicemen, but the corporal greeted her every conversational gambit with silence or, at most, a grunt, and continued to stare moodily at his reflection in the lighted window of the coach. From time to time a muscle below his jaw knotted and moved sharply upward or his hands formed involuntary fists at his sides.

Abigail's curiosity grew with each rebuff. She studied him with interest.

Perhaps, she thought, he is returning to the front and is troubled at leaving his family. Or perhaps he has a Problem. In any event, it will do him good to talk about it and get it off his mind.

But her charitable impulse seemed doomed to failure. He remained unconscious of her scrutiny, nor did her struggles to remove her coat serve to make him aware of her. When her filmy scarf became entangled with the brooch of her glasses he ignored her frantic efforts to loose it. Only after she had sighed once or twice in gusty exasperation did he come to her rescue with a be-lated offer of help. He then went so far as to put her coat on the rack above their heads.

("Nice manners in spite of himself," Abigail observed in her notebook.)

But when she attempted to press the contact by suggesting that there was room on the rack for his own barracks bag so he might stretch his legs, he vetoed the suggestion with startled vehemence, and withdrew to further contemplation of his brood-ing reflection.

At last she was able to stand it no longer. Clearing her throat with two or three genteel coughs, Abigail groped in her handbag for the throat lozenges she always carried, just in case.

Although her companion did not glance up, courtesy fore-bade that she indulge without offering refreshment to him.

"Won't you have one?" she asked, shoving the box under his nose.

Her words seemed to jerk him back from a great distance. He eyed the box suspiciously as though he could not grasp its mean-ing, and Abigail thought he might strike it from her hand. Then, slowly, his face relaxed.

"Why, thanks!" he said, and accepted one of the lozenges.

Abigail, now tacitly the hostess, was at last able to put her questions of polite interest.

In her notebook Abigail reported her indifferent success, let-ting A stand for Abigail and S for the soldier.

"Answered personal questions briefly.

"A. Have you been home for Christmas?

"S. No. (Long pause.) I'm going home now.

"(Should have been eager and excited instead of moody. Something on his mind!)

"A. Where is your home?

"S. Ohio. (No town mentioned.)

Abigail attempted to set him an example by volunteering her own destination—Lebanon.

"(Seemed willing to talk about me.)"

"Is Lebanon your home?" the young soldier asked.

Abigail confessed that it was not and went into detail, trying to inject a note of lightness that might gain his confidence.

"I live in Wisconsin. I'm going to Lebanon to care for an aunt—or rather, I'm happy to say, an aunt by marriage. Aunt Harriet's a terror and her fifth nurse has just given notice, so I seem to be elected."

"That's too bad." The young soldier sounded genuinely sympathetic. "Is she very ill?"

"She got flu at the beginning of the winter, but she was doing nicely until temper set in."

"Temper!" She had caught his interest. Abigail mentally blessed Aunt Harriet and her eccentricity.

"She broke her leg two days ago, trying to kick her last nurse down the stairs. At Aunt Harriet's age—she's almost eighty—that probably means she'll be laid up for quite a time!"

The corporal smiled, a spontaneous, boyish grin that was quite engaging. Satisfied that she had at last broken through his reserve, Abigail allowed herself a few more anecdotes of her deceased husband's colorful aunt before she tried once more to bring the conversation back to her companion.

"Became monosyllabic again on subject of himself:

"A. How long since you were home last?

"S. Two years.

"A. In Pacific all that time?

"S. Mostly.

"A. Suppose your family can hardly wait!

"S. Probably.

"(Visible withdrawal, almost annoyance. Wrong thing to have said? Why?)

"A. Married?

"S. No.

"A. But surely there's some girl—someone special?

"S. No! (Almost rude. Undercurrent of violence?)

"End of conversation."

The corporal yawned, begged Abigail's pardon, and as though firmly shutting a door between them, closed his eyes. His breathing became too quickly regular. Abigail knew that she was, for the moment, defeated.

She shut her own eyes, and eventually dozed.

"Interlude (About 5:30 A.M. Train had just stopped in Richmond, Indiana. Behavior: furtive throughout.)"

During the night, Abigail swept up to near consciousness each time the train stopped and the lights in the coach were turned on. Toward morning, during one such stop, she became abruptly wide awake, sure that the young corporal was staring at her. With an effort she kept her eyelids from fluttering open and after a long moment she felt him relax.

From beneath lowered lids she watched him take a wallet from his pocket and draw from it a snapshot and a folded oblong of blue paper. For a silent interval he held the picture before him, as though committing it to memory. Abigail could see nothing but the back of the small pasteboard and it was all she could do to refrain from shifting her position so she could at least watch the soldier's expression.

At last, quietly, he laid picture and paper together and eased a tear across them both. Again and again, his hands moving without haste, he tore the pieces across, reducing them methodically to a heap of scraps on his knee which he then scraped together and transferred to the pocket of his blouse.

Abigail allowed herself to change position and to draw a deep breath as in sleep. As though he had suddenly made up his mind, the soldier bent over, picked up his barracks bag and, stepping carefully over Abigail's feet, headed up the aisle to the men's room at the far end.

Abigail felt a tingle of more than interest. As soon as he was out of sight she stooped to search the floor beneath his seat. Surely one of these myriad tiny scraps had fallen without his being aware of it. Wishing that she had a match, she turned over or lifted to the light to examine a number of crushed cigarette papers with stale tobacco spilling out, a chewing-gum wrapper, a ticket stub. In the end, triumphantly, she had retrieved two small scraps of the blue paper and an infinitesimal piece of the heavier glossy picture.

("Two scraps of blue notepaper—obviously feminine handwriting—sloping script. One, torn across fold, contained parts of two words, one above other: '. . . urt y . . .' and '. . . orry . . .' (Worry? Sorry?) The other, only '. . . leas . . .'")

The corporal came back down the aisle before Abigail had finished her study of the piece of snapshot—a dark blob that might have been part of a girl's hair, a dog's shaggy coat, or a bit of background shrubbery. Her glasses were still clamped to her nose and Abigail, realizing that she had no time to remove them and pretend to be still asleep, hastily shoved the scraps into her bag and brought forth a book which she opened at random.

By the time the young soldier had stepped across her to his seat she was engrossed in her reading, but not so completely that she neglected to make out the name on his barracks bag (Cpl. J. R. Manning) before he turned the lettered side away and replaced the bag between his feet.

The pocket of his blouse, she observed, no longer bulged.

"Second stage: (5:45 A.M. to 6:38—arrival in Dayton. Friendly, loquacious, eager to talk about himself.)"

Abigail was startled when, after a few moments during which he seemed to be appraising her and her choice of reading matter, the young soldier addressed her of his own accord.

"What are you reading?" he asked in an undertone which deferred to the sleeping passengers around them.

Abigail turned the lurid paper jacket toward him so he could see the title, *Smile for a Suicide*. A Daliesque design of an intricately carved knife and a grasping hand rising from a pool of blood promised a gory treat for the reader.

"I'm afraid my tastes aren't very highbrow," she apologized, also whispering. Her companion did not look disapproving. In fact, he seemed eager to talk now, but as though he were uncertain how to proceed. In an effort to encourage him, Abigail followed his own lead.

"Do you ever read detective novels?"

He greeted the question with enthusiasm. From this point in her recapitulation, Abigail endeavored to record in its entirety the odd conversation that had been carried on wholly in whispers in the dim, somnolent coach.

"S. You bet! (Boyish slang strange contrast to earlier formal reserve!) Matter of fact, I've always wanted to try my hand writing one. Probably sounds silly, but out there on the edge of the jungle with Japs all around—well, the only way I could get my mind off—well, off the present was to figure out ways of committing a perfect crime. (Paused, added hastily:) For a book, of course!

"A. Not at all silly.

"S. (As though trying to justify himself for some course already decided on.) There was one fellow on Iwo who wrote. Always wanted to talk his stories out first, see if he had his plot line straight. Smitty had good ideas, all right, but even after he'd kicked them around in his mind a long time we'd often be able to show him places he'd gone off the tracks, things he'd overlooked or figured wrong. He used to say you could never tell about a plot until you'd tried it on the dog.

"(Seemed to be merely making conversation, yet I got feeling the whole thing was tremendously important to him. When I smiled he hurried on as though afraid might change his mind.)

"S. Now take this plot I've been working on. I keep thinking of such foolproof ways of killing a person I can't see how I'd—how the criminal would ever get caught! But I suppose there's something I've overlooked and it wouldn't fool the police—or a reader—for a minute.

"A. Think it might help if you 'tried it on the dog'?

"S. (Suddenly eager. This was what he'd been aiming at!) Would you mind? Maybe you'd be able to tell me whether it would work—whether I could find some neat way to catch the murderer, I mean—after he's committed this foolproof crime! If it wouldn't bore you?

"A. Not at all. Never forgive you if you didn't!

"S. (Began lightly but with undercurrent of tension.) It's just this: Suppose one man hated another because he'd taken his girl away from him— (Stopped abruptly, went on with less assurance as though choosing each word with extreme care.) Or, well, some motive—I haven't quite figured that out yet—and he wanted to get rid of him. And suppose this man he wanted to kill—

"A. Hadn't you better call them X and Y?

"S. What? Oh—oh, yes! Good idea! Well, X wants to kill Y. Now suppose X knows that Y takes a certain medicine—something in capsule form. X knows he takes these capsules pretty often and that if one of them is emptied and refilled with some poison, sooner or later Y will take it, and die.

"A. How could he be sure someone else wouldn't get pill?

"S. Oh, X knows no one but Y uses this particular stuff. And by time Y gets to that one capsule, you see—if X had put it in bottom of jar—X could be hundreds of miles away, living in another place. Might not even hear about actual death. There'd be no trace of poison left in food Y had eaten or in dishes—nothing to indicate where he'd gotten it, so even if death were recognized as poisoning, no one could ever prove a thing!

"A. Of course they'd trace purchases of that particular poison.

"S. (Scornful. Did he glance instinctively at barracks bag?) No criminal would be so stupid as to get it by any means that could be traced!

"A. You've set yourself a nice problem, but there's where your fictional sleuth has advantage over police in real life. You, as author, have to create loopholes and then lead your detective to them.

"S. But how? In order to have a case at all, you know, police have to prove means, motive, and opportunity. Should think a murder committed in this way would make such proof impossible!

"A. You could have your criminal overlook some trifle, or let his own awareness of guilt trick him into giving himself away. In a great deal of fiction, murderers are brought to justice because can't let well enough alone. They execute what could be perfect crime and then their own fear and guilt lead them to kill again and again until finally they slip up.

"(Far from seeming grateful for suggestions, soldier looked almost resentful, as though making mental resolve to avoid every solution offered. Had the feeling he neither expected nor wanted me to find flaw in his plot; that he was already satisfied and anxious to drop subject.)

"A. Perhaps you can get him on basis of motive. If Y had taken his girl away, should imagine someone would suspect revenge or jealousy no matter how carefully he tried to cover up.

"S. (Startled, defensive.) No one could prove he ever really cared—not unless he let it show. People do change their minds, you know!

"A. Suppose he'd be very careful to destroy any letters—things of that sort—that would point to him!

"S. (Looked at me sharply a moment.) Well, it's just an idea, after all. If I write the story I can take care of all that. You change in Dayton, don't you? We're almost there.

"(Seemed anxious to get rid of me. Withdrew into earlier preoccupation. I felt uncomfortable, as though I'd failed him. Just before train stopped, wrote my name and home address on slip of paper and gave it to him.)

"A. I'm counting on you to write that book so I'll know how you decide to work it out. Drop me card when you finish—perhaps I can help you find a publisher. (Then asked his name.)

"S. (Stammering.) Jer— G-George! George Rascinski! But don't bank too much on that book. Don't suppose I'll ever really write it!"

It was then that Abigail Potter's vague uneasiness came to a sharp and unpleasant focus. George Rascinski! But the name on his barracks bag was Manning!

On an impulse, just before she started down the aisle, Abigail laid a hand on the corporal's arm.

"Oh, but you must!" she said earnestly. "When an idea for murder takes hold of you, I've found that the best thing to do is write it all out on paper. And I don't really think a detective would find it hard to trap his man, no matter how carefully you laid your plot! Yes, Corporal—Rascinski, I am sure you really ought to write that book!"

She had left him staring, his mouth slightly open and looking, Abigail recalled with satisfaction, as though a pet canary had bitten him! She regretted that she could not have seen his face when he discovered that she had left her book on the seat beside him, the book with the hand and dagger in a pool of blood and the name of Abigail Farringdon Potter, as author, on the cover.

I

Abigail Potter read three newspapers regularly and she read them well. Every morning, between seven thirty and eight, she washed and wiped her coffee cup and saucer, her two spoons, the paring knife with which she cut her grapefruit and the bone-handled knife with which she spread her single slice of toast; emptied her coffee grounds and the cleaned-out half grapefruit rind (with the shell of an egg on Sundays) into a paper sack; and then settled herself in her faded tapestry chair by the front windows to read the *New York Herald Tribune* which came in the morning mail.

In the evening, it was her deep leather armchair near the fire and the *State Journal*, but always her method was the same. Starting with the obituaries and working backward through the paper with closest attention to accounts of sudden death, Abigail read avidly, a pencil poised to mark items of exceptional promise. Occasionally she would tear out a murder account that offered something new or special, and later would trim the torn edges and paste it in her bulging scrapbook under its proper alphabetical heading: "Accidental," "Poison," "Shooting," "Suicide (?)," and so forth.

These two papers marked the official beginning and end of Abigail Potter's day. In the hours between, she wrote. Each day, in a fine script that never became cramped after thousands of words, she turned out a prodigious amount of material.

Those who watched eagerly for the biennial detective stories over her own name would have been amazed to learn that an equal number of psychological mysteries by a certain A. B. Gail originated from the same pen; while readers who devoured lurid crime tales in *Murder Monthly* and *Headline Horrors* were unaware that their favorite author, Pottingail, also published, under still another name, a series of delightfully baffling mysteries for boys and girls, featuring the juvenile detective Red Harris.

The two city papers, in combination with her overflowing scrapbooks, Abigail considered tools of her trade. The third newspaper, a small-town weekly, might have seemed, then, an inexplicable departure. In the three years she had been reading the *Glen Falls Gazette* not one murder had occurred in that small Ohio town.

Abigail refused to admit, even to herself, her motives for having subscribed to the *Gazette* shortly after she returned from her visit to Lebanon. Instead, she justified her interest in the eight-page sheet as a sort of comedy relief. To one conscious of the frequency and brutal extent of big-city crime it was refreshing to pick up a paper that faithfully reported among items of special interest that "Mrs. W. C. Abernathy submitted to dental work last Tuesday," or that "Bill McKenna's three heifers, reported stolen, were discovered by the pilot of an airplane behind some bushes at the extreme north edge of Bill's pasture."

Yet every Saturday Abigail suffered a fresh disappointment as week after week passed and no citizen of Glen Falls departed this life under suspicious circumstances.

It was not that Abigail really *expected* sudden death to follow as a sequel to her encounter on the train. It was certainly not that she hoped for it! Yet, remembering the young corporal's early reticence and his overeager intensity after he had embarked on the outline of his supposedly fictitious plot, Abigail could not believe she had been mistaken in her conclusions. Whether he would ever have carried out his plans or not, she was sure that at the time they met he had been planning murder.

Frankly curious, she had found out from the conductor who helped her off the train that the yellow stub in the clip above the soldier's head proclaimed Glen Falls as his destination. Had it been Xenia, or Dayton, or Washington Court House, the episode might very well have ended there. But Abigail's Aunt-by-marriage Harriet had lived all of her youth and most of her middle

age in the little town of Glen Falls, and even after twenty-five
years in Lebanon she had kept up her subscription to the home-
town paper.

So it was that, shortly after her arrival, Abigail had learned
through the pages of the *Gazette* that a Corporal Jerome Manning had returned to Glen Falls the previous Tuesday while
George Rascinski was overlooked in a manner scarcely typical of
small-town editors.

He isn't really going to murder anyone. Of course he isn't!
Such a nice young man! Abigail's reasonable self had argued. But
there had remained a nagging *what if—?* that would not be stilled.

And so Abigail had become a Constant Reader. During her
visit, which had been prolonged through Aunt Harriet's linger-
ing disability and final unlamented demise, and for three years
after her return home, Abigail had read the *Gazette* each week
with an odd mixture of hope and trepidation.

To understand the contradictory emotions that warred within Abigail Potter it is first necessary to understand Abigail Potter.
Or perhaps it is only necessary to record that at the age of twenty
she had married Jonathan Potter in an attempt to escape the
joyless tyranny of a puritanical father, and had succeeded only in
plunging herself into the even less agreeable confines imposed by
a narrow-minded and intolerant husband.

Perhaps because she had never been in the habit of discard-
ing a bad bargain, perhaps because divorce had not yet become
fashionable, Abigail had stuck out her marriage for thirty-two
years. But duty had been unable to stifle imagination. Her ad-
vice to the soldier on the train may have been more personal
than objective when she urged him to write out of his system
his murderous impulses, for when death finally relieved her
of Jonathan Potter, as well as of his financial support, Abigail
had approached a publisher with a literal trunkful of murder
mysteries in manuscript, which had earned a ready market. It
was probably mere coincidence that in all of them the murder
victim was a man—sometimes middle aged, sometimes older—
and that these victims shared a certain intolerance, a paucity of
viewpoint, and a scorn for the feminine mind.

That had been eight years ago, eight years during which Abigail had lived a life of the spirit violent enough and abundant enough to have satisfied any lesser soul for two times fifty-two years of deprivation. But for Abigail vicarious living was not enough. She had a boundless enthusiasm for life, an insatiable interest in the affairs of others, and a curiosity about humanity as a whole that could not be satisfied through imagination alone. And although it is true that a murder actually took place in Frenchie's Corner Bar at the very moment she was having a dress fitted next door, and although at another time a beautiful blonde had been stabbed by her lover less than a block from where Abigail, unwitting, waited for her bus, Abigail never knew of these occurrences until she read of them the following day.

Unlike Samantha Vernay, her favorite of her various detectives, Abigail had no nose for sudden death to place her propitiously in the center of tragic and exciting events. Although she longed to live the adventures of which she wrote, Abigail had never seen a murdered man, had never witnessed a crime, had never even been called for jury duty.

In the mysterious soldier on the train she had seen her chance. For three years she had watched and waited, torn between a very real distress when she recalled that the soldier whom she was casting in the role of murderer had been human and likable— and had trusted her—and a foolish hope that this time, armed with knowledge no one else could be expected to possess, she might find herself in a position to render valuable aid in the solution of an actual murder case.

Suppressing her instinctive sympathies for the troubled corporal, she had painstakingly built up a case against him in a crime that common sense told her would never be committed. For three years she had been aware of every major factor in her hypothetical murder: the name of the murderer, the method, and, in all probability, the motive. She even had reason to suppose that she had deduced the name of the prospective victim. Only the final link was wanting, the culmination of the murder plot.

On Saturday, April 12, 1948, Abigail lingered even longer than usual over the Glen Falls death notices of the week just past before, reluctantly, she laid the Ohio paper aside and forced her mind to concentrate upon the *New York Herald Tribune*. No lack of death notices there, from natural causes and otherwise.

Then, as she scanned the obituaries, she stiffened and her sharp nose almost quivered. Beneath the heading "Deaths Elsewhere," a brief paragraph announced the demise of a well-known Detroit industrialist and financier, Harrison Hawkes, "suddenly, while visiting at the home of Mr. and Mrs. Arthur Snyder of Glen Falls, Ohio." An inquest, the item concluded, would be held on Saturday.

Abigail Potter removed her glasses and released them with a snap that sent them careening up their trolley to swing agitatedly against her bosom. Her light blue eyes gleamed and then sobered.

Rapidly she calculated. The unfortunate death of Mr. Hawkes had occurred Thursday evening, too late for inclusion in the Glen Falls paper, which was not equipped to deal with emergency deadlines. For a more complete account, then, she must wait until the following week unless, of course, she telegraphed to some nearby Ohio town that would carry the story in its daily sheet.

Even as this practical idea occurred to her she discarded it, realizing that at the earliest no further papers could reach her for twenty-four hours, whereas if she herself went by train—

Before the thought was finished, Abigail went into action, telephoning to the railroad, throwing a few necessities into her suitcase, running across the street to make arrangements for the care of her furnace and her seventeen canaries.

I'm being silly! she thought. What possible connection can Harrison Hawkes have had with Corporal Manning-Rascinski?

Yet excitement swelled in her breast. She felt as a backwoods worshiper of the theater might who, after faithfully attending all the productions of the local school and reading with yearning hundreds of plays, sees at last the possibility that he himself may be cast in a leading role upon the legitimate stage.

But Abigail Potter, though a romantic, was also practical. If she were not to be dismissed by the police as a meddlesome crank she would have to be able to back up her accusations with substantial proof. In the final analysis her entire case rested on the unlikely premise that the soldier on the train had been Jerome Manning and not, in actual fact, George Rascinski with a borrowed barracks bag. Wishful thinking and a fertile imagination had built up a plausible case in which she could play a stellar role, but she would need a great deal more evidence than she yet had to convince even her own rational self that the sudden death in Glen Falls was anything but a coincidence.

You're chasing a mare's nest, Abigail Potter! she snapped at her own protesting reason, but there's no harm in taking a little trip—just to look around!

Less than two hours after the discovery of the pertinent obituary Abigail, scarcely winded and with minutes to spare, launched herself up the steps of the train that would carry her on the first lap of her pilgrimage to Glen Falls.

She was able to secure a vacant seat. She folded her coat neatly and placed it beside her to discourage any last-minute travelers, and then she snapped open her suitcase and produced a fat notebook, two pencils—a red and a black—and the copy of the *Herald Tribune* that had released her pent-up energies.

In her first quick reading only two phrases had leaped out at her—"Glen Falls, Ohio," and "inquest." Now, adjusting her spectacles, Abigail turned again to the obituary and read it more carefully. A small, troubled frown creased her forehead. The case she had long and optimistically thought of as the Glen Falls Murder had failed to burst upon the world according to her preconception, and Abigail was disturbed.

That one Harrison Hawkes, a man in no way connected in her mind with the principal actors, should have been the victim of the plot was of course a regrettable accident. What troubled Abigail was not the identity of the murdered man so much as the locale of his death.

She read the words again: "—while visiting at the home of Mr. and Mrs. Arthur Snyder." Her bewilderment increased and she felt, an irritation with Mr. Hawkes for having disturbed the pattern of the puzzle into which, for thirty-eight months, she had been laboriously fitting pieces.

Immediately she tendered a mental apology to the dead man. It was more likely, if less flattering, to assume that she herself had made a miscalculation. There was nothing to be done but to start over. To this end, she carefully removed and polished her spectacles and perched them again in her nose before, pencil in hand, she opened her notebook.

As in all her working notebooks, Abigail had given her investigations a title, elaborately lettered in red on the first page:

THE GLEN FALLS MURDER
by
Jerome Manning
(alias George Rascinski)
and
Abigail Farringdon Potter

There followed, transcribed from the joggled notes she had made on the Lebanon bus, a complete account of her meeting with the soldier, annotated with her own impressions, underlined in red and labeled, prudently, "Not Evidence."

After the introduction and apologia, Abigail had settled down to business. On the left-hand pages were pasted clippings from the *Glen Falls Gazette*, each with its proper date. Opposite these, in her careful handwriting, Abigail had written her deductions.

The first item, culled from Aunt Harriet's copy of the *Gazette* a few days after the meeting on the train, stood alone.

"Cpl. Jerome Manning, who has been in the Pacific Theater for the past nineteen months, arrived Tuesday to visit his parents, Mr. and Mrs. Nelson Manning, of 39 Prescott Avenue. This is Cpl. Manning's first leave since 1943 and we regret that the serious illness of his father prevents it from being the joyous homecoming it would otherwise have been. Welcome home, Jerry Manning!"

On the right-hand page Abigail had commented, "No mention in this issue of the *Gazette* (January 16, 1945) of George Rascinski who also traveled to Glen Falls on Tuesday (?)!"

There followed several more pages of script under the general heading of "Comments."

"Let S = soldier (Manning or Rascinski).

"Let X = victim.

"I. Motive: Jealousy or revenge. X took Girl away from S.

"A. Girl probably married to X.

"1. If Girl had merely become engaged to X, S would not harbor thoughts of murder until he had relinquished all hope of winning back Girl's affections.

"2. Marriage undoubtedly took place within past 19 months (while S was overseas).

"3. Marriage probably took place in the very recent past, else S's hatred would not remain so strong.

"B. In order to conceal motive S must:

"1. Express pleasure in Girl's marriage.

"2. Not appear to avoid X or Girl.

"3. Establish in minds of observers that his present feeling for Girl is friendship rather than hate, jealousy, or love.

"4. Establish appearance of friendship for X.

"5. Destroy any letters or pictures of Girl which might betray his true feelings or past relationship. (See Exhibit 1.)"

Here Abigail had pasted the three scraps she had retrieved on the train.

"Summary. ∴ S may be expected to appear, during his visit, at one or more gatherings at which X and Girl are also present."

Abigail wrote her "therefore" as a pyramid of dots, as she had been taught to do in high-school geometry some forty-five years before.

"II. Means: Poison capsule substituted for medicinal pill.

"A. S may have had poison already in his possession. (In closely guarded barracks bag? This would be very difficult to trace.)

"III. Opportunity: Presupposes a certain intimacy with X.

"A. S must know—or, at any event, have reason to suppose—that X is in the habit of taking certain medicinal capsules.

"B. S must assure himself that this medicine is habitually taken by X alone.

"C. Must be assured of free access to X's home and/or medicinal supply.

". . . Girl and X may be any married couple with whom S associates during his stay."

These deductions, filling three pages on their own account, were followed by further clippings from the *Gazette*. In order of their entry, together with Abigail's conclusions, they were:

Issue of January 23. "Mrs. Nelson Manning and son, Jerome, enjoyed Sunday dinner at the home of Mrs. Dora Weston of 15 Glen Road. Other guests were Mrs. Eloise Demarest, Dr. and Mrs. John Werner, and Mr. and Mrs. Philip Koestler."

"Comments: Mrs. Demarest and Mrs. Weston probably widowed or divorced, else why were their husbands not also present. Mr. Manning, Jerome's father, apparently still sick.

"N.B.   Dr. and Mrs. John Werner (?)

          Mr. and Mrs. Philip Koestler (?)"

Issue of January 23. "Miss Millicent Brannum, 116 Fairview Drive, entertained a group of friends at a supper party on Friday before the Country Club Dance. Among those present were: Miss Harriet Jonson, Miss Mable Hurst, Mr. and Mrs. Philip Koestler, Mr. and Mrs. Daniel Morgan, Mr. and Mrs. Arthur Snyder, Fred Snyder, Vincent Blackwood, Cpl. Jerome Manning."

"Comments: M.H., H.J. unmarried (Miss)

"N.B.   Mr. and Mrs. Philip Koestler (?)

          Mr. and Mrs. Arthur Snyder (?)

          Mr. and Mrs. Daniel Morgan (?)"

The issue of February 2 had provided further social notes:

"Guests of Mrs. Eloise Demarest, 37 Prescott Avenue" (apparently next door to Manning house, see Clipping I) "attended the Minstrel Show at the Opera House on Thursday, followed by a buffet supper at her home. Guests were: Mr. and Mrs. Philip

Koestler, Mrs. Dora Weston, Miss Millicent Brannum, Miss Harriet Jonson, Miss Mabel Hurst, Vincent Blackwood, Cpl. Jerome Manning, Mr. and Mrs. Arthur Snyder, and Fred Snyder."

"Bringing together," observed Abigail's notes, "all with whom S has had social contact—except for Mrs. Manning. (Was she not invited or is her husband's condition worse. And if the latter, why would her son attend the gathering?)"

Over the date of February 2, one item stood alone:

"Cpl. Jerome Manning left on Sunday to rejoin his outfit."

(No comment.)

Although it had completed her list of names, the departure of Jerome Manning from Glen Falls had not put a stop to Abigail's research. In the months that followed she had read each issue of the *Gazette* exhaustively. Gradually she had been able to eliminate most of the troublesome interrogation points and had acquired, in addition, a surprising fund of information about the people she had elected to follow.

No detail was too trivial for her notice if it concerned anyone with whom Corporal Manning had had dealings. She had observed a moment of silent sympathy for the young soldier and for his widowed mother when she came across the announcement of Nelson Manning's death in August, 1945. She had worried a great deal when, two months later, his mother took a trip to Washington to visit her son, "who has been in Walter Reed Hospital for the past ten weeks."

As a sideline that Abigail hoped might prove useful if she should ever have occasion to visit Glen Falls, she had compiled a list of women who ran rooming houses: names gleaned from the classified ads or, more frequently, through pure deduction as the address of one unmarried female after another had duplicated that of oft-mentioned matrons. Two pages at the back of her case history were devoted to the interests of all such possible landladies: their activities in such community organizations as the WCTU, the Library Association, the Wednesday Afternoon Sewing Circle, and so on. Abigail, a Methodist by birth, a Baptist by marriage, and a regular attendant of the Congregational church by preference, had not blushed as she noted the church affiliations of each of these potential landladies, and she was prepared to espouse whichever branch of the Protestant religion seemed most likely to further her cause.

By April, 1948, when she actually found herself on the train, Abigail knew that as soon as she reached Glen Falls she would inquire first for a room with Mrs. Dora Weston. Mrs. Weston had the obvious advantage of being linked socially with the principals in the case. In addition, a coincidence of names had led Abigail to hope that she was also a close relative of Tom Weston, the sole representative of the Law in Glen Falls—a relationship that could undoubtedly be put to good use.

On the whole, Abigail had been proud of her detective work. She had felt justified in eliminating one after another of the married couples whom she had checked with a question until only one remained. Yet now that Harrison Hawkes had succumbed at the home of Mr. and Mrs. Arthur Snyder her confidence was shaken. According to her calculations, the victim of Corporal Manning's revenge should have been Philip Koestler or, if not Mr. Koestler himself, then a member of his family or a visitor to his home. Abigail had to face the fact that, if this were indeed the Glen Falls Murder, she had somehow gone astray.

Turning the pages of her notebook slowly she reviewed her comments and deductions with what she hoped was an open mind. The Morgans had been crossed off, justifiably she was sure, when their daughter Susan celebrated her fourth birthday with a party at her nursery school. ("the Morgans must have been married long before S left Glen Falls.")

Similarly, Dr. Werner and his wife had fallen by the wayside when they "quietly observed their twentieth wedding anniversary," and the Snyders had been scratched only after "Arthur Snyder and his son, Fred, traveled to Columbus last week to attend the Ohio-Northwestern football game."

Abigail read again all the items referring to the Snyders. She nibbled at her pencil point abstractedly. If Fred Snyder, who was old enough to attend country-club dances ("see Clipping, p. 6") and go to football games, was the son of Mr. and Mrs. Arthur Snyder, his mother could scarcely have been Corporal Manning's estranged sweetheart!

Abigail's original conclusion had been supported and strengthened a few weeks later when the *Gazette* social notes had reported the observance, by Mr. and Mrs. Philip Koestler, of their first wedding anniversary. This item, in conjunction with everything else, had seemed to Abigail so conclusive that she had entered four exclamation points beside the pasted notice.

"Comment: This sets the date of their marriage only a few weeks before Cpl. Manning's return. Small wonder it was fresh and sore in his mind and that bitterness filled his heart! Perhaps Girl—Mrs. Koestler—did not even let him know in advance!"

From that day, Abigail had considered that Philip Koestler's days were numbered. Although she had faithfully continued to preserve every item relating to any of the people she knew to have associated with Jerome Manning, she had found no further references to cast doubt on her conclusions.

Occasionally she had been disturbed at the knowledge that the Koestlers were real people and not merely characters in one of her own novels, but she had been quite able to rationalize her failure to warn them. Without ever admitting to herself that their danger might be only a product of her own imagination, she had worked up a strong resentment against Mrs. Koestler, "who had treated a nice young service man so shabbily," and had evolved in her mind the picture of a lovely-to-look-at but cruelly fickle girl and of her husband, a handsome and self-centered 4-F whose life was maintained by (and whose death would be the result of) daily doses of thyroid, insulin, or medicinal capsules for a weak heart. "They are not Nice People," had been her instinctive attitude. When, as it sometimes did, her conscience had suggested that her fears had some foundation, after all, she had reasoned that if she were to write and warn the Koestlers they would not believe her anyway.

"Look at this crazy letter!" Philip would say to his wife. "Some crank, no doubt!" And he would laugh ungratefully and fling it into the nearest wastebasket.

Abigail's lips tightened. She preferred not to be thought of as a crank, even by a man whose opinions she valued as little as she did Philip Koestler's. Even while she believed him to be doomed, even though at times she had been able to visualize quite clearly the small bottle of pills with its burden of death sitting unsuspected in the Koestler medicine chest, she had bided her time in silence.

And yet—her thoughts came back inevitably and resentfully to the ultimate fact—the poison pill had not been in the Koestler medicine chest at all! Contrary to all her logic, the death of Harrison Hawkes had occurred in the home of Mr. and Mrs. Arthur Snyder! The fact that he had succumbed mysteriously while visiting one of the couples who had been associated with Corporal Manning gave Abigail small comfort, though the tie-up made it easier to believe that this death was that for which she had been preparing. She was chagrined because with all segments of the puzzle spread before her she had apparently overlooked a key piece and had tried to force another in its place.

As the wheels clacked along the rails, Abigail brooded and at last, less than an hour before she reached Chicago, she fell upon the only possible explanation. In a firm, triumphant script she concluded the premurder portion of her investigations with a red-penciled note:

"Comment: Harrison Hawkes, although a house guest of the Snyders, undoubtedly was entertained at the home of Mr. and Mrs. Philip Koestler on the evening of his death and there, in some manner, gained access to the Koestler pills."

By the time she had transferred to the day coach out of Chicago her plan of action was complete, and self-confidence had been restored. Only then did she put aside her notes and allow herself to dwell upon the possible outcome of her intervention in the affairs of Corporal Manning.

I feel like a traitor, she reflected. But either he did it, or he didn't. If he did, he *should* be brought to justice.

And if he didn't? her conscience probed.

If he didn't, Abigail assured herself firmly, my investigations can do him no harm.

In the meantime, she could not overlook the fact that if Corporal Manning-Rascinski were a murderer he would not appreciate her interference.

If I were writing this story, Abigail reflected, and Samantha Vernay were in my position, I should have her step off the train into the arms of Jerome Manning. And wouldn't that be a nasty jolt—for both of them!

On the whole, she was just as glad that real life was not likely to duplicate fiction. She had the soldier's own word for it that, if guilty, he would have put as great a distance as possible between himself and the scene of the crime, with every intention of remaining there.

With no misgivings, Abigail curled up like a child on the unyielding seat, and although it was barely midafternoon she fell into an instant and untroubled doze.

II

Darkness had moved in before Abigail reached her destination. There were no other passengers for Glen Falls, and the platform was deserted as she climbed from the train. No red cap hastened up to take her bag. No taxi stood in the parking lot. For a treacherous instant, Abigail felt unsure of herself, and knew a fluttering desire to clamber back to the security of the lighted coach. Taking herself in hand, she set her bag foursquare on the boards beside her and turned her back to the train.

Are you a rabbit, Abigail Potter? she demanded. The scorn in her own voice served to stiffen her spine. Anyone would think, she went on sternly, that you were expecting Glen Falls to turn out with a band to welcome you!

It was disconcerting, however, to realize that for all practical purposes and in spite of all her preparations, she and Glen Falls were strangers to one another. If, at this moment, she were to bump into Dora Weston or Philip Koestler, she would not recognize them.

A light was burning somewhere at the far end of the shanty-like station. Feeling as though she were stepping into the pages of one of her own books, Abigail took a firm hold on her suitcase and started toward it.

The grizzled station agent did not look up from the worn copy of *True Western* that lay open among the timetables and bills of lading on his flattop desk, but he answered her questions intelligibly, if with a minimum of words.

"Can you tell me where I might find a room for the night?" Abigail asked, after waiting in vain for several moments to gain his attention.

The agent scratched his unshaven chin ruminatively.

"Might try the Ee-light Calf," he observed at last.

Thanks to her habit of reading even the advertisements in the *Gazette*, Abigail knew he was referring to the Elite Café, "best food in town closed Wednesday afternoon."

"Which way do I go?" she asked.

The agent wet his thumb and turned a page before making a double gesture with his forefinger, pointing first west and then south.

"One and one," he directed sparingly.

Abigail picked up her bag and followed this sketchy blue-print. At the corner she was encouraged by the lighted window of a pool hall and a vista of neon signs and street lights to her left.

"Dayton Street!" she told herself, pleased that she did not need a street sign to give her the name of the principal thoroughfare. Her step was brisk as she covered the second block and approached the murmuring heart of Glen Falls' night life.

The Elite Café was beyond the moving-picture theater, and groups of people were beginning to pour out from the first show as Abigail walked by. She scanned their faces eagerly, feeling against all reason that at any moment she might see one she knew, hear spoken a familiar name. Few of them, she noticed, turned into the Elite, and Abigail followed the crowd, slowing only to glance through the streaked plate-glass front of Glen Falls' only restaurant. The "best food in town" was apparently less popular with customers of the Elite than bottled beer; the stained and uncovered tables were less well attended than the bar.

Abigail had no strong conviction against beer. If her investigations proved it necessary she could even, she felt sure, continue to breathe in an atmosphere where cigar smoke had long since triumphed over oxygen. But for tonight, at least, she had no wish to make the experiment. If the Elite Café ran a hostelry for transients in addition to dispensing food and beer, its proprietor would be the last to recommend any of the rooming houses she had in mind.

The drugstore at the next corner looked cleaner and more promising. Abigail made her way to the soda fountain, which was surrounded two and three deep by refreshment seekers. Taking advantage of a lull she spoke, holding her suitcase prominently and managing to look and sound like a very old lady who has traveled a grueling distance.

"I wonder," she quavered, "if you could suggest a place—" (Not too far away? she thought, and then rejected the qualification, reminding herself that as yet she had no idea of the relative locations of the addresses she knew.) "—a place where I could get a quiet room for a day or two, preferably in a private home?"

In the manner of small towns, a number of people at once added their suggestions to that of the soda clerk. With an exultant triumph Abigail heard mention of several familiar names.

"How about Mrs. Pickett?" (Unitarian, Abigail briefed herself. WCTU.)

"There's Miss Orton—" (Librarian. Methodist.) "Her roomer left Monday."

"You might try Mrs. Danvers."

"I think Miss Sawyer—"

And then, through the confusion, Abigail heard the name she had most hoped to hear.

"Mrs. Weston's sister left this afternoon, so her spare's empty."

"But Dora's so far out—"

Abigail promptly qualified her needs.

"I was hoping to get something on the edge of town—quiet, you know."

The woman who had mentioned Mrs. Weston spoke with decision.

"Then you'd like Dora Weston's. Why don't you telephone from here and then I can drive you over. I live out that way."

"Oh, no!" Abigail protested. "I thought a taxi—"

"Nonsense! We have no such thing. You must let me take you. I insist."

She insisted, in fact, to the point of calling Mrs. Weston herself and making all the arrangements.

"Dora, dear, this is Hilda. About that room of yours—"

Hilda paused once or twice to ask a question of Abigail. "Did you want meals, too? Dora is an excellent cook." Abigail bobbed her head, trying not to gloat. "Is two dollars a day all right? It's a very comfortable room."

Abigail waited with strained patience while Hilda, unmindful of the fact that she was using a public phone and that as a close neighbor she must see Mrs. Weston in person daily, went into a detailed description of the movie she had just left, combined with enthusiastic rejoinders to Dora, my dear, that she must on no account miss seeing it for herself. From the frequency and length of her enforced pauses, Abigail deduced that Dora Weston was quite a talker in her own right. Her satisfaction grew apace.

Luck, she thought, is certainly with me! Luck and foresight, she qualified immodestly. Without foresight she might have been already settled in a dingy and isolated room for transients above the smoky Elite Café.

The garrulous curiosity of Abigail's good Samaritan, who introduced herself as Hilda Werner (the doctor's wife!), continued as she helped Abigail to her car and fitted the suitcase at their feet. Abigail took great pleasure in answering her freely, if not factually. The sooner she became a known and accepted part of the village the faster her task would proceed. By tomorrow, she was sure, her presence in town and the reason she had given therefore would have spread throughout Glen Falls.

"I'm here for a little holiday," she explained. "I've always wanted to see Glen Falls. My husband's aunt lived here most of her life—Harriet Potter, her name was— Oh, you've heard of her? I'd supposed it was so long ago. Yes, nearly twenty-five years. Aunt Harriet always spoke very lovingly of this little town. . . . No, I've never been here before. . . . Yes, Aunt Harriet died three years ago. She was eighty—"

"You must talk with old Mrs. Osborne," Mrs. Werner exclaimed. "She must have known your aunt and she'll be delighted to meet you. And Seth Wetherby, at the post office, is simply a

storehouse of memories about our little town and everyone who
has ever lived here. He'll be able to tell you a great deal—"

She seems to think I've come on a pilgrimage of loving memory, Abigail thought, amused. But then, she reminded herself,
glancing at her companion, she's too young really to have known
Aunt Harriet.

She was pleased to find that mention of Aunt Harriet's name
wafted her at once from the orbit reserved for tourists and admitted her to that more intimate region accorded those who belong. Perhaps, posthumously, her acid-tongued aunt by marriage
might prove a valuable ally!

"The edge of town" was less than a mile from its center. Abigail, who had envisioned a much longer trip, had had no time
to prepare herself to meet, in the flesh, the second of the people
whose names appeared in her notebook. Hilda Werner stopped
her car in front of a large stucco house and Abigail could only
think exultantly, three years ago Corporal Manning had dinner
in this very house, before the door was flung open and Dora
Weston welcomed her in.

Mrs. Weston was plump and hospitable, in the flesh, indeed,
but rather charmingly so. Her ample figure was squeezed into a
bright green flannel robe which zippered up the front with the
appearance of a train track mounting up a steep and hilly grade
through verdant fields. Abigail liked her on sight, and pushed
back a nudging impulse to say, frankly, "I'm so glad to meet you
at last—after reading so much about your activities!"

Instead she observed, "It's very good of you to take me in on
such short notice. I should have made arrangements in advance,
but I had thought of course there would be a hotel."

"In Glen Falls!" Mrs. Weston snorted.

"This is Mrs. Potter, Dora. Her aunt was Harriet Potter who
used to live here."

"Harriet Potter!" Mrs. Weston seized upon the name. "Wasn't
she a dressmaker? I'm sure I've heard Eloise Demarest speak of
her. Miss Potter used to do all the sewing for the Baker girls—
Eloise was a Baker. Eloise often says they don't make clothes today as Miss Potter used to do! Why, I do believe your aunt made

Eloise's wedding gown! You must meet her—you'll have so much to talk about!"

(Eloise Demarest, 39 Prescott Avenue, where Harrison Hawkes died!)

"Indeed we shall!" Abigail muted her triumph with fervent appreciation.

It's too good to be true, she exulted, half an hour later as she nestled in the huge old-fashioned fourposter with its modern innerspring.

This bed, she told herself solemnly, is in the home of Mrs. Dora Weston, of Glen Falls, Ohio. I, Abigail Farringdon Potter, am going to sleep in this bed—and tomorrow, having intimated to Mrs. Weston that, like herself, I am a good Presbyterian, I am to go with her to church where I shall certainly meet her dear friend Mrs. Manning, who is also a Presbyterian—and the mother of Corporal Jerome Manning. At the very first opportunity, I shall be introduced to Mrs. Eloise Demarest for the purpose of reminiscing at length about dear Aunt Harriet and, one hopes, other things. And, through Mrs. Demarest, I shall undoubtedly be able to arrange an introduction to Mr. and Mrs. Arthur Snyder, who live at the same address and at whose home Harrison Hawkes died—she made a rapid calculation—died just two nights ago!

The inquest, she remembered, was to have been held today. In the morning, of course, she must get hold of the newspapers, although she knew they would have little to tell her that she did not know already. "Death at the hand of person or persons unknown" would be the only possible verdict.

Abigail smiled a secret smile as she reminded herself that even now Chief of Police Tom Weston was undoubtedly questioning suspects and trying in vain to establish a motive for the murder.

I'm the only one, she reflected complacently, who knows that there *is* no motive for the death of Harrison Hawkes, that the murderer got the wrong man! The only one except, perhaps, Jerome Manning, she amended, wondering if, wherever he now was, he too had read of Hawkes' death. She fell asleep with a

smile on her lips as she thought of the shock and disappointment
the revelation must have been to him.

On Sunday mornings, Abigail customarily slept until eight
thirty and on her first morning in Glen Falls she had no difficulty in adapting her subconscious to the change from Central
to Eastern Standard Time. No sounds issued from the rest of the
house, however. After she had crept to the bathroom and taken
a considerately subdued sponge bath and had lingered long over
the familiar processes of dressing and of combing out and adjusting the "switch" with which she augmented her own thinning
hair, Abigail found herself, at nine thirty, with nothing to do in
a strange and still somnolent house.

Her interior, trained to punctuality, was outraged. By the
time she at last heard sounds of movement from Mrs. Weston's
bedroom she had decided, firmly, that she would simply have to
insist upon *two* slices of toast and perhaps an extra egg.

When Dora Weston finally emerged, however, genial in her
emerald robe, she began rapidly to assemble a lavish breakfast of
Canadian bacon and scrambled eggs. Abigail found her irritation considerably appeased. Under Dora's directions, she spread
a flowered cloth on the kitchen table and laid places for two, her
nose meanwhile approving the truly superior aroma of coffee.

To her surprise, she found that tomato juice was a welcome
change from her usual grapefruit and that scrambled eggs à la
Dora Weston could compete favorably with her own two-and-a-
half-minute-in-the-shell variety.

Have I been getting in a rut? she asked herself anxiously.
By way of refuting the disturbing possibility she added a dash
of cream and a scant spoonful of sugar to her coffee, which for
forty years she had taken black—and, as a long-term policy, she
resolved to scramble her future egg on every alternate Sunday.

"I don't know why I always end up rushing like mad of a
Sunday morning," Dora Weston apologized placidly, spreading
jam on her third slice of toast. "My friend, Charlotte Manning,
always stops by for me—and I'm never ready. It makes her furious!"

Abigail choked and took a hasty sip of coffee. Charlotte Manning, the Mrs. Manning, of the Jerome and Glen Falls Mannings!

"I hope she won't mind if I go along—" she began.

"Not at all! Mrs. Manning has a big car, plenty of room for one more. You mustn't let her intimidate you, by the way. Charlotte is not very—outgoing—but she has a heart of gold. Poor dear, she's had a great deal of trouble. Her husband died two years ago and her only son—she simply worships Jerry—never came back from the war. She's terribly lonely, but—"

Abigail's heart pounded suffocatingly.

"You mean—her son was killed?" she asked. Such a possibility had never entered into her calculations.

"Oh, no. Jerry was wounded, but not seriously. I just meant that he has never come back to Glen Falls. Of course, when his father died, Jerry was in the hospital, but it does seem strange that even after he was released— Of course," she added charitably, "he has a very good job on the coast and I'm sure Charlotte wouldn't want him to come back permanently, not when he'd have to work for Arthur Snyder or go into some other field—" She stopped apologetically, becoming aware of Abigail's bewilderment.

"Oh, of course you don't know what I'm talking about! You see, Jerry's father, Nelson Manning, owned the Midwest Foundry here. Jerry's grandfather started the business and built it up and Nelson always counted on passing it on to Jerry when he retired. Then, during the war, and just when business was booming, mind you, what with war contracts and all, this Arthur Snyder came to town and started a rival business. Before long Nelson sold out to him—lock, stock, and barrel. We never quite understood, although, of course, he got a very good price.

"Anyway, Charlotte never got over it. She can't stand Arthur Snyder, always said there was something crooked about his methods—you know—that Nelson didn't really want to sell at all. Of course, it was right after that Nelson took sick and some people thought more than likely he knew his health was failing and that's why he sold out."

"But if he had a son to carry on?" Abigail protested.

"I know, it did seem queer, but there it is. Anyway, as I was saying, Jerry's got a good engineering job on the coast and he's never been home since the Red Cross got him an emergency furlough back in nineteen forty-five, a few months before his father died. Nelson was in the hospital then and didn't even recognize his son part of the time. All he could talk about was getting the foundry back for Jerry. He died that same year, Nelson did—of a broken heart, Charlotte says, though if you ask me, that's rubbish!"

Abigail's thoughts were churning. When she had spoken to him on the train, Jerome Manning must have been returning on that emergency furlough. That would have been enough to explain his preoccupation, his ill-concealed anxiety. Later, when he had begun to talk freely, it could have been in an effort to keep his thoughts away from his father's illness. The guilt, the desperation she had read into his manner might have been due to anxiety and dread rather than to a criminal resolve.

Though it meant the collapse of three years' plotting, Abigail felt almost relieved at the possibility that she might have been mistaken about the young corporal's guilt.

And yet, there was still the matter of the name. No amount of personal anxiety should have made it seem necessary for the young soldier to give a false name. Abigail had as yet no proof that her companion on the train actually had been Jerome Manning, but until she could see a picture of him she felt impelled to assume that George Rascinski did not, in actual fact, exist.

Harrison Hawkes had died in Arthur Snyder's house. And Arthur Snyder was the man who had pushed Jerry's father out of business, robbed Jerry of his inheritance, contributed to his father's failing health!

Suddenly Abigail saw an explanation for the locale of Hawkes' death. What if Jerome Manning's murder scheme had been used to get revenge on his father's enemy? She had assumed from the torn scraps of letter, from the hypothetical motive the soldier himself had suggested, that his hatred had been born of jealousy, but perhaps she had taken too much for granted.

And then a second and more startling possibility caused Abigail to sit bolt upright. Jerome Manning had devised a perfect and untraceable means of murder. Abigail was convinced that when he spoke to her on the train his hatred was directed against a rival in love, but if he had arrived home to find his father critically ill and his mother filled with bitterness toward Arthur Snyder, might he not have attempted the death of Snyder as well as that of Philip Koestler, who had married his sweetheart?

The more she thought about it, the more convinced Abigail became that Jerome Manning must have planted two lethal capsules. One had done its deadly work but the other—

Philip Koestler was *still* in danger! Philip Koestler must be warned!

Agitatedly she pushed back her chair and stood up.

"I'll just stack these dishes," Dora Weston was saying, "and then trot up and change my clothes."

Abigail's jaw dropped. How could Mrs. Weston talk of dishes at a time like this! Immediately she recognized the absurdity of her thought, as well as the helplessness of her position. Unless she worked fast, another death might occur yet she could not speak, could not even mention the name of Philip Koestler whom she supposedly did not know.

"I'll wash them up while you dress," she forced herself to offer.

"Indeed you won't!" Dora Weston countered. "We'll do them with the dinner dishes this noon when Charlotte's here to help. She always eats with me on Sundays and today my son, Tom, will be here, too—his wife is out of town—so you see there's not a particle of sense your fussing with the dishes. You just sit down and look at the morning paper—it's likely tucked inside the front screen—and I'll be ready in a jiffy."

Abigail, completely bemused, watched the rounded green mass that was her landlady disappear up the stairs. She was trying to understand why two guests for dinner constituted a logical reason for not washing the breakfast plates and wondering, too, if the company dinner was to prepare itself while she and Mrs. Weston worshiped.

At least, she reminded herself, I was right about Tom Weston: he is Dora's son, and since he is also the chief of police I may be able to get his co-operation. He will be in a position to warn Philip Koestler before it's too late.

Dora Weston's jiffy was considerably more than that. Abigail had time to find and read the account of the previous day's inquest in the paper, but as Mrs. Weston subscribed to a Cincinnati journal in preference to a Dayton paper the report was brief—only a few lines with a Dayton dateline on an inside page. (Dayton, Abigail presumed, being the county seat.) Short though it was, the item contained quite enough to satisfy Abigail who already knew so much more than had been brought out at the inquest. Two facts only were new to her: that death had been caused by cyanide poisoning, and that Mr. Hawkes' collapse had occurred shortly after dinner, which he had eaten in the Snyder home.

"Authorities," the account continued, "have as yet been unable to trace the poison or determine how the fatal dose was administered, as all food served was shared by everyone present."

The jury had returned a verdict of "death at the hands of person or persons unknown."

There followed a résumé of facts that had been more fully covered in previous issues, and a summary, which Abigail considered quite irrelevant, of the life of Harrison Hawkes and of his importance on the national industrial scene.

The loud double blast of a horn sounded on the street outside, repeated after a short interval with more impatience.

"That'll be Charlotte!" Dora Weston called frantically from upstairs. "Tell her we'll be right out!"

Abigail opened the front door and relayed the message before she hurried to put on her coat and hat. She did not wish her acquaintance with Jerry's mother to begin by keeping her waiting, yet she hesitated to go out alone and introduce herself. She compromised by peering with interest through the net curtains. Mrs. Manning drove a large and well-preserved sedan of a flamboyant green, a color that appeared to have little in common with the severity of the driver who sat, straight backed, behind the wheel. Abigail, whose eyes were very keen for distant objects, observed approvingly that there was nothing sporty or flamboyant about

Mrs. Manning Her close-fitting brown hat was innocent of arti-
ficial fruit or waving plumes. As far as Abigail could discern, she
wore no make-up to soften the austere lines of her face.

Charlotte Manning's first words, when Abigail and Dora
Weston finally joined her, made no more concession to tact in
the presence of a stranger than her appearance did to fashion.

"You're improving, Dora. Only fifteen minutes late today!
We may be able to catch the last of the sermon as well as the
benediction!"

"I'm sorry, Charlotte." Her friend's irony seemed not to ruffle
Dora. "Mrs. Potter, this is my dear friend, Charlotte Manning.
Mrs. Potter is staying with me for a few days, Charlotte. She's a
Presbyterian, too, and her aunt grew up in Glen Falls. Perhaps
you knew her—Harriet Potter, you know, the one that used to
sew for the Baker girls. We've been having the most delightful
visit and simply let time slip away."

"Time always slips away from you, Dora," Charlotte Manning observed, but not unkindly. She nodded to Abigail. "I hope
you don't mind being crowded; this seat's a bit narrow. Dora, you
get in first so Mrs. Potter won't get tangled with the gearshift."

She spoke brusquely, but her gray eyes were kind. Her mouth,
Abigail thought, did not look like one accustomed to smiling;
the descending lines at each corner of her straight lips seemed to
anchor it in an uncompromising line. Abigail felt herself drawn
to that face, surmising that the lines that marked it had been
carved through stern self-repression rather than by bitterness or
temper. For no reason she could name she did not take advantage
of the hand Mrs. Manning stretched across to help her. Abigail's
mission to Glen Falls held little of friendliness to the Mannings
and Abigail was not such a hypocrite that she could accept a
hand which was offered in trusting good faith.

Mrs. Manning drove swiftly along side streets and eased the
big car neatly into a parking space near the church. Abigail, with
Dora Weston on one side and Charlotte Manning on the other, was
rushed up the walk like a tardy schoolgirl. There was no opportunity for conversation though Abigail, impatient for progress,

thought that Dora Weston could at least have inquired after her friend's absent son.

Abigail's impatience could find no fault, however, at the speed with which fate furthered her purpose after church.

On the way home, apparently by a prearrangement of which Abigail had no knowledge, Charlotte Manning stopped her car in front of a bungalow not far from the center of town.

"My daughter's," Dora explained as she heaved herself out of the car. "Won't you run in with me and say good-by?"

Charlotte Manning turned off the ignition.

"I'll just wait here," Abigail suggested, but Dora pushed her firmly from the car.

"Indeed you won't. I want you to meet Janet. We'll just be a minute—long enough to get the dinner."

Bewildered, Abigail allowed herself to be escorted to the door, wondering if it were traditional in Glen Falls for mothers to stop in after church to cook dinner for their daughters before going home to prepare a meal for guests of their own, and whether neighbors customarily dropped in to say good-by rather than hello.

A moment later she was overcome by an Alice-in-Wonderlandish sense of unreality as Dora Weston pushed open the door of the little house and introduced Abigail to the pasty-faced, bespectacled young man who jumped up to greet them.

"Mrs. Potter," she said quite calmly, "I want you to meet my son-in-law, Philip Koestler!"

Abigail's mouth opened and closed without a sound, but she retained enough presence of mind to extend her hand. She was not surprised to find that Philip Koestler's felt cold and moist in her own.

Clammy, she described it mentally, and could see the touch of death already upon his sallow features.

Words of warning struggled to arrange themselves in her mind: "Be careful!" "Throw away your medicine!" "Your life is in danger!" His obvious ill health made her tremble lest he had already taken the deadly pill.

Philip Koestler's wife came in then, wiping her hands on the apron which protected a full-skirted velveteen dress.

"Hello, Mom—Mrs. Manning." She acknowledged her mother's introduction of Abigail with a smile. Abigail studied her curiously.

Janet Koestler was not unattractive, but she was far from the *femme fatale* that Abigail had envisioned. Already she was on the rounded side and in a few more years, Abigail was sure, she would have spread until she rivaled her mother in avoirdupois. A pleasant enough person, Abigail decided, but hardly the sort to inspire a jealousy killing!

Even more difficult to understand was how Janet Koestler, née Weston, would have allowed so unprepossessing a character as Philip to blot out the memory of a charming young man like Jerome Manning.

"The dinner's all ready, Mom," Janet said.

"Janet and Philip are leaving tomorrow," Mrs. Weston explained. "Philip has a fine job out in Phoenix—for his health, you know. We'd planned a special farewell dinner today, but then Philip's boss asked them over—practically a command performance—and since Janet had already gotten this wonderful roast—"

"We'd much rather have had you here, but you know how it is, Mom! And we'll be over to see you this evening, of course."

"One of these days I'll be wanting to come back—and it won't hurt to keep the boss's good will," Philip finished.

He had taken a small pasteboard box from his pocket as he spoke and, to Abigail's dismay she saw him shake two small pills into the palm of his hand.

"I'd better just take a couple of these digestive pills before I go. I know the boss's dinners!"

Abigail's rush across the room was instinctive. As Philip Koestler raised his hand to his mouth she careened into him, knocking box and pills from his grasp and scattering the contents far and wide.

"Oh!" she gasped, searching frantically for an explanation for her weird behavior. "How stupid of me! I—I thought I saw a moth!" Tardily she clapped her hands together to the right of Philip Koestler's ear.

Philip and Janet laughed uncertainly. Charlotte Manning snorted. Dora Weston charitably launched into an unconvincing diatribe against the ravages of moths. Only Abigail was not in the least disconcerted. Philip Koestler's pills were scattered beyond recall and she was sure, from his ill-concealed annoyance, that he had no substitute supply.

But perhaps he had other capsules! A man in poor health might rely on a variety of specifics. New anxiety swept over her. Impulsively, she stooped and began to brush her hands across the hearth, sweeping the scattered pills into a pile until Janet, embarrassed, fetched a broom and finished the job.

Then, Abigail displayed her dusty hands.

"I—I wonder if I might trouble you—" she hinted.

Dora Weston indicated directions. Abigail could hear the buzz of their puzzled comments as she made her way to the back of the house.

Once in the bathroom it was the work of minutes to examine the medicine cabinet, to empty and dispose of a small bottle of pills and two pharmacist's boxes containing capsules.

With a great weight off her mind she rinsed her hands and returned to the living room.

In the car, sharing with Dora Weston the weight of a large roaster of meat and potatoes, she indulged in a mood of immoderate self-satisfaction. She suspected that both Philip Koestler and his wife thought her slightly demented, but their opinion concerned her not at all. She was not likely to see either of them again, in any event, and whether they approved of her or not she had done her duty. Philip Koestler's life was safe!

III

At the dinner table Abigail divided her attention between the excellent roast beef and a silent and curious appraisal of Dora Weston's son.

He's the lad I've got to convince, she thought. In spite of her success in meeting and becoming intimate with key people in her case she had gained no whit more of actual evidence against Jerome Manning. Her hypothesis, as it stood, would certainly not convince a jury much less a policeman who was a friend of Jerry Manning's.

Tom Weston's frame was large like his mother's, but solid where Dora's was flabby. His square face sharpened to a queerly shelving jaw as though his chin had been molded in wax and left too long in the sun. Nothing in his easy manner hinted whether he would be skeptical, easily convinced, or pigheadedly opposed to Abigail's disclosures.

Now that the danger to Philip Koestler had been averted she had no desire to test Tom's credulity prematurely. She was quite content to listen quietly to the general talk, confident that sooner or later the conversation would turn to the subject that occupied her thoughts.

The moment came after Tom had followed his mother into the kitchen with a stack of plates.

"How's your murder case, son?" Mrs. Weston asked. Abigail strained unashamedly to hear Tom's answer through the open kitchen door.

"It's not my case any more, Mom. The sheriff took over right after the inquest. This business is rather out of my line, but I'm stringing along, of course."

Apparently Charlotte Manning had also overheard. She brought the subject into the dining room.

"Perhaps you read of the death of Harrison Hawkes?" she asked Abigail.

Abigail thought it safe to admit that she had.

"You remember my speaking of Eloise Demarest—the one that knew your aunt?" Dora, coming in with a sauce dish of peaches in each hand, picked up the recital. "It was her house Mr. Hawkes was staying at when he died—of cyanide poisoning, mind you—right here in Glen Falls! Tom is chief of police and they called him right away. My! Far as I can see they'd do better to let Tom handle the whole thing. The county sheriff's doing his best to prove Eloise's son-in-law, Arthur Snyder, killed him, just because he's the only one that knew Mr. Hawkes before he came to Glen Falls. We've never heard of anything so absurd, have we, Charlotte?"

Charlotte Manning, Abigail noticed, did not spring vehemently to Arthur Snyder's defense.

"No," she said, after only a slight hesitation. "I'm sure Mr. Snyder wouldn't *poison* anyone!"

Abigail was aware of a slight stress on the verb.

"Of course he wouldn't!" Dora Weston emphasized indignantly. "Arthur's a perfect lamb, wouldn't hurt a fly. And as for Eloise, or Maida—why, the idea is ridiculous!"

"And that, I suppose, leaves Fred!" Tom suggested dryly.

"I'd rather think it was Fred!" Dora snapped. "That young whippersnapper!"

"Why are you so sure it was—one of those people?" Abigail asked. "I should think Mr. Hawkes could have gotten the poison somewhere else?"

Tom shrugged.

"Wish we could prove he did! I'd like nothing better than to find out he got it through the mail in a box of chocolates—or took it on the plane coming down—or that someone crept into the house and slipped it in his soup. But it just won't wash! There's not a trace of anyone who ever knew him, except Snyder, and he never left the house from the time he got there Thursday morning until he died that night."

Charlotte cut in sharply.

"I think we're treating this affair in very poor taste," she observed. "It's not a parlor guessing game, but a most unfortunate occurrence that affects our friends directly. The police are doing all they can, I'm sure, and we're hardly justified in making accusations against anyone, even in jest!"

"Good for you, Charlotte!" Tom Weston applauded.

Abigail regarded Charlotte Manning with uneasy respect. She felt uncomfortable at the very thought of accusing this loyal woman's son of murder. Her suspicions had never seemed so distasteful.

But you still don't know that Jerry did it, she warned herself. You have no proof!

She was glad when the talk shifted to other and less disturbing topics.

Tom left as soon as dinner was over. Under other circumstances, Abigail would have been glad to remember her status as a paying guest and retire to her own room, but at the risk of imposing on Dora's hospitality she excused herself only long enough to fetch her crocheting before she rejoined Charlotte and Dora and settled herself firmly in the living room.

Casually she produced the lacy doily over which she had struggled long and with dogged purpose and began to ply her hook. At once she was rewarded.

"What a lovely pattern!" Charlotte exclaimed, coming to sit beside Abigail.

"If you are interested in crochet, Mrs. Potter, you should see some of the lovely things Charlotte has done," Dora Weston contributed on cue. "She won first prize at the state fair last year with an exquisite bedspread. And her tablecloths!" She spread out her hands and breathed an ecstatic sigh.

Abigail responded with enthusiasm. She did not explain that it had been the announcement in the *Gazette* of Mrs. Manning's crocheting triumph at the state fair that had motivated her to take up the art.

"I'd love to see them! I'm just a beginner, but I'm very fond of crocheted pieces. Perhaps you could even help me—" She held out her work and added, truthfully, "I seem to be all thumbs."

The straight lines of Charlotte Manning's mouth showed an ability to curve upward.

"I used to feel that way myself, but your thumbs will soon turn back into fingers. You'll get so you hate to put it down."

Abigail made a mental reservation that so irritating a pursuit would never gain such a hold on her.

"You really ought to see some of Charlotte's work," Dora persisted. "I know! You can drive her back to your house with you this afternoon, Charlotte! Then I can ride along and stop in to say hello to Eloise."

"Now, Dora, I'm sure Mrs. Potter—"

"Oh, but I'd love to!" Abigail said quickly.

"Then it's all settled." Dora made up Mrs. Manning's mind with decision. "I'll just get my hat. I haven't seen Eloise since their trouble, and I'm sure she needs every friend she has at a time like this. It's right next door to Charlotte's so I can walk back with you, Mrs. Potter, whenever you're ready."

This is too easy, Abigail thought, aware that Charlotte Manning was the logical person to verify or explode her theory. She might begin by admiring crocheted luncheon cloths, but Abigail was confidant that she could soon get Mrs. Manning to talking of her son—and talk would lead logically to snapshots.

Never had Abigail admitted that deep in her heart she did not really believe in the investigation to which she had committed herself, but as she sat between Charlotte Manning and Dora Weston in Charlotte's green sedan she began to prepare herself for the collapse of her adventure. It had been absurd to believe that a young man who contemplated murder would have discussed his plan with anyone, just as it was beyond reason to have imagined he could actually have carried through those plans as outlined. Soon Charlotte Manning would produce a picture of her son. Abigail would see that it bore no resemblance to the young soldier she had met on the train—and her house of cards would fall to the ground.

To her astonishment, Abigail discovered that she was not unhappy at the prospect. She liked Glen Falls and the people she had met there; she liked and admired Charlotte Manning. Even if Jerome Manning is someone I never saw before, she reflected, I may as well stay on a while. After all, someone did kill Harrison Hawkes and perhaps I can even help the police to track the murderer down.

And then as Charlotte Manning led the way into the pleasant living room of the Manning home, Abigail was confronted with the confirmation of her premise.

Upon the mantel stood a framed photograph, the picture of a young man in uniform whose eyes met Abigail's with a friendly and trusting directness. She had no difficulty in recognizing the young corporal of the train.

Oh, no, she thought. She wondered if she had spoken aloud for Charlotte was looking at her strangely. Abigail closed her eyes and pressed her fingers to the indented bridge of her nose.

"I wonder if I could trouble you—for a drink of water?" she murmured and realized that she really did feel faint.

Charlotte's arm was firm about her as she helped Abigail to a chair, but she did not linger with vain flutterings. Abigail let her head rest against the cushioned back, listening to the firm haste of her hostess's departing steps, to the distant sound of a faucet turned on full. She tried to collect her whirling thoughts.

Oh, dear—it's been such fun till now! she wailed in silent protest. She looked again at the picture, almost expecting that the candid young eyes would have turned bitter and reproachful. The pursuit was no longer a game, a problem in murder to be worked out on paper and Abigail, in that moment of shock, discovered that all her instinct was to run with the hare rather than to hunt with the hounds.

It's all been a mistake, she thought, a dreadful mistake! I shan't have anything more to do with it!

The doorbell pealed as Charlotte came back with a tumbler of water.

"Feeling better?" she asked. "Excuse me, I'll just see who's at the door."

Abigail took a long drink of the cool liquid. The horror of her knowledge began to fade before her new resolve to wash her hands of the whole affair.

Jerome Manning has gone away as he said he would, she reasoned. Whatever hatred he once felt must have been wiped out. In any case, he will never come back. No one need ever know!

She felt much better. When Charlotte returned, Abigail was sitting back comfortably, prepared to enjoy without reservations the hospitality of her new friend.

Mrs. Manning carried an opened yellow envelope which she laid, without comment, on the mantel beneath her son's picture.

"You look much better," she observed. "I'm sure a cup of tea—"

"I'm quite all right," Abigail assured her. She was unable to decide from Charlotte's expression whether the telegram had brought good news or bad. "Please don't bother."

"No trouble at all. I've put the kettle on," Charlotte answered matter of factly. "And now, if you're sure you want to see my needlework—"

Abigail was grateful that her hostess showed no curiosity over her brief attack of weakness. Charlotte chatted of trivialities as she spread out her crocheted bedspread and table linen for Abigail's inspection and, aside from refusing to allow her guest to help in any way with the tea things, she made no reference to her indisposition.

Over her second cup of tea Abigail found herself confessing that she herself preferred to create with words rather than with crochet cotton and discovered, to her surprise, that Charlotte Manning was familiar with the books of A. B. Gail and delighted to meet their author.

I do like her, Abigail thought. She's a forthright person, but goodhearted! I certainly shan't do anything to cause her pain.

A door slammed somewhere in the back of the house, punctuating their growing intimacy and, although Abigail did not suspect it, putting an end to her interlude of serenity.

"Aunt Charlotte! Yoo-hoo!" a girl's voice called. A moment later someone pushed open the swinging door from the kitchen. "May I come in?"

"Maida! Of course!" Charlotte's voice was warm. "Mrs. Potter, this is my very dear friend and next-door neighbor, Maida Snyder."

Abigail blinked, grasped her glasses' chain for support, and blinked again. Maida Snyder was strikingly beautiful—and young! This can't be Arthur's wife, Abigail thought. This can't be—

"How do you do, Miss Snyder?" she ventured.

"Mrs. Snyder," Charlotte corrected. "I should have introduced you properly."

Abigail floundered.

"But—you seem so young!" she said.

She noticed that both Maida Snyder and Charlotte were staring at her and she felt even more foolish and upset. What she had meant, of course, was not that Maida seemed too young to be married—she must be twenty-five, at least—but that she was obviously too young to have a full-grown son.

You fool! she chided herself, as the truth forced itself upon her. Fred Snyder is Arthur Snyder's son, but not Maida's! This is the girl whom Jerry had loved—and in his absence she had married a man twice as old as herself, the man who had ruined Jerry's father! There was no longer any reason to doubt that Jerome Manning had planted only one lethal pill, and that in Arthur Snyder's house, where Harrison Hawkes had somehow got it by mistake!

But, she reminded herself sternly, you're not going to do anything about it, Abigail Potter!

"Mrs. Weston told us you were here," Maida was saying. "I understand your aunt used to live in Glen Falls, that she was the family seamstress when Mother was a girl."

"Maida's mother is Eloise Demarest," Charlotte explained. "You must meet her while you're here."

"That would be very nice," Abigail agreed without sincerity. Only a short while before how eagerly she had hoped for just such a lead!

"Will you be staying long?" Maida asked.

Abigail decided that the question had been polite rather than interested, for almost before she had finished explaining that her plans were indefinite, Maida had turned to Charlotte Manning.

"Have you had any more news?" she asked, adding frankly, "I saw the boy from the Western Union."

Charlotte Manning nodded.

"It was from Jerry. He's really coming this time—leaving tonight!"

Stunned, Abigail saw Maida's hand reach out impulsively for the older woman's and saw a look pass between them, of shared pleasure and of something more than pleasure—almost a deep thankfulness.

"I'm so glad," Maida said. "So very glad!"

Charlotte's visible emotion was fleeting. Drawing her hand away, she apologized to Abigail.

"You must excuse us," she said. "Jerry is my son—and Maida's very dear friend. He hasn't been home since—since his father died."

"You must be very happy," Abigail responded, but her thoughts were tumultuous.

What could it mean? Why was Jerome Manning coming home—now? He must have seen the newspapers, must realize how dangerous it would be for him to return right after the sudden death of Mr. Hawkes!

With a sensation of skidding downward in a faulty elevator, Abigail corrected herself. The only danger to Jerome Manning lay in her own knowledge, her own presence in Glen Falls!

If I go away, if I say nothing, no one will ever know!

Yet how could she leave until she knew why Jerry had chosen this particular time to come home? His attempt to murder Arthur Snyder had failed; fate had decreed that the man he had planned to kill was not to die. Did Jerry think, then, that he could come back home, freed of his hatred and guilt, to resume his old life? Or—and with all her generous heart Abigail wanted to believe this—or was he returning, consumed with remorse, to make a full confession?

She looked again at the portrait as if for guidance, but the pictured face seemed only very young and unformed. Taken at some time before Jerome Manning had entered Abigail's life, the photograph gave no clue to the man he had become.

All murderers, Abigail reminded herself, were young once. Most of them had mothers who loved them, too. Yet once one has stepped across that threshold that separates a man who will kill from one who will not—can one ever really go back?

What if Jerome Manning was coming home to try again?

You know too much to stop now, Abigail Farringdon Potter, she told herself grimly. The time for conjecture is past. Either Jerome Manning is innocent and you must find the means to prove it, or he is a killer, a menace to society!

In the recesses of her mind she knew now that the only truth she really longed to find was the unlikely evidence that Jerry Manning was not, after all, a murderer. But even if her fears were proven correct it did not follow that she must then betray him.

If he has repented, she assured herself, if he has given up his deadly scheme—

At any rate, the sooner she got on with her investigations, the better. To this end, she smiled disarmingly at Maida Snyder and waited for a break in her reminiscences of the hair-pulling feuds she and Jerry had waged when they were small.

"I'm very anxious to meet your mother," she said. "Perhaps I could run over for a few minutes now, just until Mrs. Weston is ready to leave. It would save her the trouble of stopping here for me."

Maida smiled regretfully.

"I do wish you could," she said, "but, if you don't mind, some other day? As I explained to Mrs. Weston, Mother has been far from well, and Mr. Hawkes' death—you've heard about it, of course—on top of everything else has simply been too much for her. May I call you in a few days?"

Abigail, who had begun to take it for granted that doors would be opened, realized that she had walked full tilt into a brick wall.

"I quite understand," she said. "It was thoughtless of me to suggest it, under the circumstances. The whole affair must have been a severe shock to all of you. So distressing—"

Maida grimaced.

"It's more than distressing. We're all under surveillance, you know. Number one suspects!" She shrugged, as though attempting to dislodge a disagreeable and persistent insect. "Oh, well, I suppose it will all blow over soon."

In spite of her attempted lightness, Abigail sensed that Maida was desperately afraid. She had to remind herself that the Law was not infallible, that not often but occasionally, people were convicted unjustly on circumstantial evidence alone. It had never occurred to her that an innocent person might be called upon to pay for Jerry's crime. Either, she had thought, she herself would betray what she knew or the murder would go forever unsolved. But if someone else were to be arrested for Hawkes' murder she would no longer have the right to keep quiet, even if Jerry Manning stayed away as he had planned.

And then she remembered, with relief, that Jerry was not going to stay away. If the police built up a case against Maida or her husband sufficient to arrest either of them, Jerry would be there to come forward, to confess his guilt. The decision was out of her hands.

But *would* Jerry come forward and confess?

That night Abigail tossed restlessly in the high fourposter, trying vainly to guess the reason for Jerry's return. To forget? To confess? Or—to try again? If the latter, Arthur Snyder was still in danger. And what of herself? Abigail shoved the disturbing doubt aside.

Within twenty-four hours the game she had played with herself for so long had become a frightening reality. She longed only to run back into her ivory tower and slam the door.

A fine mess you've made of things, Abigail Potter, she accused herself, blushing again as she remembered Philip Koestler's quizzical scrutiny as he had passed her in Mrs. Weston's hall that evening. He had surely discovered her depredations in his medicine chest!

Let that be a lesson to you, she told herself. A good detective never jumps to conclusions. She had acted impulsively, scattered his harmless pills and destroyed his innocent medicines—and for nothing! Philip Koestler had been in no danger after all!

Now that she knew definitely that it was Arthur Snyder for whom Jerry had intended death from the beginning, the necessity of gaining admission to the Snyder house had become, in Abigail's mind, the only possible avenue of further investigations. She did not know what it was she hoped to learn there, but she retained sufficient faith in herself to believe that if she could but get her foot across the threshold she would be able to set a course from there. Surely someone in the household held the key, the evidence she must have if she and Arthur Snyder were to remain alive and safe.

When it came to making plans for effecting that entrance, however, Abigail bumped into the unyielding wall. Short of surreptitious entry in the unlikely guise of a female electrician or forcing herself in behind a menacing gunlike bulge from the hip pocket, Abigail could see no immediate hope of advance through that last essential door.

IV

Abigail fell asleep without solving her problem, but during the night her subconscious mind continued to worry it. When she awoke the answer was waiting.

Abigail, you're an old fool! she pronounced. You go all melodramatic with elaborate ruses and absurd disguises and completely overlook the obvious!

Aunt Harriet had been a friend of Eloise Demarest's, hadn't she? What could be more in order than for Abigail, learning of the disaster that had befallen Mrs. Demarest's household and of her indisposition, to pay a little call? She would take some flowers! Or, better yet—

With sudden decision, Abigail pushed back the bedclothes and got up. In her suitcase was a cameo brooch, the only article of Aunt Harriet's that Abigail had kept, not because it had belonged to Jonathan's crotchety aunt but in spite of it. Now, however, Abigail took it out of its tissue-paper wrappings and slipped it into her handbag. She and Aunt Harriet, Abigail reflected, had never really liked each other. Surely Aunt Harriet, wherever she was, would be far happier to know that something of hers had returned to Glen Falls to keep her memory alive.

"Aunt Harriet used to speak of you often, Mrs. Demarest," Abigail rehearsed without a blush. "Toward the end she slipped back into the past." (This, at least, had been irritatingly true.) "She told me over and over of her life in Glen Falls. I think she was never really happy anywhere else. And then she would mention you—how lovely you looked in the wedding gown she made

for you. 'After I am gone,' she used to say, 'I want Eloise Demarest to have my cameo brooch.'"

Mrs. Demarest might think it odd, but if Abigail knew human nature she would be flattered and touched.

After lunch Abigail dressed with extreme care, choosing her
black wool as the most suitable in which to pay her respects to a
house of sorrow. She felt a twinge of regret as she adjusted a fresh
white collar and realized that never again would she fasten it at
the throat with the pink cameo.

Abigail had no difficulty in retracing the few blocks she had
been driven the afternoon before. She scuttled along the sidewalk as though at any moment she might be stopped and chided,
and as she pulled the old-fashioned doorbell of the Snyder house
her hand trembled. She murmured a childish prayer as she waited. "Please don't let Maida come to the door!"

When the handle turned she drew herself up primly.

She couldn't be so rude as to turn me away, she reassured herself, clutching the brooch.

Her prayer was answered. Not Maida but a mild-mannered,
slightly stooped man with receding gray hair stood in the doorway.

"How do you do?" Abigail began nervously. "I'm Abigail Potter. My aunt was a very dear friend of Mrs. Demarest's—and as
long as I happened to be in town—"

The man threw the door open.

"Come right in! I'm sure Eloise will be delighted to see you!"
His hand was thin and cold in Abigail's.

He's afraid, Abigail thought. I wonder who he thought I was?

Arthur Snyder did not look like a ruthless man of affairs but
rather, as Dora Weston had described him, like one who would
hesitate to swat a fly. His face was lined; his gray eyes sat deep in
his head and were shadowed with fatigue. Abigail would not have
put his age at more than fifty, yet she noticed that he moved like
a tired old man.

Does he suspect? she wondered. Does he have any intimation
of how narrowly he himself has escaped death and in what peril
he still moves and breathes?

"Won't you sit down," Snyder said, sweeping a camel's hair top-coat from a chair in the hall and draping it over the newel post. "I'll tell Eloise you're here."

His step, as he started up the stairs, was slow and heavy.

I'm in! Abigail gloated. The truth lies somewhere in this household and I intend to find it!

Somewhere in the back a door opened. Abigail heard light quick footsteps.

"Arthur! Arthur! He's home! He—"

The voice broke off as Maida stepped into the hall.

"Why, Mrs. Potter!" Her expression betrayed her astonishment.

Abigail stood up, fingering the chain that held her glasses.

"Mrs. Snyder, how nice to see you again!" she exclaimed, untruthfully. "I do hope you don't mind my coming so soon—I shall only stay a minute. I have a little something for your mother —a brooch that my aunt wanted her to have—"

Almost pleadingly Abigail held out the cameo.

Maida's words were courteous, but Abigail could not fail to sense her withdrawal and annoyance.

"Your aunt—wanted mother to have this brooch?" Maida repeated. Abigail suspected indignantly that Mrs. Snyder did not believe her.

"Why, that's very good of you, Mrs. Potter, really! Won't you let me take it to her? As I told you yesterday, Mother is far from well. Perhaps tomorrow or the next day—"

"Oh, there you are!" Abigail and Maida turned as Arthur Snyder spoke from the stairs. "You won't mind going up, Mrs. Potter? Eloise prefers to entertain in her own—"

Maida crossed to him swiftly and spoke in an undertone. An expression of bewilderment and distress flickered across his face. Then he continued down the stairs, leaving Maida standing there, gripping the banister.

"Eloise seems to be resting at the moment, Mrs. Potter," he reversed his field smoothly. "She isn't at all well and I'm sure you will understand that I hesitate to disturb her. She has gone through so much—"

For a moment Abigail contemplated charging past him up the stairs and then, as she met Maida's steady gaze, she wilted and backed toward the door.

"Of course!" she murmured, feeling behind her for the knob. "Please give her my best regards. I'll come again—if I may?"

Even as she spoke she was appalled at her own insistence. Singleness of purpose is all very well, Abigail Potter, she warned herself, but you've lost all sense of proportion! Immediately she sought to justify her behavior. I'm only trying to help them, after all. Why do they have to make it so difficult?

Arthur found the knob for which her hand groped and held the door open for her. His eyes seemed to question Maida's before he answered.

"I'm sure you may. Eloise will be terribly disappointed when she learns—" The apology seemed to be addressed to his wife rather than to Abigail, but Maida did not yield.

"I'll give her this," she said, and Abigail became aware that somehow Maida was holding the brooch in her own hand. "It was very kind of you—and your aunt—to think of Mother. We will get in touch with you soon."

A smile frozen on her lips, Abigail found herself once more on the steps. With a solid click the heavy door closed behind her. She was further from her goal than ever—and now she did not even have her beloved brooch. She could have wept for vexation.

She was sure of only one thing. Eloise Demarest wanted to see me, I know she did, she fumed. Arthur Snyder came from her room with every intention of taking me to her until that little—until that *girl* stopped him!

Abigail was not in the habit of using strong language, but she managed to inject a masterly amount of venom into the innocuous noun. That *girl* was at the root of the whole business! If she had not led Jerry on and then tossed him aside for a man over twice her age that nice young soldier would never have been driven to murder and Harrison Hawkes would not have died.

She's even keeping her poor sick mother a prisoner—shutting out anyone who might bring a little pleasure into her drab existence—turning away the niece of a very dear friend, Abigail told herself angrily, and then chided herself for thinking like a character in one of her own novels.

In spite of the rebuff she had met, Abigail was reluctant to retreat. Her attention focused on a narrow brick walk that led off at right angles to the main one and curved around one side of the house.

Obviously there is a side entrance, Abigail thought, a service door. I wonder—

Without conscious decision she started along the narrow walk and around the corner of the house. She looked up at the second-floor windows as she went, almost persuading herself that she would see some signal of distress, perhaps a handkerchief being waved.

If I only knew which was her room, she thought, I could wait until Maida steps out—

"Hello!"

Abigail let out a little shriek. What must this man think—to find a perfect stranger wandering about the house, staring up at the windows! Absurd to pretend that she had lost her way, in broad daylight!

And then, as she looked at him, her breath caught in a gasp of pure terror. The man who had greeted her so casually was the corporal of the train!

In spite of his civilian clothes, in spite of the scar that creased his face from temple to jawbone, in spite of the tired eyes that had once been alive and boyish, it was Jerome Manning, the person in all the world Abigail least wanted to meet!

She could not tear her gaze away. She could find no words. She could only stand and stare, her heart pounding, waiting for him to remember. He, for his part, seemed to expect her to make some explanation of her presence. For a long moment they eyed one another until, with a muttered excuse, he stepped past her toward the Snyder house. Without knocking, he opened the French doors at the side and walked in.

Well! Abigail breathed fervently. On legs that buckled like candles in the sun she tottered back to the front gate.

He didn't recognize me! I would have known him anywhere—but he didn't recognize me!

Relief swept over her. She began to giggle nervously as she hurried up the street.

As swiftly as it had come, the impulse to laughter died. Jerome Manning was in Glen Falls and Abigail's reprieve could be, at best, only temporary. At this very moment, indeed, he might be asking questions of Maida and Arthur Snyder about the old lady he had seen poking about. As soon as he heard her name, as he inevitably must, he could not but remember all the circumstances.

Abigail Featherbrain Potter, she dubbed herself scathingly. You not only had to give him your name before you left him on the train—you had to leave him one of your books to impress yourself on his memory!

If only she had come to Glen Falls under an alias. But no, she corrected herself, the major portion of the progress she had made so far had been solely because of her relationship to Jonathan's aunt. Had she elected to sail under false colors she might still be becalmed in mid-ocean and yet, to complete the simile, unless she furled her flag at once and sailed away, she might never reach harbor at all.

One way was still open. Jerome Manning's premature return, combined with her expulsion from the Snyder home, had put an end to her own hopes of solving the murder—yet she might yet save the life of Arthur Snyder if she went at once to the police— to Tom Weston—and told him all she knew. After that, if something happened to her, or to Arthur Snyder, Tom would know where to look. It was even possible that through her sincerity and the completeness of the notes she had kept, she might be able to convince him without definite proof and could enlist his aid in obtaining the evidence she lacked.

At least, she resolved, my secret will not die with me! I will *not* behave like the stupid characters in my books who withhold vital evidence and lay themselves wide open to lethal attack.

Dora Weston was not at home when Abigail returned. The house was very quiet, and Abigail jumped when the grandfather clock on the stair landing struck three times as she passed. She tried to tell herself that it was absurd to feel on edge because

Jerome Manning was in town, but she could not shake off a sense of urgency. Stopping only long enough to get her notebook from the locked suitcase beneath her bed, she tiptoed through the silent hall and hurried back down the stairs.

At the front door she came to an abrupt stop. A car, which she recognized as Charlotte Manning's ancient green sedan, had drawn up before the house. Abigail saw Jerome Manning climb out and turn to speak to someone in the back seat. Certainly the coincidence of his presence could have nothing to do with her, but Abigail had no desire to run into him again.

Cautiously, she backed away from the door and, as heavy steps crossed the porch, she turned and fled through the kitchen, where the lunch dishes were still stacked unwashed, out the back door, and across the lawn. Not until she had put a tool shed, an alley, and a neighboring garage between herself and the house did her breath stop jerking. Feeling like a starched tablecloth after a torrential rain and knowing that her face was at least as bleached, she headed for town, making her way through alleys and side streets until she judged herself to be opposite the business section of Glen Falls.

She discovered the office of the police on the main street, wedged between a barber shop and the offices of the *Gazette*, and above the Railway Express. An arrow painted on the wall directed her up a flight of steep stairs; grasping the handrail firmly, Abigail followed it. But at the top, although she rapped loud and persistently upon the frosted glass, the door remained shut. Her zest for the chase had been considerably damped by an absurd case of jitters. She longed only to unload her responsibility onto other and more capable shoulders, yet not even a negligible minion of the Law appeared to relieve her.

Most inefficient, she fumed. What sort of protection is it that locks up and goes out to lunch while decent people are in danger of being set upon and murdered!

That it was already well past the lunch hour only increased her irritation. Still fuming, she stepped out onto the sidewalk again—and retreated in a flurry. Across the street stood Charlotte Manning's unmistakable green sedan!

The labored beating of Abigail's heart corroborated the swift vision of Jerome Manning, still in the driver's seat. For an instant their eyes met before Jerry's glance flicked away. Abigail discovered that she was shaking.

He *is* following me, she thought. Like a startled rabbit she sought cover as he opened the car door and stepped out onto the sidewalk in front of the Elite Café across the street from her.

From the *Gazette* offices next door came the clack of a typewriter and the laugh of normal people at their work. To Abigail, trapped at the foot of a dingy stairway leading upward to a locked door, those sounds meant safety. Only if she could duck out onto the sidewalk and into the *Gazette* office before Jerome Manning could cross the street might she postpone her fate. Surely, among people, in a busy newspaper office, she would be safe.

With thudding pulse she made the dash and attained the shelter. Not until the door slammed shut behind her and a girl looked up, startled, from her desk did Abigail consider how precipitate had been her entry. She paused to catch her breath and to glance behind her. The green sedan was empty. Jerry was nowhere in sight.

"I—I wonder if I might use your telephone," she gasped, as the girl smiled inquiringly.

The girl obligingly indicated the phone on her desk and offered Abigail her chair.

She's looking at me, Abigail thought, as though she expected me to ask for smelling salts or a shot of brandy. She did feel a little weak and accepted the chair gratefully. The girl hovered near, obviously expecting Abigail to put through some call of greatest urgency and, with her hand on the phone, Abigail wondered whom she could dial.

She took a deep breath.

"I wonder if you can tell me where I might find the chief of police," she said. "His office is locked and I must see him at once." The girl's concern turned to eager interest.

"Have you tried his home—or, wait a minute!"

She disappeared into an adjoining room. The noisy industry of the typewriter was halted. Almost at once the girl returned with two hundred pounds of tousle-headed editor-reporter and a couple of teen-age hangers-on.

"Anything I can do?" the man asked. His black eyes poked holes in her as he directed his gaze downward. He was a man to inspire confidence, Abigail decided, but there was only one in whom she wished to confide.

"I'm trying to find Officer Weston," she repeated.

"I saw him with the county sheriff this morning," one of the boys ventured.

The other contradicted him promptly.

"The sheriff left an hour ago and Tom wasn't with him," he stated. "I saw Greenough drive off when I took a break for a coke."

"You might try the Ee-light, across the street," the big man suggested. "It's sort of unofficial police headquarters. If Tom's not there come back and I'll call around. He could be at the fire station gabbing with the boys or over at the jail—he hauled in a drunk last night. Or perhaps Snyders would know. He gets out there a lot these days."

"Thank you," Abigail said, a little disturbed at the idea of crossing to the Elite Café alone. "Just across the street, did you say?"

She injected a note of uncertainty and helplessness into the question. At once the girl took her arm sympathetically and offered to escort her.

"Watch the phone for me, Jimmy," she directed one of the boys. "I'll just be a minute."

"A minute, two cups of coffee, and a cigarette!" Jimmy responded genially. "Okay, Sally, I'll watch it."

Mrs. Manning's car still stood at the curb. Abigail veered away as they passed, but no one took a shot at her from behind it. No one, in fact, appeared to be anywhere near. With Sally's hand firm on her arm she arrived without mishap at the door of the restaurant.

"There's Tom!" Sally observed.

As Abigail's eyes adjusted to the dim interior she saw the chief of police squatting atop a stool at the bar which, on closer inspection, proved to be more of a fly-specked counter. Tom looked, Abigail thought, less like a man seeking conviviality than one upon whose back rested the weight of the universe. His huge arms rested on either side of an innocuous cup of coffee, that was nested in a saucerful of cigarette butts. Abigail suspected that he had not lifted it for some time, if at all.

"Thank you so much!" she said, dismissing Sally, whose face fell. Tom Weston glanced up as Abigail struggled to mount the stool beside him. Recognition made way for enthusiasm.

"Why, Mrs. Potter!" he exclaimed. "How nice to see you! Here, why don't we move to a booth where you'll be more comfortable. I've been wishing I could talk to you!"

Abigail, taken aback by the warmth of his reception, agreed. Why, she asked herself, should Tom Weston be wanting to talk to me? Not but what it will make my job much easier!

She slipped off her coat and clutched her black notebook while Tom ordered two fresh coffees and squeezed himself into the seat across from her.

"Say!" he began then, "I got thinking yesterday after I got home—your name sounded familiar. Are you the Abigail Potter who writes those books—*End of a Perfect Debut* and *Smile for a Suicide*—all those?"

Abigail was forced to admit that she was.

"Swell!" Tom's broad hand slapped down upon the table and he leaned back as though a knotty problem had at last been solved. And now, Abigail thought ruefully, he'll ask for my autograph, and when I try to tell him what I know he'll discount everything as being merely the product of an author's imagination. Bother!

"I read all your books," Tom went on. "I think they're swell. I've never met a real author before—"

Here we go! Abigail thought. She murmured her thanks and waited for him to produce paper and pen.

"I suppose you work with the police a lot, to get your material? I mean, maybe you've actually helped solve some crimes?"

He paused and Abigail realized with incredulity that he was looking to her with a touching expectancy. It would have been too bad to let him down, so she smiled modestly.

Tom leaned across the table and lowered his voice.

"I don't know how much you've heard, Mrs. Potter, but I'm in a tough spot. A police officer in a small town doesn't come up against real crime very often—we're not trained for it. We have traffic violations, petty larceny, peeping Toms, a few cases of assault and battery—stuff like that—but never anything serious. And now there's this murder, and a national figure at that, right here in Glen Falls! Just between you and me, Mrs. Potter, it's too hot for me to handle!"

"But I thought the county—" Abigail began, but Tom Weston cut her off.

"The sheriff's worse, if anything. He's taken some course in police work and he's all full of procedure and methods—all that sort of business. But he doesn't know the first thing about people. Not about our people, at any rate. He turns up what looks like a motive, he finds a possible source of poison, and there you are! He's all ready to arrest a man that couldn't possibly be guilty of murder. Why, Arthur Snyder would no more kill—"

"He really suspects Arthur Snyder?"

"I'll say he does. Greenough's gone back to Dayton right this minute to swear out a warrant—and there's not a thing in the world I can do to stop him! After all, he *is* in charge!"

Abigail's hand rested on the cover of the black notebook. Tom Weston was asking her opinion! He was looking for an explanation that would save Arthur Snyder, and she was the one who could give it to him. But, with the opportunity before her, she hesitated.

All she had to offer was a strong suspicion, a suspicion without an ounce of tangible proof. If she should tell her story Tom would be in a position to go after the evidence to support or disprove it, but did she have the right to accuse Jerome Manning as long as there was any possibility that he was innocent? If she could only get into the Snyder home—find out for herself—

She looked at the chief of police speculatively. Here, if she could handle it right, was her entrée! Maida Snyder could not turn her away if she came accompanied by the Law.

"I think," she began, choosing her words with care, "that I might tell you how Harrison Hawkes was killed."

"*What!*" Tom's exclamation caused several glances to be turned in their direction. He hastily removed the hand he had stretched out to grip Abigail's. "What are you saying?" he demanded in a more discreet tone. "That you *know* who killed Hawkes? But how—"

"I do not *know*," Abigail corrected. "I *suspect*. But with your help I am sure I could find proof, one way or the other."

"But whom do you suspect? Tell me that—and if there's any proof, I'll find it! You don't mean—Arthur Snyder?"

Abigail shook her head, her lips pursed.

"No," she said, "not Arthur Snyder. But the proof lies in his house. There, and in the memory of the people who live there. I've been hoping to be sure before I said anything, but unfortunately Mrs. Snyder seems to have taken a dislike to me." Her voice reflected her sense of injustice. "My aunt was a very dear friend of Mrs. Snyder's mother, but I have been refused admittance even though I understand that Mrs. Demarest is eager to see me."

"Do you mean you've already been working on this case— that you really think you can break it!" Tom Weston's voice carried a mixture of incredulity and respect.

"That," admitted Abigail, "was my real reason for coming to Glen Falls."

Tom Weston banged the table again, triumphantly.

"And you won't tell me whom you suspect?" he persisted.

Abigail shook her head. This was her investigation, and with the renewed hope that she might follow it through by herself she had lost all desire to share the responsibility. The almost reverent admiration in Tom's eyes was a heady draught to one at whom no officer of the Law had ever before glanced twice, and Abigail was determined to justify that admiration.

She was not, however, foolhardy. The holster, so prominently slung about Tom Weston's hips, was reassuring, and Abigail had no intention of losing its protection.

"Perhaps," she suggested, "if I could go out to the Snyder's with you I could find the proof I need. A few questions—a little freedom to look around—"

Tom frowned thoughtfully.

"Maida wouldn't let you see her mother, you say? I wonder—"

Decisively, he pushed himself out of the booth.

"Well," he said, "let's go. I think I can get you in, all right—but I'd feel a lot better if I knew what you were looking for."

And so would I, Abigail echoed silently.

V

Seated in the police coupe beside Big Tom Weston and feeling secure in the solid heartiness of his presence, Abigail relaxed and drew a deep sigh. Her eyes sparkled and she felt no qualm when he stopped the car in front of the impressive residence from which, an hour earlier, she had been politely ejected. Charlotte Manning's sedan was not in evidence nor had Abigail seen it when she and Tom left the Elite Café, but Abigail was no longer concerned with Jerome Manning's whereabouts. At last she had gained the inside track.

Satisfaction moved her to generosity. She determined to allow her ally a small part, at least, in the investigations. Certainly it would be easier for Tom Weston to prowl through medicine chests and cupboards while she concentrated on obtaining the information she must have.

"I'm going on the assumption," she confided, "that Harrison Hawkes took poison in a medicinal capsule. While I talk to Mrs. Demarest, you might be rounding up all such pills and finding out all you can about where they are kept, who uses them, and how often. It would help, too, if we could establish that Mr. Hawkes did use someone else's medicine—and under what circumstances."

Tom slapped his great hand on the steering wheel.

"Now, why didn't I think of that!" he commented. "The only thing that's held Greenough up has been finding out where and how Hawkes got the poison. There wasn't a trace in anything he ate or drank. In fact, he didn't eat much dinner and nothing that everyone else didn't eat, too—and he only drank water. Fat chance of disguising cyanide in that! But medicine, especially a capsule! I think you've got something there!"

"If you do find pills that belong to someone in the Snyder house, pills that no one else was in the habit of taking—and that haven't been used up over a period of three years—then I believe I can tell you who killed Harrison Hawkes."

"You don't mean—Arthur?" Tom asked suspiciously.

"No, indeed. In fact, I'm certain the poison was actually intended for him!"

Tom froze, half in and half out of the car. "You mean, it being Hawkes that died was just an accident?"

Abigail nodded.

"But then—why, there wouldn't be any motive at all! Not for Hawkes' death, I mean!"

Taking her arm, he sailed her up the walk as though he were a gust of wind and Abigail an autumn leaf. Without waiting for an answer to his authoritative knock, he pushed open the door and pulled her in behind him.

"Arthur! Hey, Arthur," he called. "It's me—Tom!"

Abigail could see that already, in Tom Weston's mind, Arthur Snyder had been tried and found not guilty. Tom's raised voice boomed reassurance.

A dark young man with sharp features and a scowl answered the summons. He flung open a door to the right of the hall and confronted Abigail and her escort.

"Don't you think you've snooped around enough for one day, Tom?" he demanded. "Haven't you hounded us enough?"

"Don't be like that, Fred." Tom was obviously ill at ease and defensive. "I can't help it if it's my job. I know your dad didn't kill Hawkes. The only reason we're here now is because Mrs. Potter, here, thinks she can prove it!"

Fred's questioning gaze followed the motion of Tom's head toward Abigail and his belligerence thawed a bit.

"A way to prove— Well, say, that's different! Come on in!"

He smiled disarmingly and laid a hand on Tom's arm.

"Sorry I yelled at you, but we're getting pretty fed up. It's been a hell of a note, just because old Hawkes decided to pull a suicide in our house and you guys plunked for murder. I'm glad you've come around to my way of seeing it! Poor Dad's been about on the rocks!" He still eyed Abigail speculatively. Tom remembered to make the introductions.

"Mrs. Potter, I guess you haven't met Fred Snyder, Arthur's son. This is *Abigail* Potter, Fred, who writes—"

Abigail caught Tom's eye and shook her head slightly. Tom tried to cover his break with a cough and lamely patched up the introduction.

"Mrs. Potter's aunt was a close friend of Mrs. Demarest's, and Mrs. Potter would like to pay her respects. If it's all right, you might just take her up while I have a word with Arthur."

"Dad's not here, and neither is Maida. I don't know when they'll be back, but if there's anything I can do—"

"I just want to look around a bit. With an eye to proving your dad's innocence, if that makes any difference!"

Fred hesitated.

"It makes all the difference, of course—but, I don't know. I'll be glad to show you anything I can."

He led the way up the stairs, his long legs finding it more convenient to take the steps two at a time. Tom held Abigail's arm solicitously. It's a wonder, Abigail fussed to herself, that I ever manage to get around at all, living alone as I do with no one to grab me every time I move!

The house, she observed, was even larger than it had appeared from her previous glimpse. The doors on each side of the entrance hall were closed, and Abigail was unable to form any impression of the lower rooms, but at the top of the wide staircase the house branched out into a broad hallway that stretched away in both directions with doors on either side.

"At least eight rooms upstairs," Abigail estimated, following Fred to the left. "Maybe more."

Fred knocked on a door at the far end of the hall and received, after a moment, permission to enter. As he threw open the door light rushed into the hallway, light from the setting sun, which shone through the floor-length windows across the end of Eloise Demarest's room. The late sun's rays were deepened and turned more ruddy by reflection from the walls and woodwork, which were papered and painted in shades of glowing pink and deeper rose, set off by rich velvet drapes of cedar hue, which framed each bank of windows and were looped across the top. It was a room of startling, almost saccharine pinkness. Even the telephone beside the bed was camouflaged as a pink-skirted lady.

In the middle of the pinkness, her impeccable gray coiffure propped against a mound of pink cushions, her body enfolded in an old-rose dressing gown, lay Eloise Demarest.

"Someone to see you, Eloise!" Fred announced. "Mrs. Potter—says you knew her aunt."

His tone in addressing his grandmother-by-marriage was brusque. Abigail sensed an unspoken antagonism. He's handsome enough, she concluded, but too arrogant, too sure of himself. Too bad he didn't inherit some of his father's manners.

Mrs. Demarest extended one thin hand warmly, ignoring Fred.

"Do come in, Mrs. Potter! I'm so glad you could come back! I was terribly disappointed that you couldn't stay this afternoon so I could thank you for the brooch. So sweet of your dear aunt to remember me, though I can't imagine why she should! I was just a girl when she sewed for us. I scarcely remember her, I must admit—except that of course she was an excellent seamstress. I've never found anyone else nearly so good! I must ask Maida to show you my wedding gown. Exquisite workmanship! One of the last things she did for me."

Abruptly she broke off and her tone became irritable as she addressed Fred.

"Are you going to stand there all day? I don't suppose you could fix a cup of tea for Mrs. Potter?" She turned back to Abigail. "So inconsiderate of Maida and Arthur to go off like this when they know I'm not well. I suppose I shall have to depend on Fred to open a can of soup for my supper, and likely as not he'll let it boil! Tell Maida I want to see her, Fred, the moment she comes in!"

Without a word, Fred went out and shut the door.

"Insolent puppy! He was courting Maida himself before she married Arthur," Eloise remarked parenthetically. She patted the arm of a boudoir chair covered with large pink roses that stood beside her bed. "Now, tell me all about yourself! I'm positively hungry for companionship, shut away up here. Maida tells me you write mystery stories. So exciting! Do you know, I think she believes you brought me the brooch just so you could get into the house—because of the murder, you know! Lots of people do—scandalmongers and sensation seekers. Maida doesn't let me see anyone, not even my dearest friends."

"Perhaps she's afraid they'll tire you," Abigail suggested lamely, "knowing you are ill."

Eloise Demarest raised a limp hand and let it fall upon her breast.

"I am always ill," she said wearily. "My heart, you know. But Maida knows I love company. It's the only pleasure that is left to me. No, she's afraid of what I'll say. I know too much! But of course," she amended hastily, "I've already told the police everything. 'What could I do?' I asked her. 'I couldn't very well refuse to answer when they asked!'"

"The whole affair must have been very distressing," Abigail prompted.

Eloise's voice became less complaining and the listless eyes showed a trace of animation. She obviously relished the prospect of elaborating on a topic that Maida's zealous guardianship had given her no chance to discuss.

"It was too awful," she said. "A moment before he had been talking to us, quite pleasantly really, and then suddenly he clutched his stomach and his eyes got glazed. He just said something about 'terrible pain'—Arthur and Fred both started to help him out of the room and then he just sort of jerked and fell. I couldn't bear to look, but I can still hear the thud as he hit the floor"—Eloise's eyes shone with ghoulish pleasure—"and then everything was very quiet. When I opened my eyes just a little bit, he was dead. He was quite, quite dead!"

She shook her head with solemn relish.

"How terrible!" Abigail breathed, sincerely. Eloise's enthusiastic word picture had made something inside of her shrivel to a small point of horror. It might have been Arthur Snyder, she thought, that nice man! I wonder if Mrs. Demarest would be equally unmoved if it had been? I wonder how she really feels about her son-in-law?

"I understand the police are suspecting Mr. Snyder," she ventured, and Eloise was off again.

"So stupid of them," she agreed, but Abigail was sure she was not deeply disturbed. Was it because she did not believe that Arthur would actually be tried for the crime—or because she did not care? "Of course, it does look bad—Arthur's quarrel with Mr. Hawkes, and his having cyanide and all—but then, not even a baby could really suspect Arthur of committing murder. Why, he won't even set a trap for mice!"

There it was again, the apparently universal faith in Arthur Snyder's humane and moral instincts. If I were writing this story, Abigail reflected, Arthur Snyder would certainly be the gentleman to watch. At the moment, however, she was more interested in Eloise Demarest's startling disclosures.

"Do you mean that Mr. Snyder had access to cyanide?" she repeated incredulously.

"Oh, yes!" Eloise explained readily. "At the foundry, of course—something to do with hardening steel. I can't understand why they don't use something safer. Maida and I were both shocked when Arthur showed us through, but Fred and Arthur both work with it all the time. But of course, as I told Sheriff Greenough, that doesn't mean Arthur would bring any home. I'm sure I'd never have slept a wink if I'd ever had the least idea—"

"You say Mr. Snyder and Mr. Hawkes had a quarrel?" Abigail was beginning to see why the police might be excused for regarding Arthur with suspicion. "When? What was it about?"

Eloise regarded Abigail with delight.

"Do you know, I believe Maida was right after all! Are you *really* going to write a book about us—and all this? I can't see why Maida should be so upset, even if you are. I shouldn't mind at all myself—"

She went back to her story without waiting for Abigail's vehement denial.

"It was before dinner that night," she reported. "Mr. Hawkes and Arthur were in the little study, just off Arthur's bedroom. They were talking so hard they didn't hear the gong go, so I just went to the door to tell them. And then, of course, when the police asked me I had to repeat what I'd heard—although I knew it didn't really mean a thing—just a manner of speaking, you know. Maida was furious with me, but really, there was nothing else I *could* do, don't you agree?"

She looked anxiously to Abigail and Abigail bobbed her head. Interpreting the gesture as agreement, Eloise continued.

"I didn't really hear what the quarrel was about, you understand, except that Arthur said, very loudly, 'I've had enough of your blackmail, and I'm through, do you understand? Spread your dirty tales if you want, but it won't do you any good! The business is in my name and I shall do with it as I see fit!'

"And then Mr. Hawkes said something, very low so that I couldn't hear"—and I'll bet she tried, thought Abigail—"and then Arthur said, 'Go to my wife if you wish. I've already told her all about it and we're quite prepared to face the music together! No, Hawkes, you're licked!'

"And then Mr. Hawkes said something about 'spread over every front page by tomorrow,' and that's when Arthur threatened him. He said—and I never heard his voice so terrible—he said, 'Blackmail is a nasty business, Hawkes. I'd advise you to drop it while you can. A good many blackmailers end up—dead!' I heard Arthur coming to the door then, so I knocked and told them the gong had rung, and Arthur and I went down together."

"And Mr. Hawkes?" Abigail prompted.

"He came down a few minutes afterward. Dinner was terribly late and it was too bad, for Mrs. Hedges had a mushroom soufflé and of course it was completely ruined. It wasn't a pleasant meal at all. Arthur looked like a thundercloud and Mr. Hawkes complained of a headache and hardly ate anything. Maida tried her best to keep the conversation going, poor dear, but it was all a dismal failure.

"I'm sure I wasn't much help, what with wondering what Mr. Hawkes had to blackmail Arthur about and whether it would all come out in the papers the way he said and what it would do to us if it did. It must have been something terrible—and if Maida knew about it I do think she might have discussed it with me, for after all this is my home and how we should be able to keep it if Arthur should get sent away, I don't know. I always thought he was such a fine man—and very well-to-do, of course, which is why I encouraged Maida to marry him. Fred hasn't a bean of his own, and of course that schoolgirl crush on Jerry Manning was most impractical when he was overseas and might not even come back and his father's business losing money hand over fist until it didn't look as though he'd be able to support Maida even if he did come back."

"It doesn't sound like a pleasant meal," Abigail agreed, herding Eloise back to the subject.

"Indeed it wasn't. Fred didn't even come down until we were almost through, though he'd been in his room the whole time and must have heard the gong, and he raised a terrible row because all the food was gone. And on top of everything else, Mrs. Hedges refused to stay late. Help is so independent these days— simply impossible! And such wages as they ask! Mrs. Hedges was the only one Maida could find to help out while Mr. Hawkes was visiting. 'Seventy thirty I'm supposed to be through,' she said, 'and seven thirty I leave.' And off she went. Maida and I had to clear the table and wash up."

"Was it after that that Mr. Hawkes died?"

"We were all back in the living room," Eloise admitted. "Fred was mixing drinks and Mr. Hawkes came in and said he'd just like a glass of water. It was right after he drank it—or not long— But of course they tested the water and the glass and there was nothing there."

"Do you think he could have taken something for his head-ache—perhaps used the water to wash it down?" Abigail suggested, excitement mounting.

"He might have. He asked me, as we were leaving the table, if I had anything, but of course my sedative wouldn't have done him any good, being very mild, you know, on account of my heart. I told him to ask Maida. She never takes anything herself, but she might have given him something from the downstairs medicine chest. Fred usually keeps something there—for hang-overs, you know."

Abigail thought it scarcely likely that Mr. Hawkes would have accepted medicinal relief from Arthur, if Arthur had indeed made the threats Eloise had quoted, but the question had to be asked.

"You don't think Mr. Snyder might have given him some-thing? Doesn't he have any special sedative of his own?"

"Arthur? Oh, yes! He suffers terribly from migraine. He has a special prescription and he's always most particular to keep it filled. But I'm sure he wouldn't have offered it to Mr. Hawkes. Arthur has a perfect fit at the thought of anyone else getting hold of it—even keeps it locked up in the safe in his room— You'd think it was poison, he's so peculiar about it.

"I remember once he sent Maida to get his prescription filled and she mislaid the box. I've never seen him so angry, and wor-ried, too. Accused Maida of 'criminal negligence' and all sorts of terrible things! And then, that very evening, Maida remembered where she must have left it—in Jerome Manning's car when he brought her home from downtown. It was while he was home on furlough a few years ago—and she went over to the Mannings and looked and sure enough, there it was slipped down behind the front seat—and all that to-do over nothing at all! At least, Arthur had the grace to be ashamed of himself for the scene he'd made!"

Behind the seat in Jerry Manning's car! The casual words echoed in Abigail's mind. Means, motive, and now, opportunity!

It only remained for Arthur to admit that, on the evening of Harrison Hawkes' death he had given him a capsule to relieve his headache, and the last piece of the puzzle would fall into place. Abigail could understand why Arthur had not already volunteered the information that would have been the final damning link in the chain of evidence against him.

Does Arthur suspect, Abigail wondered, that the medicine he gave Hawkes was the cause of his death, or does he simply realize that to admit that he had given his guest a capsule to which he alone had access would have been to sign his own death warrant? Who would have believed his only possible defense; that the capsule, if indeed it had contained poison, must have been meant for him? Coming on top of the overheard quarrel, the circumstantial evidence against him would have been overwhelming.

"I'm sure the question of a sedative never came up in the police questioning, and until you mentioned it I'd quite forgotten that Mr. Hawkes asked me. You don't think, do you—I mean, I suppose Arthur *could* have—oh, dear, I suppose I *ought* to tell the police!"

Eloise sounded disturbed and doubtful, but Abigail got the impression that she would be glad to throw out the suggestion that would draw the noose more tightly about her son-in-law's neck. Abigail drew away with barely concealed distaste.

"I don't think I'd say anything to the police," she advised. "After all, you don't *know* that Arthur gave Mr. Hawkes anything. It might have been Fred—" and then, as she saw a calculating gleam in Eloise's eye she added hastily, "or your own daughter. As you said yourself, either Maida or Fred might have given him something from the downstairs medicine chest. If the police began to ask questions along that line and found that it was Mrs. Snyder who had prescribed for his headache—well, it might look very bad for your daughter!"

The fright in Eloise's face told Abigail that the warning had struck home. Abigail stood up abruptly.

"As a matter of fact," she said, hoping to give Eloise something to think about, "in spite of the quarrel you heard, I not only know that your son-in-law did not kill Mr. Hawkes, but I know who did—and I intend to prove it! I strongly advise you not to spread your accusations any further."

Eloise gasped and turned pale. As Abigail started toward the door she became piteous.

"Oh, please don't go! It's been so pleasant talking to you. It would never occur to Fred to keep me company or even to ask if I wanted anything. Maida might as well have left me completely alone in the house, sick as I am. It was most inconsiderate—"

Abigail cut short her complaints with scant patience.

"I really must go. I'm sure your daughter will be back before long."

"But you will come again soon, won't you? Promise!" Eloise let a limply pleading hand trail over the edge of the pink coverlet. "And—I do think it's wonderful that you're going to help Arthur! It would be so terrible for all of us if he were sent to jail! You must tell me everything you find out! You have no idea how lonely I get. You will come again soon, won't you?"

"I will if I can," Abigail said, with mental reservations, "but I don't expect to be in Glen Falls much longer."

That, at least, was true. As soon as she found Tom Weston and told him how to solve his crime her business would be completed. After Eloise Demarest's significant revelations it was impossible to believe any longer in Jerome Manning's innocence.

He was such a pleasant boy, she lamented. Oh, dear! I never realized that criminals could be so nice!

In the face of the circumstantial evidence against Arthur Snyder she could not allow sympathy to seal her lips, but she determined that never again would she long to play the heartbreaking role of detective.

There was no one in the upper hall and the house was silent. Abigail knew that the only decent thing to do was to go downstairs at once to find Fred Snyder, but the sight of so many closed doors piqued her curiosity. Perhaps, she persuaded herself, behind one of these doors Tom Weston is conducting a search for the capsules, unaware that they are locked in a safe in Arthur's room.

On an impulse, she tapped at the nearest door. There was no answer.

Abigail Farringdon Potter, she chided. You're behaving outrageously!

Nevertheless, she turned the knob and peeked in.

The rosy glow of a spacious bathroom met her eyes. The walls were a pale pink; the shag rug on the floor and the towels above the tub were of a deeper rose; even the bathroom fixtures were pink. Abigail, noting that one door led to the room she had just left, backed out hastily.

Pink! she snorted. No imagination!

The door on the other side of the bath revealed an obviously unlived-in bedroom. A night stand by the bed held an ash tray, a cloisonné cigarette box, and two novels such as a hostess might leave at the bedside of a guest whose tastes she could not hope to guess. The tops of dresser and vanity were bare, as were the drawers and the closet.

Completing her survey, Abigail withdrew, convinced that this was a guest room—perhaps the very one where Harrison Hawkes had slept. If he had, however, all traces of his presence had been removed. There was nothing for her here.

I wonder, she thought, if Mr. Hawkes appreciated the rose-colored bathroom he shared with his hostess's mother?

Between the guest room and the stairs Abigail, after first knocking timidly, found only a small sewing room, which offered nothing. At the head of the stairs she hesitated, and then crossed to the door that adjoined Eloise Demarest's on the south. The master bedroom, she reasoned, was likely to be one with a southern exposure. In addition, Abigail felt that her presence in the hall on the far side of the stairway would be difficult to explain, whereas if she were merely on her way from Mrs. Demarest's room to the stairs, Fred would not think it odd if he came upon her suddenly.

That he might think it more than odd when she walked into his room, she did not stop to consider. Fortunately, he was not there to protest.

The room was in the chaotic condition that some men can achieve with no apparent effort. A tennis racket had been flung on the unmade bed, canvas shoes and heavy wool socks sprawled beneath it, and gym shorts and a number of ties had been dropped in confusion on a chair. Copies of *Life* and *Esquire* lay about the room, but nowhere did Abigail see either books or a bookcase. In addition to being unmannerly, Fred Snyder's taste offered little to appeal to Abigail. She was glad to withdraw and carry her search elsewhere.

Next to Fred's room she found the study, probably, she decided, the one to which Eloise Demarest had referred. The book-lined room was not connected with Fred's, but on the opposite wall a door stood open into an enormous bedroom: the master bedroom, without a doubt.

Abigail stepped into the study, her pulses quickening. Surely, either in this room or in the bedroom beyond she would find the safe, which perhaps still held the bottle of pills, harmless now but evidence nonetheless.

Hurriedly, Abigail looked behind the framed pictures of pastoral scenes in the study and then in back of the full-length mirror and the family photographs that lined one wall in the bedroom. Disappointed, she directed her attention next to the woodwork, which was severe and unornamented, offering little hope of a secret panel. Finally, but without much hope, she searched the dressing room and bath which connected the large southeast bedroom with a smaller, more feminine room at the northeast corner. The Snyders' private suite, Abigail noted, was ideally arranged. From the moment one stepped into the study it was possible to pass from one room to another in complete privacy.

Does Maida, Abigail wondered, sleep in her own room? Or is it merely an attractive upstairs sitting room as it appears to be? In any case, she reminded herself angrily, it's none of your business, Miss Gimlet Nose!

It seemed unlikely that Arthur's safe would be concealed in rooms that were patently Maida's, so Abigail retraced her steps. In the study she paused, frozen. The Snyder suite, although arranged for visual privacy, was apparently far from soundproof. Through the wall that separated the study from Fred's room, Abigail could hear Fred's voice and sounds of movement. Then anything she did could have been heard equally well by Fred!

Suddenly acutely aware of what she had been doing, how impossible it would be to explain her actions, Abigail began a slow but frantic retreat toward the hall door. Just as she had attained the safety of the corridor, the door of Fred's room opened. Abigail drew back barely in time to avoid being run over by Tom Weston.

"Oh, there you are!" he boomed without tact. "I wondered where you'd gotten to! What did you find out?" His voice dropped to a conspiratorial whisper on the question as Abigail's frantically flapping hand shushed his enthusiasm.

"The pills we need are in Arthur Snyder's safe," she whispered. "One of them contained poison, but you'll probably find the rest quite harmless. You get Arthur to admit that he gave one of his sedative capsules to Harrison Hawkes the night he died— and I'll give you your murderer."

Tom's jovial face became grave.

"You mean, it was Arthur after all?"

"Tom!" Fred's voice hailed them from his own room behind them. "I hope you're about through with your snooping! The folks are just turning in the drive."

Oh, dear, Abigail thought, realizing that it was too late to avoid Maida. She wondered what charges could be brought against a policeman who conducted a search without warrant— and what would be done to an old lady who paid a call against express orders.

With an effort to make the best of it, she placed her hand on Tom's arm and drew him toward the stairs, stepping out firmly with her head erect à la grande dame.

"How about those pills?" Tom insisted, holding back.

"They're just pills—now. I'll explain later, when I can, but for the present don't say anything to the rest. And *please* don't say I'm helping you—"

She broke off as the front door opened. Maida came in first. Behind her came Arthur—and Jerome Manning. Jerry was looking directly at her and this time there was recognition in his face.

"Well, Mrs. Potter!" He greeted her heartily. "So we meet again!"

VI

Abigail was grateful for the support of Tom's arm as she negotiated the last few steps to the lower hall. Jerry's greeting had set her to quaking like a blanc mange until it seemed impossible that Tom, at least, could remain unaware of it.

Why had Jerry chosen to admit their previous acquaintance? Even if his words hid a threat, he undermined his own security by admitting that he recognized her. She had only to smile, to say, "Why, Mr. Rascinski—fancy meeting you again!" to expose his deceit and involve them both in explanations that could only be damning to Jerry.

She had, in fact, opened her mouth to speak before she was struck by a second and startling possibility. What if Jerry's apparently stupid greeting had been a clever ruse to determine what she knew, how much she had remembered? She *had* encountered Jerry earlier that day, if unofficially, outside the Snyder's house. For her to connect him at once with the soldier she had met so briefly three years before could be a fatal mistake.

Abigail closed her mouth again and forced her face to remain a polite blank. Only her fingers betrayed nervousness as she twisted the loop of chain that pinned her glasses to her breast.

Are you a coward, Abigail Potter? she demanded scornfully of herself. In some remote corner of her brain a small and unflattering subconscious replied, *yes!*

Tom Weston hurled himself upon Jerry, pounding his back and pumping his hand in exuberant welcome. Maida's only acknowledgment of Abigail's presence had been a glance of frustrated exasperation, after which she had apparently determined to ignore her.

It was Arthur Snyder who drew Abigail into their midst.

"Did you say you and Mrs. Potter have already met?" he asked Jerry.

"Not really," Abigail interposed hastily. "We—ran into each other a while ago, outside the house."

She was watching Jerry's face and was sure she could read relief, a kind of softening of the jaw line, as his firm hand enveloped hers, but he did not let the subject drop.

"Are you sure we haven't met before?" he persisted. "Several years ago?"

Abigail shook her head.

"If so, I'm afraid you'll have to refresh my memory. I'm usually fairly reliable about names, but I don't recall yours—and faces always elude me."

She waited tensely to see whether he would accept the challenge and elaborate. He did not.

"Put me down as just another of your fans," he said lightly. "As a celebrity you must be besieged by admirers. It was conceited of me to suppose that you'd remember one."

So that's how it's to be, Abigail reflected. She was immensely pleased with her own performance. If Jerry were convinced that she had no memory of their previous meeting, he was not likely to regard her as a menace. For the first time since she had become convinced of his guilt she felt secure, secure in the very presence of the enemy.

"Take off your coat," Arthur urged, dropping his own on a chair by the door and reaching to help Jerry.

Jerry shook his head. "If you don't mind, I'll go right over and tell Mother that everything's settled. She'll be waiting."

"Why don't you bring her back with you?" Maida asked, speaking for the first time. "We'll have a drink to celebrate—just the four of us."

Her invitation pointedly excluded Tom and Abigail. Abigail was perfectly aware that she was expected to leave, but she could be remarkably obtuse upon occasion.

There was an uncomfortable silence, broken reluctantly by Arthur.

"Are you sure you won't stay and join us in a highball, Mrs. Potter? Tom?" he asked.

"Thank you," Abigail replied. "That would be very pleasant."

She could not miss the look of baffled fury that Maida directed at her husband, the slight, puzzled movement of Arthur Snyder's left eyebrow, but she was impervious. Jerry Manning would be back shortly and until she had found an opportunity to warn Arthur it was her duty to guard him.

"Well, let's go in and sit down," Maida suggested, making the most of a difficult situation. "Jerry and Aunt Charlotte should be along soon."

She led Abigail into the living room and motioned her to a comfortable chair. To her dismay, Abigail realized that Tom had detained Arthur in the hall and she would have to face Maida alone.

"I suppose you talked to my mother," Maida observed with resignation.

Abigail nodded unhappily. Now that she had talked with Eloise she was better able to sympathize with this poor harassed girl, loyally trying to protect her husband, bewildered by the evidence that was piling up against him. Maida could hardly be blamed for wanting to keep her mother's damning story from being spread abroad—and Abigail was forced to admit that her own conduct had been anything but endearing.

"I want to apologize—" she began, but Maida spoke simultaneously.

"I'm afraid I've been very rude, Mrs. Potter," she said, her words coming in a rush. "I don't know whether you're a reporter—"

"Oh, no!"

Maida looked relieved, if not entirely convinced.

"Well, I wasn't sure," she said. "Mrs. Manning told me that you're a writer—of detective fiction—and then, after Mother had said she scarcely remembered your aunt, well, your story of the brooch seemed rather—"

"I admit I exaggerated Aunt Harriet's acquaintance with your mother," Abigail felt bound to confess, "but I assure you it wasn't out of idle curiosity. I wanted to see Mrs. Demarest, to find out—"

"I hope you'll discount anything Mother had to say about—about Mr. Hawkes' death," Maida hurried on. "Since you've talked with her I may as well be frank. You see, Mother isn't well. Excitement is apt to get her confused and she—she imagines things."

"Mrs. Snyder," Abigail interrupted gently, "please don't be afraid of me. I'm glad your mother helped me to understand the strength of the case against your husband, because—"

"So she did talk about it!" Maida reached out desperately across the small end table between them and her fingers dug into Abigail's wrist.

"You mustn't believe a thing Mother says against Arthur," she repeated urgently. "She doesn't realize—"

She broke off as Arthur Snyder himself came in with Tom. "How about those drinks, Arthur?" she asked, too brightly, getting up and moving away from Abigail.

Abigail kept a dubious eye on Arthur's activities as he rolled out a portable bar and began to set out an array of bottles. Tom promptly took the chair Maida had vacated and leaned across the little table to speak to Abigail in an undertone.

"Where's Fred?" he demanded, first.

Abigail shook her head.

"I don't think Maida and Arthur like the idea of my being here," Tom went on. "Can't we let them know what we're doing?"

"I'd rather not," Abigail cautioned, "until I can explain everything to you. Just watch out for Arthur, whatever happens!"

"I asked him about the pills—" Tom began before her warning had sunk in. He stopped and stared at her indignantly. "'Watch out for Arthur!'" he repeated. "But you said—"

"What will you have, Mrs. Potter?" Arthur interrupted. "A highball? Brandy? A liqueur?"

Abigail had essayed a highball once at a publisher's tea and had found it not to her taste and, which was more to the point, disturbing in its effects. But brandy, she recalled, was often given to elderly people and sick animals.

"Oh, brandy, thank you!" she answered gratefully.

"How about you, Tom?"

"I'll have the same."

Maida's voice, bitter and reproachful, cut across the width of the room.

"I thought it was against regulations for a policeman to take a drink while on duty!"

Tom reddened and studied the toes of his highly polished boots.

"I'm not here officially, Maida," he protested. "Gosh darn it— You ought to know I'm on your team! I know Arthur's not guilty!"

"I'd be more inclined to believe you if you'd waited until we got home before you began to snoop."

"It's my fault!" Fred interrupted her from the doorway. "Tom explained why he was here, Dad, and I told him to go ahead. He's trying to clear you!"

Maida turned to vent her exasperation on Fred.

"So I suppose you let him prowl around to his heart's content!"

Fred continued to address his father.

"I stayed right with him, Dad, until I saw you come. I knew you had nothing to hide."

Arthur Snyder's head lifted and the small furrows between his eyes smoothed out.

"That's right, son!" he said. "I'm sorry, Tom, if we've been rude. I should have known—"

"What's everybody drinking?" Fred asked. "You relax, Dad. I'll look after the bar."

"Why should I watch Arthur, if he's innocent?" Tom demanded, leaning close to Abigail once more. He had obviously been brooding over her warning.

"He's in danger!" Abigail whispered fiercely.

She noticed with satisfaction that her explanation took immediate effect. Tom turned his head to stare at Arthur with an intensity and concentration that excluded everyone else in the room.

Fred, setting out glasses and opening bottles, spoke without turning.

"You'd better go up and unruffle your mother, Maida. She's been sulking ever since you went out."

With a murmured excuse, Maida went upstairs.

"Brandy for Mrs. Potter," Arthur observed. "I'll get some ice for our highballs."

The moment Arthur started out of the room, Tom rose and followed as though attached to his ward by an invisible string. Abigail reached out a hand to detain him and then decided against trying to explain *sotto voce* that Arthur was in no danger until Jerry returned. In any event, as long as Tom was guarding Arthur so conscientiously, she would be free to keep an eye on Jerry from the moment he came in. Between them, and for this afternoon at least, Arthur Snyder would be safe.

Fred brought Abigail her drink in a small tulip-shaped goblet. As she grasped the fragile stem of the glass and eyed the contents, he looked doubtful.

"Shall I get you some water?" he suggested.

"Oh, no thank you!" Abigail assured him. "I'm not thirsty."

She thought Fred look startled. As Arthur, still trailed by Tom, returned with a bucket of ice cubes, Fred returned to the bar and made some low-voiced comment. Both men glanced slightly in her direction, Abigail noticed, and Arthur chuckled. Abigail set her glass firmly in the exact center of the small table beside her chair.

Tom, carrying his own similar glass of brandy, lowered himself once more into the chair beside Abigail and in a moment Arthur came over, holding a highball glass filled with ice and an amber liquid.

"I'm afraid we've seemed rather inhospitable," he apologized to Abigail, with a slight trace of embarrassment. "Things have been rather—well—"

"I understand," Abigail said. "But I'm sure everything's going to be all right. Chief Weston is really trying—"

"I'm sure he is." Arthur smiled briefly at Tom. He stared moodily into the depths of his glass, swirling it so that the ice tinkled gently. "But I'm damned if I see— Pardon me!"

He passed a hand across his forehead in a tired gesture.

Abigail, watching his strained, sensitive face, felt a deep pity for him, pity that overcame her reluctance to betray Jerome Manning. Arthur was so obviously bewildered and helpless in the mesh of circumstantial evidence that was closing about him that she longed to give him more concrete encouragement. Did she dare, she wondered, tell him her theory, ask him directly about the pills—or was that better left for Tom?

Before she could decide, she heard voices on the stairs: Eloise's querulous tones above Maida's anxious ones.

"—perfectly able to come down! Just let me hold your arm. Bored to extinction up there. If there's going to be a celebration—"

"But, Mother, your heart!"

"A lot you care about my heart, going of all afternoon and leaving me alone. If it hadn't been for that nice Mrs. Potter—"

They appeared in the doorway, Maida supporting an apparently half-fainting Eloise on one arm and a fuzzy pink-striped afghan on the other. Arthur and Tom both sprang to help her get settled on the couch. Only Fred remained aloof, a smile of skeptical amusement on his thin lips.

"So, you've decided to come out of your ivory tower!" he observed.

"I have no intention of being isolated as though I had cholera, if that's what you mean," Eloise retorted. She patted ineffectually at the cushion Tom had shoved behind her back and then appealed to Maida.

"I do wish you'd thought to bring my own little pillow. This thing is such a lump!"

"I'll get it," Arthur volunteered.

Fred laid a detaining hand on his arm.

"You stay where you are, Dad. I'm young and healthy."

Abigail heard him taking the stairs two at a time, but the scornful glance he had directed at Maida's mother before he left made Abigail sure that his willingness was to spare his father rather than out of love for Eloise.

What a strange relationship, she thought, finding Fred's devotion to his mild father strangely out of keeping with his barely disguised hostility toward the rest of the household. He obviously doesn't approve of his father's wife and mother-in-law, she thought. I wonder why he lives with them?

Arthur provided Maida with a highball and the gathering lapsed into an awkward silence as the celebration in honor of Jerome Manning awaited his return. Tom's big hand pushed the base of his glass in slow circles on the table beside him; Arthur abstractedly tipped his drink back and forth so that the tiny clinking of the ice cubes alone broke the stillness.

A tapping at the window at her back made Abigail jump. Maida hurried to the French doors to admit Charlotte and Jerry Manning. As Arthur went over to greet them Tom, like a faithful watchdog, stood up and followed at his heels.

"I'm so glad you came over!" Maida said, drawing Charlotte into the room. "We thought we ought to celebrate because Jerry's back—and everything is settled."

Abigail watched, puzzled, as the unemotional Charlotte Manning put an arm around Maida and grasped Arthur Snyder's hand. (But I thought she hated him!)

"I can't thank you enough, both of you," Charlotte said, looking at Arthur.

Arthur cleared his throat.

"Well, well!" he said gruffly. "Thanks enough to see Jerry, here, home again and looking so fit. He certainly doesn't look like a man who was at death's door not so many years back! Come on in, Jerry!"

Eloise, her strength apparently regained, rose from the couch and went over to the bar.

"I think," she said, demanding their attention, "that I will have a small brandy—just this once—for my heart. And because," and she smiled piteously at Charlotte, "even in the midst of our trouble, we are all so happy to have dear Jerry home!" She waved toward Abigail. "Oh, Charlotte, dear, do you know Mrs. Potter? She's helping the police to solve our crime!"

Dismayed, Abigail looked to Jerome Manning and saw his eyes resting on her with an expression at once startled and, to Abigail, terrifying. She averted her own eyes quickly, feeling as defenseless as a small animal whose covering bush has been lifted unexpectedly away.

Tom's glass, she noticed, had been left dangerously near the edge of the table. In an attempt to hide her confusion, Abigail reached out and drew it back to safety. Eloise was advancing toward her on her way back to the couch, carefully balancing her drink. Will she elaborate her statement, Abigail wondered. She breathed a silent prayer and felt a tremendous relief when Fred changed the subject with his entrance.

"Well, Eloise! It didn't take you long to regain your strength! That doesn't look like blackberry wine to me!"

With a gesture of disgust he dumped an armload of pink pillows on the couch.

Eloise chose this moment to weave slightly and clutch at her breast. Then, steadying herself for a moment against the small table between Tom's chair and Abigail's, she lifted her head with dramatic determination and took a few hesitant steps.

"Let me help you!" Tom said, springing to her aid.

Instantly, Eloise was the center of as much attention as even she could have desired. Abigail met Fred's eye and was at first indignant and then amused to see that he was grinning, a wry, infectious grin that compelled her to smile back. Eloise Demarest's dramatic play had been incredibly like that of a spoiled child who has been denied the center of the stage.

Abigail watched Tom help the invalid to lie down again, saw Maida tuck the afghan around her mother's legs. Jerry, leaning over the back of the couch, chided Eloise affectionately and even Charlotte Manning hovered near.

Fred waited with obvious impatience until Charlotte had arranged the pillows at Eloise's back and the others had resumed their seats. Then, putting an end to Eloise's scene, he raised his glass.

"What are we waiting for!" he demanded. "We're gathered together to celebrate Jerry's return to the bosom of his family. Let's drink up before the whole thing, liquor included, goes stale!"

He drained his glass. Abigail, reaching for her own, discovered that the only glass on the table was the one she had just

moved back from the edge. Hers, which had been standing far-
ther back, was already empty in Tom's hand.

"Oh, well, brandy is brandy!" she thought. She took a small
taste and then choked as though she had swallowed liquid fire.
Tears came to her eyes.

Ugh! she thought, why do people drink liquor in any form!
She would have to hope that a sip or two would preserve the
amenities. No one was looking at her anyway. No one, that is,
except Jerome Manning, she corrected herself with a recurrence
of her gnawing unease.

At her side Tom Weston made a sound. Abigail turned to him
and then froze. His eyes were wide and startled, his big hand
clutched at his throat. The noises he was making were half stran-
gled, horrible in their physical distress. The empty glass fell from
his hand, his mouth contorted in a silent fight for breath, and his
hands clawed at the arms of his chair.

Abigail screamed, a small thin scream that was lost in the
sudden confusion as Tom Weston collapsed, sickeningly still.

In a stride Jerry was at his side. White and shaken, Arthur
followed and together they bent over Tom as Jerry listened for
his heart.

Abigail could hear Eloise moaning, "Oh, my God! My God!"
over and over.

"Loosen his tie!" Charlotte rapped out. "Jerry, call John Werner." And then Maida's flat, expressionless statement.

"It's no good, Aunt Charlotte. There's nothing Dr. Werner
can do for him now."

After her first frightened bleat, Abigail sat still, staring at the
glass in her hand—at the harmless drink that should have been
Tom's. And the brandy that he had swallowed—

She could not meet Jerome Manning's eyes, but she could feel
him watching her and she knew that her knowledge and fear were
plainly visible.

(What would Samantha Vernay do? What must I do—now?
she thought helplessly.)

Arthur, his face waxen, seemed to be trying to squeeze his
temples together with shaking fingers. As though automatically,

Jerry stooped to retrieve the fallen glass. In that moment Abigail's indecision vanished. Stronger than fear, stronger than pity, a ruthless determination took possession of her.

"Don't touch that glass!" She was startled at her own decisive command, a command that froze Jerry in mid-air, his hand still foolishly outstretched toward the floor. "Leave everything exactly as it is," she finished, "until the police arrive!"

In the silence that followed, Abigail knew that every eye was upon her. Even Eloise, sobbing hysterically among her pink pillows, turned a streaked face toward her, morbid interest replacing grief and shock.

Fred leaned against the mantel, apparently unmoved although his face was pale and set. He gave Abigail a brief nod of grudging commendation. Abigail saw a flicker of respect in Charlotte Manning's eyes and open disapproval in Maida's defiant gaze.

Arthur was the first to move. As though with a great effort he straightened his shoulders and, without a word, started toward the hall.

"Arthur! No!" Maida's cry cut after him like a whiplash, rising, protesting.

Arthur paused only a moment, without turning.

"Mrs. Potter is right," he said in a tired voice. "There is nothing else to be done."

Suddenly Maida stamped her foot and the tension that held her gave way to rage.

"Why can't she leave us alone!" she wailed. "I'm sick of her interfering—"

"Maida, my dear, you don't know what you're saying!" Arthur protested, but Maida stormed on.

"Jerry saw her this afternoon snooping around the house! What business had she there? And why did she force her way in this afternoon when she knew we didn't want her? I don't believe she even has an Aunt Harriet!"

"Oh, indeed she has, Maida," Eloise interposed anxiously. "I recognized Miss Potter's brooch immediately, and besides—"

"Aunt Harriet or no Aunt Harriet," Maida finished, appealing to Arthur, "she has no right to tell us what to do! Haven't we

been through enough? No one in this room killed Tom, or anyone else—but you know what the police will think!"

"We will have to notify them," Arthur repeated quietly.

"All right!" Maida flared. "Call them! But before they come I
intend to take every one of these glasses out to the kitchen and
wash them—and Mrs. Potter can't stop me!"

She was almost in tears as she bent to pick up Tom's glass
from the rug.

There was a swift movement as Arthur caught her arm and
pulled her back. Abigail reached down just as Maida, her hand
imprisoned, kicked furiously in the direction of the goblet. Ignoring the pain in her wrist, which had caught the force of Maida's
blow, Abigail deliberately took her handkerchief and spreading
it over her hand she took the stem of the glass in her fingers and
stood up triumphantly.

"Nice try, Maida!" Fred spoke jeeringly.

"Don't be afraid, my dear!" Arthur said, holding her to him.

Suddenly, with a stifled cry, Maida pulled away and dropped
into a chair, hiding her face on the arm. Her body shook with
frightened, silent sobs as she fought to regain control.

Abigail was embarrassed. She realized, with Maida, that Arthur's fingerprints would be on the glass but so, perhaps, would
Fred's and Tom Weston's own—and Jerry Manning's undoubtedly would not. Yet she was determined to save it for the police so
that they could determine the poison that had been used. This
time, surely, it would be possible to trace it to its source.

Jerry made no move to stop her. He sat at the foot of Eloise's
couch, apparently withdrawn from the proceedings, his gaze intent on a cigarette, which he revolved, unlighted, between his
fingers. Charlotte, behind him, rested a hand on his shoulder and
once, perhaps in response to some slight pressure, Jerry reached
up and laid his own hand over hers for an instant.

Abigail felt sick with remorse. She had promised herself to
keep an eye on Jerry's every movement, but his steady gaze had
made her uneasy, afraid to watch him too closely lest she put him
on his guard. If she had not failed, Tom Weston would not have
died.

(A fine detective you've turned out to be, Abigail Farringdon Potter!)

As Maida's sobs slowed, Eloise spoke from the divan.

"I've been trying to tell you, Maida—if you'd just listen— Mrs. Potter is trying to help you! She says she knows Arthur didn't kill Mr. Hawkes and she's trying to prove it! If you ask me, she's the only one around here that's shown any sense at all!"

Maida lifted her head and faced Abigail.

"Is that true?"

Abigail nodded. When she spoke, her tone was steadier than she felt.

"The poison that killed Tom Weston," she said with dignity, "was in *my* brandy! Tom drank the wrong one by mistake. *Someone*," and she allowed herself to meet Jerry's eyes defiantly, "someone tried to kill me because of what I know. So you see, I have a right to demand that you telephone the police at once!"

An incredulous gasp greeted her statement.

"Are you sure?" Arthur demanded.

Even Fred whirled from the fireplace to face her, his jaw dropping with astonishment, and Eloise gave vent to a small moan of terror.

"Please call the police," Abigail repeated through set lips.

Decisively, Arthur put Maida from him, and this time she made no attempt to hold him back. No one spoke while he was gone. Abigail was sure that each of them listened, as she did, to the whirr of the telephone dial in the hall, to Arthur's clipped words as he got his connection. Not until he had replaced the receiver in its cradle did anyone move.

Charlotte, her lips folded tight, was the first to stir. She removed the afghan from Eloise's knees and spread it gently over Tom's still form.

"Someone will have to tell Dora," she observed grimly, as Arthur rejoined them. "I suppose she will know how to reach Tom's wife."

Eloise sat up eagerly.

"I think I should be the one to break the news to dear Dora," she suggested. "If someone will drive me over—"

"Mother!" Maida's reproach was shocked.

"I'm her best friend—and it will be so much easier for dear Dora if this terrible news is broken gently. It's a painful task, but I feel it is my duty—"

"Indeed you shan't, Eloise," Charlotte interrupted bluntly. "You are not well enough. I'll go, and Jerry will drive me."

"But the police—" Abigail protested. She was determined that Jerry should have no opportunity for flight. "You must stay here until they come! Why don't you telephone—"

For the first time since Abigail had met her, Charlotte's tone was unfriendly.

"This is not the sort of news one telephones. Surely, Mrs. Potter, you don't suspect me—or my son—of Tom's death! Come, Jerry!" At the door, Jerry turned and spoke to Abigail.

"I'll take full responsibility for our actions, Mrs. Potter."

No one spoke to Abigail after the Mannings had left. Feeling a pariah, she watched Arthur and Fred, under Maida's direction, lift Eloise and carry her, pouting and protesting, up the stairs. Without a glance at Abigail, Maida followed with the pillows.

Abigail was left alone with what had been Tom Weston. His legs stretched grotesquely from beneath the bright afghan, which hid his contorted face.

Shuddering, Abigail turned away.

There but for the grace of God, she thought, conscience stricken. Yet even though she knew that Jerome Manning had tried to kill her, she could not hate him.

(It was your own fault, Abigail Potter! You drove him into a corner! You left him no alternative. What else was he to do?)

Sick at heart, she longed only to walk briskly away from that house of death, never to return. The impulse carried her out of the house, and with no idea of where she was heading, Abigail started down the street.

The bright glare of afternoon was fading into dusk. Abigail had walked several blocks when she heard a young couple giggle as they passed and turning back to look after them she saw that they had likewise turned to look at her. Puzzled at their mirth, she walked on more slowly, her head a little higher, until she became foolishly aware that in her left hand she still carried the brandy glass, wrapped about the base in her handkerchief and extended in front of her.

Humiliated and chagrined, she was about to fling the glass into the nearest bush when reason stayed her hand.

Abigail Farringdon Potter, I'm ashamed of you she rebuked herself. Running away, indeed! You're the one who insisted that the police be called. You're the one they'll want to see. Besides, if it weren't for Tom Weston you'd be the one lying under that pink afghan right this minute. Don't you owe him something?

With new determination she turned and retraced her steps, hurrying a little as she heard the scream of sirens wailing to a stop far down the street.

I've got the evidence, she told herself, clutching the empty brandy glass. Whatever will they think when I'm not there!

VII

The living room, empty when she had walked out of it a short time before, was full of uniforms. One, stretched tight across a broad chest, was plastered against a wall behind the chair where Abigail had sat. A belligerent face, crowned with a shock of carroty hair, emerged from the top of this uniform and defied anyone to attempt an escape by way of the French doors. A second policeman had planted himself beside Arthur Snyder, who sat painfully erect in a corner of the couch while still another blue-coated figure loomed over him—a gray-haired man whose air of authority was reinforced by the prominently displayed sheriff's badge upon his chest.

Maida, Abigail noticed, huddled at the other end of the couch, her eyes wide and frightened. Fred, too, had come downstairs again and was leaning against the mantelpiece. All their eyes seemed to be focused on Arthur, all of them seemed waiting for him to speak.

Three men in plain clothes, on the other hand, appeared to have divorced themselves from the proceedings and carried on their own specialized investigations like animated bits of background. With a sense of surprise that she was thus seeing real life duplicate her own fiction, Abigail identified them as photographer, medical examiner, and—bending over the bar—fingerprint expert.

To her amazement, no one looked around as she slipped into the room. The words of explanation she'd had ready were not necessary. No one seemed even to have missed her. Abigail felt a bit annoyed. Carefully, she set the brandy glass on a table near the door and waited with the rest.

"All right!" Arthur spoke at last, his tone flat and hopeless. "I should have known he'd have had a copy made. He always was a crooked, double-crossing—"

"Arthur!" Maida said warningly.

"—but I didn't kill him!" Arthur concluded.

Abigail stared at him blankly, aware that she must have missed something. Surely no one could accuse Tom Weston of having been crooked or double crossing.

"You'll have a chance to prove that!" the sheriff challenged coldly. He nodded to the uniform beside Arthur and, as though acting on cue, the policeman clapped a heavy hand on Arthur's shoulder.

"You're under arrest," he declaimed, "for the murder of Harrison Hawkes. Weston, too," he added under his breath, "though that remains to be proved."

So Sheriff Greenough had returned with the warrant for Arthur Snyder's arrest, as Tom had prophesied. But surely, thought Abigail, Tom's death puts everything in a different light. How can anyone think Arthur would have killed the man who believed in his innocence and was working so hard to prove it?

Maida sat in stunned silence. It was Fred who protested. "You can't do this! You're crazy if you—"

The sheriff, his mission accomplished, shrugged and tapped his badge.

"I've got a warrant that says I can."

Dismissing Fred and ignoring the appeal in Maida's eyes, he turned to the medical examiner.

"What do you say?" he asked. "Same as the other?"

"Far as I can see, same thing. Won't swear to it till after the autopsy." The examiner, without bothering to replace the afghan over Tom's face, produced a cigar and struck a match into sudden flame.

"Okay!" the sheriff proceeded. "Now, let's get the setup. Might as well listen to your stories, long as I'm here, but I don't guess there'll be any trouble finding the killer. Snyder, here, thought Weston was on to him so he rubbed him out the same way he did Hawkes."

His voice became furious as he whirled on Arthur.

"You poor sap! You should have known Weston was no danger to you! In spite of the evidence, he swore up and down I was wrong. 'Arthur Snyder couldn't do a thing like that!' he says, over and over. I wish he could have lived to see this photostat they found in Hawkes' safe! I wish he—well, I wish he could have lived, that's all!"

He became abruptly official. "Well, what happened? Who was here, just you three? You first!"

He jabbed a forefinger at Fred, and Fred, one hand gripping his father's shoulder, answered.

"No. Our neighbor, Mrs. Manning was here, and her son. We were celebrating—"

"Wait a minute! Mrs. Manning? And her son? Where the hell are they?"

"They'll be back," Maida answered, seeming to come out of a trance. Deliberately she moved over to sit beside her husband. "They just went to Tom's mother, to tell her—"

"Okay, okay! I'll want to talk to them, but it'll keep. Go on, Snyder."

Fred reported accurately, as far as Abigail could tell, the bare details of the gathering and of Tom Weston's collapse.

Greenough let him talk, his jaws working rhythmically, his expression bored. The photographer packed up his equipment and left. The medical examiner perched on the arm of the chair that had been Tom's and listened. No one paid any attention to Abigail. Once, she flashed a smile of encouragement to Maida, to Arthur, but she might have been invisible. No one glanced her way.

"Okay," said the sheriff when Fred had finished. "You sure that's how it was? No one but your father, here, mixed the drinks, right? No one else went to the bar—"

"But myself," Fred amended. "I was right there with him all the time."

"You were right there, except when you were handing around the drinks! Check? Check! And no one else went—"

"My mother went to the bar once, just before—"

Greenough turned on Maida.

"Your mother! Was she here, too? For crying out loud! Why can't you people tell a story straight! 'Were just you three here?' I ask, and you say, 'Just us three—and a couple more!' And then you suddenly remember Mrs. Snyder's mother. Where is *she?*"

"Upstairs, in her room. She's—not well."

"Check on that, Brown!"

The uniform by the window detached itself from the wall and brushed past Abigail.

"So your mother got herself a drink. Then what?"

Maida continued the recital.

"She was taking it back to the couch when she—she lost her balance and fell against that little table there. We all rushed to her—"

"Lost her balance. Drunk, eh?"

Abigail found herself liking Sheriff Greenough less and less.

"My mother has a bad heart," Maida answered, "as you ought to know. She's been through a great deal in the past few days—"

"You mean she had an attack?"

"Or faked it!" Fred muttered. Although Abigail had been inclined to share his diagnosis, she was dismayed at his unfeeling candor.

"Are you trying to say that your mother-in-law—"

"Grandmother-in-law," Fred corrected without rancor.

"Mrs. Snyder's mother, then. Are you trying to suggest that she faked a heart attack, staggered against that table there, and dropped a slug of cyanide in Weston's glass? Oh, please!"

"Fred's not suggesting any such thing!" Maida flared. "We're simply trying to tell you what happened. If you weren't so pigheadedly sure you know everything, you'd see that anyone—any one of us—could have put poison in Tom's glass. Mrs. Manning and Jerry had just come in the French doors in back of him. Arthur and I had gone over to meet them there, and Tom was with us. Anyone could have done it—and they wouldn't have left fingerprints on the glass, either!"

"You've mentioned everyone but me!" Fred prompted wryly. "I was upstairs getting a pink pillow for the patient's head."

"Oh, no!" Maida corrected, too sweetly. "You had just come down, Fred. You'd thrown the pillows on the couch before Arthur and Tom helped Mother lie down. After that I remember you going over to mop up the drink she'd spilled with your handkerchief. Such unusual tidiness—for you!"

Fred glared, but Maida did not drop her eyes.

"Fred! Maida! Stop talking nonsense!" Arthur rebuked them. "I know you're trying to protect me, but it's no good. You don't really suppose anyone would have put poison in Tom's glass under his very nose! Besides, you forget that the glass was right beside Mrs. Potter. She would certainly have noticed any unusual gesture."

(I wonder, thought Abigail, trying to recall those moments of confusion after Eloise's big scene. Tom certainly would have noticed nothing. He was too busy helping Eloise. And I—why, I don't even remember Fred mopping up the drink! We were all watching Eloise!)

Sheriff Greenough was making strange noises; his features were empurpled.

"Mrs. Potter!" he choked. "Who the hell is Mrs. Potter?"

"I am," Abigail introduced herself, relieved that she had been remembered.

Greenough wheeled and regarded her fretfully.

"Who are you?" he demanded. "And where do you come in?"

"This is Abigail Potter, the authoress," Maida explained. "She writes detective stories, so naturally she's been interested in our murders."

Greenough snorted.

"I give up!" he howled. "I suppose she's been helping you cook up some fantastic story to cover a plain murder. Look for the least likely person! Find the guy with the perfect alibi! Hogwash! I've had enough of the lot of you—obstructing justice, concealing evidence, refusing to answer questions. I've got my case—and I've got the right man. Once we take this into court it's going to take more than detective fiction to convince a jury that Arthur Snyder isn't guilty as hell! Come on!"

The policeman, who had not moved from Arthur's side, jerked his head and, without protest, Arthur stood up. Maida, frozen, did not move until he stretched out his hand. Then she went to him.

"Don't worry, my dear," he said, stroking her hair. "I'll be back!"

But his words did not carry conviction.

"Please!" Abigail's first attempt was little more than a whisper. She tried again with more success. "Please, Mr. Greenough, I'd like to speak to you a moment, please—alone. You're making a terrible mistake."

For a moment she thought the sheriff would strike her, but she stood her ground.

"You and everyone else!" he roared. "If you've got anything to say, tell it to Snyder's lawyer!"

Abigail swallowed twice.

"I'll advise him to sue you for false arrest," she said stoutly. "I'll tell them you refused to listen to vital evidence and that your conduct of this investigation—"

"What evidence?" Greenough demanded dubiously.

"Evidence to prove that Arthur Snyder is innocent. You see, I *know* who killed Harrison Hawkes. The same man tried to kill me to keep me quiet—but Tom Weston died instead. It was my drink that was poisoned!"

"Wait a minute!" Greenough spoke to the policeman who still waited, a hand on Arthur Snyder's arm. "Take Snyder out to the car and keep him there. We'll hold the warrant till we see where Weston's death fits in—but I'm taking Snyder along for questioning now. Mrs. Snyder, is there any place I can talk with this lady alone?"

"I'm going with my husband," Maida said distinctly. "Fred can go with us, or to his own room, I don't care. As far as I'm concerned you can have the whole house."

Greenough eyed them uneasily as the policeman led Arthur out with Maida and Fred staunchly at his side.

"You can wait at the car till I come out," he stipulated, "but I'm taking Snyder to Dayton alone. Now," he went on, turning to Abigail, "what's all this about someone trying to kill you?"

"It was my brandy that was poisoned. Tom Weston drank it by mistake."

"Hogwash! There was only one brandy glass!"

"No," Abigail corrected him. She pointed to the snifter she had set on the hall table. "That is the glass Tom drank out of. The other one, the one you've sent off to be tested and finger-printed, is harmless."

Greenough loosed a bellow of rage.

"Do you mean Mrs. Snyder deliberately gave me the wrong glass? Why, I'll—I'll—" He broke off and eyed Abigail suspiciously. "Then where was this one? And what right did you have to touch anything?"

"I was afraid it might get—broken. There was some talk of washing all the glasses before the police arrived so I—I just took this one for a walk until you came."

"Well, at least you had enough sense to pick it up without mucking up the prints!" Greenough acknowledged grudgingly. "That whole Snyder family's in cahoots, but I guess we've got him now—"

"You're wrong, Mr. Greenough," Abigail explained earnestly. "Arthur Snyder is innocent and unless you let me tell you what I know I'll advise his lawyer to sue—"

"All right! All right! Talk fast and make it good! I'll give you five minutes."

Abigail had rehearsed her story so often that she had no difficulty compressing it into the allotted time. Beginning with her meeting with the young soldier who gave his name as Rascinski, she traced the course of her long-distance surveillance, concluding with the discoveries she had made since her arrival in Glen Falls.

"You see," she said, "it was a foolproof scheme, except that he gave it away in advance. Of course he never supposed that I'd question his explanation that it was a story he'd made up, or dreamed that I'd follow it through. But you must see how everything falls into place once you know the facts—even to Jerome Manning coming home as soon as he'd learned of Hawkes' death.

"Perhaps he'd have given the whole thing up when he found out what a terrible mistake had been made. I imagine he'd have been glad to settle down and live a decent life—but once he saw me and realized that I knew the truth—well, he couldn't stop. He had to try to get rid of me, too. But once again he had the bad luck to get the wrong person. And so Tom Weston is dead."

Greenough chewed vigorously for a few moments. Gum? Abigail wondered, or tobacco? If tobacco, it could not be much longer before he would have to spit. She thought he looked as though he might.

At last he spat, but it was only a word which came out.

"Hogwash!" he said. He continued more reasonably, "Look, in the first place, if this guy had really been planning to murder someone do you suppose he'd come up to a dear old lady on the train and say, 'Look, I live in Glen Falls, Ohio, and—'"

"But he didn't!" Abigail pointed out excitedly. "That's just the point. He wouldn't say where he was going—I found that out from his seat check—and he told me his name was George Rascinski, but his barracks bag was labeled Manning. And later, when I read the Glen Falls paper, there was no Rascinski mentioned, but there was Jerome Manning who'd just come home on furlough. So then I was sure.

"You say you've talked to this Manning guy since he came back. Are you sure he's the same one?"

"Of course I'm sure. He was wounded in the war, and he looks older, but I couldn't be mistaken. Besides, he even knew my name—and spoke of our meeting."

"Well, then! That proves he has nothing to hide!"

"Not necessarily." Abigail explained about the chance meeting in the garden and her hypothesis that Jerry's greeting had been in the form of a test. "He wanted to see if I remembered him," she explained. "Of course I pretended not to. But then Eloise Demarest told everybody that I was helping the police and that I knew who had poisoned Mr. Hawkes, and then, of course, Jerry knew that he had to get rid of me. It was just after that Tom was poisoned."

"Hmmm!" Greenough shuffled his feet uneasily. Abigail was sure he was reminding himself of the legal aspects of false arrest. "Hardly likely the fellow carries cyanide in his pocket for emergencies. We might frisk him, though!" His smile at his own humor was forced. "You say you have a record of these clippings and all? Might be worth putting it to him—see how he reacts."

Abigail drew a deep sigh of relief and then, in sudden panic, realized that she had not had her notebook since Tom's death. Where could I have left it, she questioned herself frantically.

She knew she had taken it upstairs with her when she followed Fred to Eloise's room; she could not remember carrying it away. It would be there still, in Mrs. Demarest's room where she must have left it.

"I'll get my notebook right away," she promised, starting for the stairs. "I'll just turn the whole thing over to you and let you handle it as you think best." The wisest policy, she reminded herself, was to flatter the Law. "I have every confidence in your ability," she added, throwing the dour sheriff a smile in the nature of a reassuring pat on the back.

Abigail found Brown, the policeman who had been sent to check on Eloise, sprawled in a pink slipper chair smoking a cigarette and listening, without apparent ennui, to Eloise's recital of wrongs and ailments. He jumped up as Abigail came in.

"I just came for my notebook," she explained. "I think I left it here earlier this afternoon."

Brown helped her look, and Eloise assisted with alternate suggestions and repeated denials that she had ever seen such a notebook. Five minutes' search yielded nothing.

"Sure you didn't leave it somewhere else?" Brown suggested.

Abigail shook her head. It was not only that she could not admit her earlier unauthorized presence in the other rooms of the second floor but also that, since she had entered Eloise's pink boudoir she had become absolutely certain that she had not taken the notebook from this room. She remembered distinctly that she had leaned it on the floor against the flowered chair where she had sat. She would have remembered if she had picked it up before she went. It should still be there, leaning against the far side of the chair. But although she lifted the pink ruffle and peered beneath, and although Brown helpfully got down on his knees to look under the bed, the notebook was not to be found.

More disturbed than she cared to admit, Abigail murmured her thanks and apologies and withdrew, escorted by Brown.

Greenough was still standing at the foot of the stairs. With him, Abigail saw with a strange sense of reliving again an instant in time, was Jerry Manning. Would he always be lying in wait for her at the foot of stairs, she wondered—and must she, perhaps, sometime come down them alone and find him there, waiting? She put the thought aside as unjustifiably morbid.

"Hello!" Greenough greeted her cordially. He turned to Jerome. "Mrs. Potter was just telling me the amazing story of your first meeting. Strange, your running into each other again after all these years! It's a small world, isn't it?"

Jerry Manning's eyebrows drew together in apparent bewilderment.

"Our meeting!" he repeated. "Have we met before, Mrs. Potter? If so, I'm afraid you must refresh my memory."

"You haven't forgotten!" Abigail followed through doggedly. "It was several years ago, on a train. You were on your way home on furlough and you told me such an interesting story. I haven't been able to forget it!"

Jerry shook his head.

"I'm afraid you must have me confused with someone else, Mrs. Potter. I'm sure I should never have forgotten so charming a traveling companion."

"But you yourself said," Abigail reminded him triumphantly, "'So we meet again, Mrs. Potter!' How else would you have known my name?"

"Because Maida had told it to me, of course," Jerry replied promptly, raising an eyebrow as though asking Greenough's patience. "And we had met, however informally, a short time before when you were, shall we say, exploring the outside of this house."

"But you even asked me then if I were sure we hadn't met earlier—several years ago!"

"Did I?" Jerry asked politely, but his tone denied it.

"You said something about a notebook," Greenough reminded her, but not as though he retained any real interest.

"I'm—I'm sorry," Abigail apologized, beginning to feel flustered. "I had it just this afternoon, but now I can't find it."

"Well, I'm sure you will." His tone was courteous, but Abigail knew that he had shut a door in her face.

"Those notes of yours ought to make great stuff for your next book. Hope you send me a copy. Well, I gotta push along. It was nice talking to you, Manning."

Before Abigail could protest, before she could put out a hand to stop him, Brown had swung the door open, the two uniforms had stepped through, and the door had closed again behind them. With a sense of panic, Abigail started after them, but as she took a step toward the door, Jerry Manning raised his arm and barred her way.

A call for help stuck in her throat as she saw his expression, not terrifying, not threatening, but humbly pleading.

"Mrs. Potter," he said urgently, "please wait. I've got to talk to you."

Her fright must have been obvious for he added hastily, spreading his hands wide to show their emptiness of weapons, "I won't hurt you. Why would I, with Eloise in the house and Maida and Fred right outside? You've got to give me a chance!"

Something in his face choked the cry of protest on Abigail's lips—and then it was too late. Through the glass panel at the side of the front door she saw the sheriff's car start off. After it, to her complete dismay, she saw another car, with Fred at the wheel and Maida beside him, pull out of the driveway and turn after Greenough's.

Abigail backed slowly into the living room. He won't kill me here, she told herself. He wouldn't dare! Yet her heart was pounding so hard it seemed in danger of beating its way free of her body.

"Mrs. Potter," Jerry said again, more quietly, "I know what you think, but it's not true. I've got to make you believe me, and there isn't much time. If I had admitted your story to Greenough, I'd have been done for. You can see that. But I didn't kill

Tom Weston and I didn't kill Harrison Hawkes. You've got to listen to me!"

Abigail shrank back as he took a step toward her.

"Look!" he said, almost yelling, "there's the telephone—there in the hall. Sit by it. I'm not afraid. If I make one move toward you, you can take the receiver of the hook and dial anyone you want! Or, better yet, write a note—write it there on that pad—address it to the police and tell them whom you suspect. Say, 'If I am killed, arrest Jerry Manning!' Isn't that the way they do it in your books?"

"And then, of course, you would destroy the note," Abigail reminded him with a faint smile. His frantic efforts to reassure her, his proposals to protect her against himself, were fantastic. She believed that he had killed two people and she had no reason to suppose that he would boggle at one small old lady, but she found it useless to remind herself to be on guard. In spite of herself she felt fear leaving her.

"All right," she said, "what is there to say? I knew that day three years ago that you weren't writing a story and when I asked your name you gave yourself away by giving me a name that was not the one on your barracks bag. I went on from there and found out who it was you meant to kill. Since coming to Glen Falls I have even learned all about Arthur Snyder's migraine capsules and how you got hold of them.

"But your poison killed the wrong man, didn't it? And so you came back to try again. You didn't expect to find me here, did you? You knew I was dangerous to you and so you tried to kill me, too—and again you got the wrong person! Now it's too late. Eloise is upstairs. Fred and Maida will be in any minute."

Apparently Jerry had not seen them drive off and her bluff was going to work. "You don't dare touch me now!" she finished.

Jerry had sunk into an armchair by the fireplace as Abigail began her accusations. He made no move to answer. His hands clenched and unclenched on his knee; his head was bowed so she could not see his face. Not until she finished did he stir, and then only to run his fingers despairingly through his hair.

In pity and triumph Abigail thought, he never imagined the strength of the evidence I've accumulated! Now that he has learned how very much I do know, surely he must admit defeat!

"I don't know what to say," he began at last. "I haven't much time. In the first place, you must believe me when I swear that when I came home I knew nothing of Mr. Hawkes' death. I'd never even heard of him. I arrived this noon and after that, except for a few words with my mother, I was with Maida and Arthur all afternoon until I met you in the hall down here before Tom's—accident. During that whole time, not one word was mentioned about Mr. Hawkes' death nor of Arthur's position in the case. If I had heard of it, if I had heard how Hawkes died, I might have been uneasy—even though I know that I can't be responsible. But I did not know. I didn't know anything about it until my mother told me as we were driving to Mrs. Weston's after Tom's death."

Abigail snorted.

"You expect me to believe that!" she observed caustically. "You expect me to believe that after deliberately avoiding Glen Falls, with not one visit to your old home and your mother for three years, it was nothing but chance that made you decide to come back two days after Harrison Hawkes died of poison in the Snyder home!"

"It wasn't chance that brought me back," Jerry insisted, "but a telegram from my mother asking me to come. I received her message last Wednesday and, obviously, it had nothing to do with Hawkes' death as he was not even in Glen Falls at the time. As a matter of fact," he went on, in a voice so low and dead that Abigail had to strain to hear his words, "if it hadn't been for a last-minute change in my plans I would have arrived home last Friday morning, the day after Hawkes died.

"You have been right in so much—how can I prove that you're wrong in the one important fact? I did give you a false name and it was because, as you guessed, I was planning to murder Arthur Snyder and I didn't want my real name known. For months, out there in the jungle, I lay awake at night planning ways to kill him. I hated him because he had taken Maida away from me. I reasoned that if only he were dead she would be mine again." He gestured helplessly. "I can't expect you to understand. It was like a sickness, a poison working inside of me. It got hold of me until I couldn't get free. When I came home on leave I had it all worked out down to the last detail; I even had the poison with me in my bag. Then I met you. You were interested in me, and when I saw you reading a mystery it gave me an idea for putting the whole thing into words in a last attempt to test the soundness of my scheme. After I had taken it out and looked at it—and especially, after your parting words—I realized that I couldn't go through with it."

He paused, as though to weigh Abigail's reaction.

"It was like coming out of a nightmare," he said simply.

Pity troubled Abigail, pity she had no right to feel for a murderer. He looked so tortured, so miserable, sitting there that she wanted desperately to believe what he said.

"But you did go through with your plan," she reminded him. "You did substitute a poisoned capsule."

"Yes," Jerry admitted unexpectedly. "I did. When I came home I thought it was over, the hatred and the jealousy. I thought I could see Maida again, could watch her and Arthur together, could forget— But I didn't know then what he'd done to my father."

He stopped again as though searching for words.

"Mrs. Weston told me he forced your father to sell his business," Abigail prompted.

"The Midwest Foundry wasn't Dad's business; it was his life," Jerry corrected bitterly. "Did Mrs. Weston tell you what it did to him—how his health failed after that, and even—even his mind? Did she tell you that he became obsessed by the one idea of getting the foundry back? In the three weeks I was home he recognized me only twice—and both times it was to beg me to get revenge on Arthur Snyder!"

The poor boy! Abigail thought, deeply moved. Weakened as he had been by his own months of bitterness, how could he have withstood the extra burden of his dying father's hate?

"But even then," Jerry continued, "I told myself that I wasn't going to carry out my plans. And yet, subconsciously I suppose, I was acting as I had planned to act—pretending friendship for Maida and Arthur, all the camouflage I intended when I was plotting Arthur's death. Then, two days before I left, I picked Maida up downtown and drove her home, and she left Arthur's prescription in my car. It seemed like fate. Almost against my will I took that bottle of capsules, opened the wrapper, and—it seemed so easy, so foolproof—I made the substitution."

Abigail heard a car door slam outside. Maida's voice called out to someone and then Abigail heard Fred's response. Then they had not gone all the way to Dayton! With renewed confidence she returned to the attack.

"You admit you planted the poison that killed Harrison Hawkes, yet you say you are not responsible for his death. Do you mean that you're going to plead temporary insanity? Is that it?"

Her words were scornful and Jerry's eyes dilated. He, too, must have heard Maida's approach. Quickly, pleadingly, he reached out and grasped Abigail's hand.

"No," he said, "that's not it at all. You don't understand. I planted that poison, yes—but five months later when I was in the hospital, facing an operation I wasn't expected to survive, I got a letter from Maida and Arthur—from both of them—wishing me well. Arthur was still alive! I realized then what a terrible thing I had tried to do!"

Sweat stood out on Jerry's forehead. "Some merciful fate had given me a reprieve, but even then I knew I might be too late. I was afraid to die with that on my conscience—"

"What have you on your conscience?" Maida broke in lightly. Abigail and Jerry jerked around.

"You know what I have on my conscience, Maida. You must tell Mrs. Potter about the letter I wrote you from the hospital. Tell her what I told you—what I asked you to do—or she'll have me hanged for the murder of Harrison Hawkes!"

VIII

"Hanged! You?" Maida stared at Jerry as though she suspected him of trying to make a very bad joke. Then, apparently realizing that he was serious, she turned on Abigail.

"Really, Mrs. Potter, I never heard of anything so stupid! Of course Jerry had nothing to do with these deaths—any more than Arthur did. He didn't know Mr. Hawkes. He wasn't even here."

"Mrs. Potter thinks Harrison Hawkes was killed by mistake," Jerry elaborated. "She thinks he got the poison in one of Arthur's migraine capsules and that it was Arthur who was meant to die, so you see she has reason to suspect me."

"To suspect you—of trying to kill Arthur?" Maida repeated the words as though the idea were new—and unthinkable.

Is she protesting too much? Abigail wondered. She was sure that Maida was feeling for a clue, trying to grasp what Jerry wanted her to say.

"But that's ridiculous!" Maida said again, forcing a laugh. "Jerry and Arthur are devoted to each other. Why on earth would Jerry—"

"Maida!" Jerry spoke commandingly. "Don't pretend. You know why, and so does Mrs. Potter. What she doesn't know is why the poison I meant for Arthur could not have killed Hawkes—or anyone else. You've got to tell her about my letter! You *did* destroy the capsules, as I asked. I had your telegram saying that you had."

"My telegram!" Maida's face was a mass of incredulity. Her lips moved as though repeating words that conveyed nothing. Suddenly the mask broke; her lips quivered.

"I don't know what you're talking about! You can't have planned to poison Arthur! You never wrote to me at all after Arthur and I— It's all horrible—and untrue! If you're trying to make a joke, I—I don't think it's very funny."

For a long moment she faced Jerry, then her eyes filled with tears, and she crumpled and sank onto the couch. Abigail did not know for how long she had been holding her breath, but now she let it out with a reluctant sigh.

If Maida's acting, she thought, she should be on the stage! She had been hoping so desperately for verification of Jerry's innocence that disappointment gave her words a cruel emphasis.

"You gave her every possible lead," she said, "but it didn't work, did it? Perhaps you should have had a private briefing first!"

Now was the time for a murderer, cornered, to register thwarted fury, perhaps to make a last desperate attack upon his accuser. But Jerry made no move. He looked not so much thwarted as bewildered and beaten.

Either Jerry or Maida must be lying, Abigail felt sure.

"Perhaps Jerry did write that letter," she mused aloud. "Mrs. Snyder, do you hate your husband so very much? Would you have been happy to see him dead, if his death could never be traced to you?"

Maida looked up quickly.

"I love my husband," she said.

"If I hadn't believed that," Jerry told her without bitterness, "I wouldn't have written that letter."

"Then, *if* you wrote it," Abigail summed up, stressing the conditional, "and *if* Mrs. Snyder didn't receive it, who did? You said there was a telegram?"

"Yes. 'Have done as you asked.' That was all, but I stopped worrying after that. It was signed by you, Maida."

"No."

"With your name, then."

They stared at each other, Abigail forgotten.

What can I believe? Abigail asked herself. That Jerry was lying about the letter, the answering telegram? That Maida had received the letter and for some reason was denying it? Or that someone else had opened and read a letter addressed to Maida Snyder—and had ignored Jerry's plea to dispose of the poisoned capsule?

"If you really sent that letter and Maida didn't get it," she said, "there should be some way of finding out who did. Since the capsule was not destroyed, it must have been someone who would have been glad to see Jerry's plot go through, to have Arthur dead. Who would have had access to your mail, Mrs. Snyder? Who might have opened and read a letter addressed to you?"

Maida shook her head, obviously at a loss.

"I didn't mail it directly to Maida," Jerry said slowly. "I enclosed it in a letter to my mother and asked her to give it directly into Maida's hands."

Abigail's heart sang a paean of joy. He would never have named a witness if he were lying, she argued. He must know that I'll check up!

"Then your mother can tell us to whom she *did* give the letter!" she cried.

"What good will that do?" Maida asked helplessly. "No one is going to admit having opened it."

"I'll have to go to the police, of course," Jerry said. "In spite of the telegram, it seems I *am* responsible for Hawkes' death. They'll have to release Arthur."

"But, Jerry, what about you?" Maida protested.

"I think you should wait!" Abigail interposed quickly. "If you go to the police now you won't stand a chance, but if we can just find proof—"

She felt fiercely protective now, as though she must somehow atone to Jerry for the wrong she had done him in her thoughts. But Jerry was firm.

"There's no point in putting it off," he insisted. "I planted the seed of murder, even if someone else allowed it to grow in spite of me. I can't let Arthur suffer."

"Arthur isn't under arrest, yet," Abigail argued. "The police are only going to question him, not put him on the rack. We still have time. Before you give yourself up we must find out who intercepted that letter. Whoever he is, though he didn't originate the crime, he at least took advantage of it and is equally guilty. And don't forget—Tom Weston is dead because someone tried to murder me! The police can't charge you for that!"

"She's right, Jerry," Maida said quickly. "You'd better wait until we know more. Arthur wouldn't want you to save him at your own expense."

"What do you suggest we do?" Jerry looked to Abigail for guidance.

Abigail became businesslike.

"First, if I'm to help you," she began, "you'd better tell me all you can about the case against Mr. Snyder. What motive do the police give him for Mr. Hawkes' murder? I gather that's the most damning evidence against him."

The last barrier went down. Maida began to talk freely.

"If Hawkes' death was a mistake," she said, "it couldn't have happened at a worse time—nor to anyone we would rather have seen dead. That's what makes it so bad. Arthur didn't want to hate Hawkes, but he couldn't help himself. Harrison Hawkes was vile, a man who pretended friendship and used Arthur's confidence to get a hold over him and then—"

"Can't you be more specific?" Abigail suggested. "Do you mean blackmail?"

"Yes. Oh, it was the politest kind of blackmail; for a long time Arthur didn't even realize that it was. Hawkes had a government position during the war, you know, receiving bids for war material and awarding contracts. In nineteen forty-three he sent Arthur out here to Glen Falls as his agent, with instructions to buy out the Midwest Foundry. When Uncle Nelson, Jerry's father, refused to sell, Mr. Hawkes set Arthur up with a rival business and poured enough funds into the venture so he could undercut Uncle Nelson and force him to sell. Hawkes directed the whole deal and all the profits went to him, but he wanted his own name kept out of it. There was nothing shady about it," she added defensively. "Big business does it all the time. Arthur thought, of course, that Nelson Manning would remain in charge and carry on as usual—but he didn't know Uncle Nelson.

His pride was hurt; he felt he had failed when he had to let the foundry go out of the family. Arthur felt simply terrible when he realized what it had done to the Mannings, how they hated Arthur and blamed him for everything."

"Dad wasn't altogether rational at the end," Jerry apologized. "I admit I felt bitter, but I never really hated Arthur—for that."

"Anyway, soon after Arthur got control of the foundry, government orders began pouring in. Arthur realized, then, that Hawkes had been planning all along to use Arthur to cover his own war-profiteering activities. Arthur tried to withdraw—and that's when Hawkes put the pressure on."

"You haven't told us what the pressure was," Abigail reminded her.

Maida hesitated. Then the story poured out.

"It was a letter," she said. "A letter from Arthur's first wife, Fred's mother. She must have been a horrible person. Arthur doesn't speak of her much, but I know she spent money like water, gambled, ran up terrible debts. And then, when Fred was seventeen, she killed herself—with an overdose of Arthur's migraine capsules. A servant had overheard them quarreling. Arthur's fingerprints were on the bottle and on the glass of warm milk she drank. She had tried to frame Arthur for murder, but she left a note, too—a suicide note."

"But why?" Jerry protested.

"She thought she had him either way. If Arthur showed the note to the police to prove suicide, he couldn't have collected on her insurance—fifty thousand dollars—which he had to have to keep from going into bankruptcy because of her debts. In addition, he would have been tried and probably sentenced for manslaughter. You see, she wrote that she had been in the car with him the week before and that he was the driver police had been hunting in a hit-and-run death that had been played up in the papers. She even mentioned traces of blood on the car—which the police would have found. It was the first that Arthur knew that she, herself, had been guilty of that accident and the failure to report it, but it would have been his word against the word of his dead wife. You can see how neatly she fixed it!"

"Then he didn't show the note to the police?" Abigail hazard-
ed. "Was he tried for her murder?"

Maida shook her head.

"When he found her, Arthur called Harrison Hawkes, his
friend and business partner. Arthur was ready to give himself
up and take his chances, but Hawkes persuaded him not to. If
Arthur had gone bankrupt, Hawkes would have been liable for
the debts of the partnership. He didn't care about Arthur, but he
wanted him to collect on that insurance.

"I suppose Arthur was too stunned to think straight, but he
let Hawkes fix everything up to look like accident before they
called in the police. I don't know how he did it, but apparently
the coroner returned that verdict. Arthur felt terrible about it,
but he's always been glad Fred didn't have to wonder if his father
were a murderer or know that his mother committed suicide—
Fred was always devoted to her in spite of everything. And, of
course, Arthur was very grateful to Hawkes."

"But wasn't the note destroyed?" Abigail asked.

"Arthur thought so. He says that when he came to Glen Falls
as Hawkes' agent, he did it out of gratitude and friendship. It
wasn't until he discovered Hawkes' game and tried to get out that
he found that Hawkes had kept that note to hold over his head.

"By that time Arthur and I were engaged—we were about
to be married—and Hawkes threatened to make the whole foul
business public if Arthur let him down. Perhaps Arthur was weak;
perhaps he should have taken a stand then, but he wasn't sure of
me. He was afraid it might make a difference. So he let himself
be—persuaded."

"You never told me, Maida," Jerry said. "Even when I first
met him I couldn't reconcile Arthur, so quiet and gentle, with
the ruthless dealings Dad claimed he'd pulled. I—"

"I didn't know myself, then," Maida said. "I didn't know any
of this until the night—the night before Hawkes died. Arthur
told me everything that evening because," and she lifted her chin
proudly, "because Arthur had determined to defy him, to call his
bluff. He wanted me to know what we might have to face—the

scandal, perhaps even prison. He wanted to be sure I thought he was doing the right thing."

"But why? What new demands had Mr. Hawkes made?" Abigail asked.

"It wasn't that he had asked any more of Arthur, but that Arthur had come to hate everything Hawkes stood for. He couldn't forgive himself for what he had done to the Mannings. It began the night Uncle Nelson died, even before Arthur knew about the war contracts tie-up. Charlotte came straight here from the hospital—it's the only time I've ever seen her lose control. She blamed Arthur for her husband's death and repeated some of the bitter things Uncle Nelson had said during his illness. You know how he talked, Jerry—almost out of his mind, part of the time? Anyway, Arthur didn't go to bed at all that night. It brought on one of his headaches and I can remember his walking the floor in agony until way past midnight. I'm afraid I failed him, myself. I couldn't understand how he could have done the terrible things Aunt Charlotte accused him of. We never talked about it, but he couldn't help knowing how I felt and he's had it on his conscience all these years. Aunt Charlotte's been a second mother to me, yet after that night she would never set foot in this house. Arthur guessed, too, why Jerry wouldn't come home after the war and gradually he began to feel that he had robbed Aunt Charlotte of her son as well as of her husband.

"It was too late to make amends to Uncle Nelson, but Arthur determined to turn the foundry back to the Mannings, where it belonged. On the books, in the records, the business was in Arthur's name and he had a right to sell. Actually, of course, Hawkes owned everything: Arthur had nothing but a nominal salary.

"A week ago, Arthur went to see Aunt Charlotte and told her what he wanted to do. He begged her to send for Jerry." Here, Jerry nodded confirmation. "Then Arthur wrote to Hawkes that he intended to sell the business back to the Mannings and that he would send the entire sum to Hawkes. Arthur would have had very little left after the sale but he would have been a free man again, his conscience would have been clear. I was glad and proud that he had decided that way!"

"I take it that Mr. Hawkes did not agree?" Abigail guessed.

"No. It never occurred to Arthur that he would protest. After all, the war is over and this one small factory could not have made much difference. Perhaps he was just vindictive. At any rate, the very day he got Arthur's letter he flew down. That night Mother overheard him arguing with Arthur. She heard them speak of blackmail and then she heard Arthur lose his temper and threaten Mr. Hawkes. I'm sure Arthur only threatened to expose Hawkes' wartime activities, but after Hawkes died that same night, Mother got confused. And now the police have found a photostatic copy of that beastly letter in Hawkes' safe and they think—"

"A photostat?" Jerry asked quickly. "What became of the original?"

"We burned it—Arthur and I—before the police came," Maida admitted. "Hawkes had brought it with him to wave in Arthur's face, to hand over to the newspapers if Arthur made trouble. Oh, it's all so horrible! But Arthur didn't kill him, he didn't! And neither did I, though I'd have loved doing it! I was never so glad, when I knew he was really dead! And now this!"

"Arthur was willing to face all that—for me!" Jerry said, wonderingly. "Yet this afternoon, when we drew up the papers, you neither of you said a word! But I'll make it up to you, Maida. We'll get Arthur cleared, don't you worry!"

They both waited for Abigail to speak, but she could not find any words of reassurance. What if Harrison Hawkes' death had not been an accident, after all? she was asking herself. What if, as she had done once before in imagining a threat to Philip Koestler's life, she had allowed her own preconceived ideas to blind her to the truth? Certainly Arthur Snyder had ample cause to have desired Hawkes' death and it had come at a strangely fortuitous time for the Snyders.

"We don't know that the poison he took was really what Jerry put in Arthur's migraine capsule," she pointed out hesitantly.

"No one has been able to prove that Mr. Hawkes had access to that medicine, and if he didn't—"

"But he did," Maida said levelly. "I haven't told the police because that would be the final bit of evidence they'd need against Arthur—but I don't think there's any doubt that that's how he died. You see—I gave him two of Arthur's capsules that evening!"

"*You* did!" Abigail exclaimed. "But your mother told me—she said your husband kept them locked up—"

"He does," Maida agreed hopelessly. "I always wondered why he was such an old maid about them, but of course, after he told me about his wife— But he got them out that night. The quarrel with Mr. Hawkes had left him with one of his splitting headaches.

"After dinner I came into the study while he was taking his pills. The box was on the desk. We began talking, about how if only we could be sure Mr. Hawkes slept soundly, we could get hold of that letter and destroy it. Then I remembered that Hawkes had asked me after dinner for something for his headache. I knew Arthur would never let anyone touch his pills, so I sent him into the bedroom for something and while he was gone I took two of the capsules. I never dreamed of their being fatal —I just hoped they would make him sleep soundly so I could get the letter."

"So it *was* the poison I substituted," Jerry finished drearily. "What a rotten, unbelievable coincidence."

"When did you give them to Mr. Hawkes?" Abigail inquired.

"I put them on his dresser, thinking he'd take them at bedtime. When. I went back downstairs I told him and he went up soon after. I suppose he must have taken them then, because it was right after he came down again that he—died."

"What poison did you use?" Abigail probed, vainly hoping for a discrepancy. Jerry's frank answer crushed her hopes.

"It was cyanide, all right. Some of the stuff they issued in the army to key men who were sent on missions into Jap territory—in case we were captured. They promised us it would be quick and certain—and preferable to torture." He hesitated, and then added without hope, "What I can't understand is how it could still be good after three years. Wouldn't it deteriorate, or something?"

Abigail seized at the straw. "And why wasn't that particular bottle of capsules exhausted long ago? How often did your husband need his medicine, Maida?"

"I'm afraid that's easily explained," Maida answered. "Arthur always kept them in a special box, a square metal box with a sliding lid. Whenever his supply got low he'd have the prescription refilled and empty the pharmacist's bottle into his own container. I suppose one particular pill *could* have remained untouched forever."

"Thank God it wasn't Arthur who did get it!" Jerry said fervently.

"It might just as well have been," Maida pointed out dispiritedly. "Everything points to his guilt. If the police ever find out I gave Hawkes one of Arthur's capsules—"

"We mustn't let them find out!" Abigail warned.

The first thing a good detective would do, Abigail decided, would be to make a routine check on Jerry's story. Perhaps Charlotte Manning could even tell them to whom, in the Snyder household, she had given Jerry's letter. Abigail determined to go back to her room at once in the hopes of speaking to Charlotte before she left Dora Weston's.

As she reached for her coat, Fred Snyder walked in.

"I stopped at Dora's to see if I could bring your mother back, Jerry," he said. "She thinks she ought to stay over there tonight, so I told her I'd pick up some of her things. Could you help me pack a bag?"

"Of course. I'll round up everything she'll need and go along with you. I'll be back in a minute."

While they waited for Jerry, Abigail again became aware of the constraint between Maida and Fred. This time she was sure it was not because of her.

"Did you find Harcourt?" Maida asked brusquely.

Fred nodded.

"Mr. Harcourt is Arthur's lawyer," Maida explained to Abigail. "We were with him at his office most of the afternoon, arranging the transfer of the foundry, but when Fred drove me back there after they—took Arthur—he'd gone. We couldn't find him at his home, either."

"He was at the Elite," Fred said. "He's going to get in touch with Greenough. God! When I think of what they may be putting Dad through over there, it makes me burn!" He looked at his watch. "It's seven already. They've been gone an hour and a half already. They wouldn't dare to keep him overnight!"

"There's no need to be melodramatic, Fred! They can't do anything to him!" Maida reproved him sharply. "Mrs. Potter is going to help us find the evidence we need. She's already given us a lot to go on."

She gave Abigail an I-know-you-won't-let-us-down look that Abigail found very flattering, even while she felt a chilling doubt. As things stood now, no one but Jerry could save Arthur Snyder, and that only by giving himself up. Would she be able to find proof of his innocence in time? Or would it end in a choice between Jerry and Arthur—the life of one for the freedom of the other?

I'm sure they could only charge him with manslaughter, in any case, she tried to console herself, but she did not feel any happier.

"All set!" Jerry announced from the garden doorway. He carried a small overnight case in one hand. "Shall we go?"

On the way, Jerry insisted that Fred make a slight detour and wait for him briefly in front of the Elite Café. When he came out, he tossed a paper sack into Abigail's lap.

"Thought you might be hungry," he said. "It's way past suppertime."

Even as Abigail thanked him she was sure she would not be able to eat a bite.

She had no opportunity to speak with Charlotte Manning alone, but neither, she observed, did Jerry. He exchanged only a few words with her before he wrung Dora Weston's hand in silent sympathy, kissed his mother good-by, and drove off again with Fred.

Finding words to express her feelings to Mrs. Weston was one of the most difficult tasks Abigail had ever faced. What could one say to a woman whose son had died needlessly, by mistake for another—if one *was* that other! Abigail could only stammer inadequate regrets before she excused herself and hurried to her room.

There, finding that she still clutched the paper sack, she was surprised to discover that she was very hungry indeed. She found the slightly stale cheese sandwich, the cinnamon bun, and the bottle of milk with which Jerry had provided her extremely welcome.

That proves he's not a murderer, was her mental footnote. He's far too thoughtful!

The clock on the stair landing struck eight—and then nine—but no one came upstairs. Abigail was tired, but for her to get ready for bed involved lengthy preparations including the ritual of spreading her gray switch on folded papers and setting its curls with rags and pins. Until Charlotte and Dora Weston should come up she delayed, preferring to be fully dressed and tonsured in the hope of intercepting Charlotte alone in the hall. And so, sitting erect in a low rocker, she rocked—and yawned—and waited.

Downstairs the telephone shrilled repeatedly, transmitting condolences as the news of Tom's death traveled the local grapevine.

The twentieth ring was no different from the preceding nineteen, but this time Abigail could hear no prolonged rumble of conversation after Dora's heavy tread had crossed the floor. Instead, after a moment, Dora came to the foot of the stairs and called.

Uncertainly, Abigail opened her door and waited until she heard her name a second time.

"Telephone for you!" Dora announced.

Puzzled, Abigail hurried down the stairs. Dora had retired once more into the living room and had shut the double doors behind her so that Abigail might speak to her unknown caller in the privacy of the hall.

"Hello?" Abigail answered hesitantly.

"Mrs. Potter?" The voice was a frightened whisper. For a moment Abigail was quite at sea. "This is Eloise Demarest."

"Oh, yes! Yes, Mrs. Demarest!"

"I know it must seem queer, my calling you, but I don't know where to turn. Please—please come quickly! It's simply terribly important. I think—I'm sure I know who killed Mr. Hawkes and Tom Weston!"

"But can't your daughter—"

"Maida's driven over to Dayton, and Fred—I just know Fred's gone out, too, and left me all alone. There's something awful going on here, Mrs. Potter. No one answers when I call, and I heard— No, I can't say it on the phone—you'll just have to come over—please! You can't just leave me here all alone with that— that murderer about! You will come, won't you?"

Some of Eloise's panic communicated itself to Abigail. She tried to speak calmly, reassuringly.

"Don't worry, Mrs. Demarest," she said. "I'm sure Mrs. Manning will drive me. We'll be right over."

"Oh, no! Don't say anything to Charlotte! Please! You mustn't! You see—I'm quite sure that it's her son who— Oh!"

"Hello! Hello!" Abigail's fingers clutched the telephone as though she could squeeze an answer from it. At last, very faintly, she heard Eloise.

"Mrs. Potter! I'm sure—I heard—something! Oh, do come quickly!"

The telephone clicked and the deafening dial tone took over.

IX

Abigail replaced the receiver with a hand that shook. The whole thing was bizarre, incredible. Why should Eloise Demarest, in a town full of people she knew, have turned to a stranger for help? There should have been someone nearer, someone more adequate to whatever situation confronted her. The fact that she had whispered in a house she claimed was empty suggested that she had nevertheless been afraid of being overheard, yet she had asked Abigail, an unarmed old lady, to walk into that house and come to her aid.

The possibility that the call had been a trap did not escape Abigail, who had baited many such in fiction, but to suppose that Eloise had deliberately set a trap was to assume that she was guilty of the murders, alone or with an accomplice.

Quickly, Abigail tested the hypothesis and found it not untenable. Maida's mother could have had access to the letter Jerry claimed he had written to Maida. She could, conceivably, have been willing to suppress it, to allow the fatal capsule to remain in Arthur's medicine chest. She could, when she faked her heart attack that afternoon, have dropped the poison into Abigail's glass.

But why? Why would Eloise want Arthur to die? And, since Hawkes' death had been unpremeditated, why would she have felt it necessary to cover up by trying to kill Abigail? She would have had no reason to fear that Hawkes' death could ever be traced to her, nor could she have supposed that Abigail knew anything to implicate her. In addition, Abigail found it difficult to believe that Eloise would have carried a lethal dose of cyanide so conveniently on her person.

No, it was much easier to assume that Eloise was innocent, a frightened bystander who had stumbled upon the murderer's guilty secret and was now, either actually or potentially, in danger. Abigail decided that she could not ignore the frantic appeal.

And yet, she reminded herself soberly, there is no reason to be foolhardy! It may be a trap and, if so, you are certainly not so stupid as to walk into it with your eyes closed!

On the other side of the parlor doors, Abigail could hear subdued conversation. She hesitated, wanting to establish contact with someone before she left, tempted to ask Mrs. Weston if she had recognized the voice that called. But there was no reason to doubt that it had, indeed, been Eloise. The question was not whether the caller had been genuine but whether the call had really come from the Snyder house. Perhaps, in spite of her supposed illness, Eloise had phoned from somewhere else, some place from which, even now, she might be watching Dora Weston's front door, waiting for her victim to emerge.

The first step was to make sure that the call had really come from the Snyders'—and that Eloise was still there.

Abigail found the number and dialed. She could hear the distant brrr-brrr as the phone rang. There was a click, but although the ringing ceased no one spoke.

"Hello?" Abigail said. "Hello! Mrs. Demarest?"

There was no reply, but Abigail was sure that someone was listening at the other end of the line. And then, abruptly, Eloise said, "Hello?"

"Hello!" Abigail repeated. "Are you all right? This is Mrs. Potter."

"Oh, Mrs. Potter!" Eloise wailed. "Haven't you left yet? There's someone moving about the house and I thought that surely you—"

"Hadn't you better call the police?" Abigail tried reasoning.

"He'd murder me in my bed before *they* could get here! He—"

"Then I strongly suggest that you get *out* of your bed!" Abigail retorted. "I'll be over as soon as I can!"

Eloise Demarest, she decided scornfully, was no murderer. She was a quaking white mouse. As for the someone in the house, it was likely nothing but a slamming door, a creaking stair. Eloise was exactly the sort who *would* get herself into a state if left alone for half an hour.

Abigail was taking no chances, however. In a firm hand she wrote a note and propped it beside the telephone. "Mrs. Demarest is alone in the house and has asked me to go over. Abigail Potter." When she went upstairs for her hat and coat she paused long enough to choose the stoutest of her lisle stockings from the dresser drawer. A stocking filled with sand or dirt, she recalled, could be a most effective weapon. As an afterthought, she helped herself to an umbrella with a crooked handle as she passed the rack in the lower hall. Finally, after ostentatiously turning on the front-porch light, she scurried through the kitchen and out the back door.

The moon was bright and Abigail did not dare draw breath until she had reached the safety of the shadows in the alley. There, she filled her lungs again with air and her stocking with gravel. Raising the umbrella so that it formed a comforting shield above her head, she made her way quickly but deviously through alleys and side streets until she was able to approach the Snyder home from the rear.

Only a roseate glow from the curtained windows of Eloise's room on the second floor broke the somber silhouette of the big house. Abigail crept closer, wondering, now that she was here, what she ought to do. No urge for adventure could be strong enough to persuade her into that darkened mansion where danger might be lurking in every shadow, waiting to strike her down before she could reach or even call to Eloise.

I wouldn't be much good to her dead, Abigail justified her reluctance. She wondered if she should fling a handful of pebbles against the lighted window to indicate that help had arrived. She wished, belatedly, that she had phoned the police herself or, if not the police, some more available ally. Even now, although it was too late to phone, she could knock at the door of some nearby house and bring forth a citizen, preferably large and masculine, who would reinforce or take charge of the rescue squad. Anyone to go ahead of her into that silent house, turning on lights as he went, now seemed to Abigail eminently to be desired.

Here pride stepped in. Are you a mouse like Eloise she questioned herself scathingly—running for help from a danger that may not even exist? What a laughingstock you'd be, indeed, if you called in some perfectly strange man to escort you through a deserted house! Instead, she decided to reconnoiter a bit first, and to this end she circled the house warily, keeping close to the shrubbery.

A double garage, apparently built to be shared by the Mannings and the Snyders, straddled the two lots at the rear. Both doors, she discovered, were open, and there was no car in either one. Maida, as Eloise had said, was probably gone. Arthur was still in Dayton with the police; Charlotte Manning was at Dora Weston's. That left only Jerry and Fred Snyder unaccounted for.

A light glowed from an unshaded rear window of the Manning house next door and, acting on impulse, Abigail started toward it. Jerry and Fred had been together when they'd left her at Mrs. Weston's a few hours before. It was not impossible that they were still together, perhaps discussing the whole affair cozily over a bottle of beer in Jerry's kitchen. Abigail suspected that they would scoff at Eloise's terrors, but she was comfortingly sure that they would go with her to investigate.

At the edge of the driveway she jumped back with a stifled squeak as something sinuous caught around her ankle and then gave sickeningly beneath her foot. Summoning all her courage she stopped to release herself and discovered, when she examined the object that had entangled her, that it was nothing more ominous than a discarded length of rubber tubing such as might once have belonged to a shower hose. Ashamed of her jitters, she kicked it into the bushes and continued across the moonlit grass toward the gap in the shrubbery between the Manning and Snyder yards.

Beyond the hedge, she tiptoed along the side of the Manning house toward the patch of light, testing each footstep on the gravel drive and straining her ears for any sound from within. There was nothing. No least movement, no talk, no laughter. Either the room was empty or Jerry was alone.

Reminding herself that it is difficult to see from a lighted room into the darkness outside, Abigail moved back a few feet and stepped into line with the window. A pair of baleful eyes on the opposite wall made her gasp before she recognized them as belonging to a stuffed deer's head crowned with widespread antlers. Poor thing! Abigail thought sentimentally, sensing reproach in the round glass eyes.

She moved closer to the window. Below the mounted head a desk, bare of papers, a few books arranged neatly between plain metal bookends, and a fresh green blotter suggested the room of a student, an absent or not actively studious one. A chest of drawers in a far corner, topped by a tilted mirror, enabled her to see—

Abigail drew her breath in sharply. One hand flew to her throat. Involuntarily she took a step forward, then another, until her face was pressed against the windowpane. Light streamed out, but she no longer feared discovery from within. The occupant of the room could not see her. His eyes, though open, saw nothing. Jerome Manning lay sprawled across a day bed to the right of the window. A pool of blood beneath his head soaked into the tan monks' cloth cover, dyeing it crimson.

There was no one else in the room.

Abigail hesitated no longer. As she ran down the driveway she was absurdly trying to shut her mind to the horror and, at the same time, to fix each detail indelibly in her memory.

The street was deserted. No car, moving or parked, was in sight; no late pedestrian walked the sidewalk. Without conscious choice, Abigail ran across the street toward the nearest lighted house. Still with no plan in mind, she found herself beating upon the door, first with her improvised blackjack and then, as though it were a battering ram, with the point of the umbrella she had forgotten to close.

After interminable minutes the door was opened. If the umbrella had not caught against the opening, Abigail would have fallen into the room. Hastily she dropped it on the porch and darted in.

"The telephone!" she cried. "There's been another murder!"

She had stumbled into the midst of a young people's card game. Several chairs scraped back and a pile of red, white, and blue chips cascaded to the floor. Not bridge, Abigail realized. And they look like such nice young people!

She had forgotten the heavy, bulging stocking in her hand until she noticed several of the group staring at it. Embarrassed, she moved it around behind her back.

One of the men showed her to the telephone and helped her find the number of the sheriff's office in Dayton. A girl asked hesitantly if she had not better call the doctor first.

"Are you sure he's dead?" someone asked, awed.

"He—he certainly looked dead!" Abigail said, weakly. She accepted the chair that one of the young men pushed forward, and was able to give her message in a firmer tone when at last she was connected.

"Dr. Werner's number is five-three-four-two," someone prodded when she had hung up. Obediently, Abigail dialed that, too.

It was Hilda Werner, the doctor's wife, who answered.

"May I speak to Dr. Werner? This is Abigail Potter."

"Oh, Mrs. Potter, I'm sorry. The doctor's just gone out. May I give him a message?"

"If you can reach him, ask him to get over to the Mannings' immediately, please. It's terribly urgent!"

"The Mannings'! But surely—" Mrs. Werner sounded bewildered. "Are you phoning from the Mannings' now?"

"No," Abigail said. "I'm across the street."

"Oh! Well, why don't you go on back. The doctor should be there any minute."

Abigail hung up, puzzled. Hilda Werner had spoken as though Dr. Werner were already on his way, but how had he been notified? Had someone else found Jerry before she did? Abigail wondered. She'd seen no other soul around.

The room was hot. It was revolving slowly. Abigail seemed to be ringed in by a tight circle of pitying eyes in pairs: two of blue and then two of brown—and all the eyes seemed to be swinging around, too.

"Here!" someone said. A glass was shoved into her hand. Abigail gulped it thirstily, choked, and coughed. Someone patted her on the back and someone else laughed.

"That's not water!" she observed indignantly, but she felt better. The room was behaving more normally now.

"I think," she said carefully, "I had better go over to the Snyders' now. Mrs. Demarest is all alone."

"But you told the police—"

"Was Jerry Manning killed at Snyders'?"

"How did it happen?"

"Who—"

A flood of questions flowed over and around her, but Abigail only shook her head. If she were any kind of detective she would have examined the murder room and so learned at least some of the answers. Instead she had run away. She did not even know how Jerry had met his death.

If I had let him go to the police at once and left it to them to prove his innocence he would be safe in the Dayton jail now instead, instead of— She shuddered.

"Thank you for the use of your phone," she said to the group at large. "I'll wait with Mrs. Demarest until the police come."

The pairs of eyes now seemed less sympathetic than curious and unfeeling. Abigail wanted to get away. Refusing almost bluntly the overeager offers of several of the young men and one or two of the girls, Abigail walked back alone. She could feel that as soon as she had left, the pairs of eyes regrouped themselves at the front windows where they could watch developments across the street.

The Snyders' front door was unlocked. Abigail pushed it open and yoo-hooed bravely into the dark recesses. No voice answered.

Her searching fingers found a light switch near the door. Before she stepped across the threshold she pressed it down and dispelled the shadows. Glancing neither to right nor left after her first quick survey of the empty hall, she started up the stairs, turning on each light as she went. She had left the umbrella behind her on the porch of the house across the street, but she still clutched the weighted stocking in her right hand and drew confidence from it.

At the top of the stairs she called again and was relieved when Eloise opened her door a crack and called, fearfully, "Who's there?"

"It's I!" Abigail replied, scurrying the last few steps.

"Oh!" Eloise's greeting was a wail. "I thought you'd never come. I've been so frightened!"

Her face crumpled. Abigail was afraid she would collapse upon her neck.

"It's all right now," Abigail soothed, feeling strong. She pushed aside Eloise's clutching hands. "I'm here—and the police are on their way."

"The police!" Eloise stared at her. "Oh, dear, they'll be furious—making them come way over here for nothing. But I was so terrified! Fred shouldn't have gone off like that and left me all alone. Maida will simply have to speak to him. He gets more inconsiderate every day—"

"The police will hardly be annoyed with me for calling them," Abigail broke in, "considering there's been another murder, next door."

Eloise's hand flew to her mouth. Her eyes were round and startled.

"You mean—he's been shot!" With a rapid reversal of her field she began to lament loudly. "Poor, dear Fred! He should never have gone over there! I knew it! I could have told him—"

"It's not Fred who's been killed," Abigail informed her sharply. "It's Jerry Manning."

"Jerry!" Eloise stared at her as though she thought her mad. "But it couldn't be! Jerry is the murderer! I know—I heard them talking!"

"Nonsense! Jerry Manning has been killed, I tell you—" Something was troubling Abigail, something Eloise had said. "What made you think he was shot?" she demanded.

"But I heard it, when I was talking to you! I told you I heard a shot, you must remember!"

Abigail tried to recall.

"You just said you heard—something," she corrected.

"No—well, maybe—but it *was* a shot. I was quite sure— It might have been a car backfiring—but it sounded different. Sharper, you know, and with sort of an echo. And it came from over toward Mannings', so of course when you said there'd been a murder next door, I knew. And of course I thought it was Fred. Are you quite sure it wasn't?" she added hopefully.

Abigail was sure. She could not have been mistaken about the face, covered with blood though it had been.

"No," she said, "it wasn't Fred."

Eloise pushed back the pink draperies that concealed her windows and peered out.

"I think the police have come," she said. "There are lights on next door—and men moving about. Do you think— Oh! You're not going over there!" She clutched at Abigail's coat as Abigail moved toward the door. "Don't leave me alone!"

"I have to go. After all, I found him. They'll want to ask me questions."

For only a moment Eloise eyed her quilted satin robe, her heelless scuffs.

"I'm going with you!" she stated, gathering the full skirts about her. Snatching up a quite inadequate marten stole from her closet, she threw it about her shoulders and started after Abigail.

The house next door was no longer dark as Abigail helped Eloise Demarest across the lawn. Lights blazed in all the downstairs rooms. As they stepped onto the front porch the door flew open and they were pushed aside without ceremony to make room for two men who carried a still form on a stretcher between them.

Eloise stifled a histrionic sob and clutched at the arm of the dapper man who followed the stretcher.

"Oh, Dr. Werner!" she cried. "Is he really dead?"

The dapper man spoke in a surprisingly booming voice.

"Not yet, Mrs. Demarest, not yet, but unless you step aside and let me get him to the hospital he soon will be. Where's his mother?"

"Oh, poor dear Charlotte! She's with Dora, Dr. Werner. Oh, this is terrible—"

"Better call her," Dr. Werner interrupted her impatiently. "Tell her we're taking him to St. Albans in Dayton. She'd better come fast—though he won't be conscious."

"Oh, yes, Dr. Werner! I'll call her right away!"

With a flurry of pink skirts, Eloise disappeared into the house.

The stretcher had been fitted into the rear of an overlong black limousine. Dr. Werner started down the walk at a run.

"What about the police?" Abigail called after him.

"Damn the police! Can't leave a man to die, waiting on them! Should've been here by now!"

He vaulted into the front seat of the private ambulance beside the driver and the big car pulled away.

X

Abigail walked slowly into the Manning house. She found Eloise already seated at Charlotte's secretary in the living room, clutching the telephone. Abigail turned away, feeling a little ill, and wandered off down the hall. She was sure that the actual scene of the crime could be no more upsetting than the spectacle of Eloise, her eyes glittering with excitement and tears, waiting to "break the news to poor, dear Charlotte."

The door of the study stood open. The desk was still neat and untouched; the deer head above it surveyed the scene glassily. Except for an unopened suitcase on a chair and a pair of shoes, pigeon-toed beside the couch, the room was too neat, unlived in. Only the stained couch cover, sprawling now half on, half off the day bed, remained a mute witness to tragedy.

No signs of struggle, Abigail noted. He had taken off his shoes, but he was still dressed and he hadn't unpacked so he couldn't have gone to bed for the night. He must have been lying on the bed when he was attacked. Was he awake? Or had he fallen asleep?

It seemed terribly important to her to know. She hoped he had been asleep, had never known his peril.

Careful to disturb nothing, she crossed the room to the window she had looked through earlier. As she stepped wide to avoid the dragging coverlet at the foot of the bed the heel of her shoe grated on broken glass, window glass. She dropped to her knees beneath the window and found more. The bottom half of the window had been shoved up, and when Abigail lifted the half-drawn shade she saw a jagged hole in the center of the pane.

But the window was down when I looked in, she puzzled. And Jerry was already dead, so it couldn't have been that the murderer broke the window to get in! Then why—

Troubled, she searched the rest of the downstairs. Before she heard the distant wail of the police siren she had made sure that all the other windows on the ground floor were shut and locked and that the kitchen door was bolted from the inside.

The murderer must have come in by the front door, she concluded, but she was not satisfied. She could devise no theory to explain the window which had been broken in the half hour since she had left to call the police.

Sheriff Greenough, pushing the front door open without ceremony, looked anything but pleased to see her.

"You again!" he observed. "How'd you get mixed up in this one? Where's the body?"

Abigail gestured vaguely.

"Gone," she said. "Dr. Werner—"

"Gone! Didn't you report a murder? Didn't you say—"

"It isn't a murder," Eloise spoke from the doorway of the living room. "That is, he isn't dead—yet. Dr. Werner took him to the hospital. And to think that it might have been me," she added, her voice quavering, "left all alone in that house!" Then she brightened. "Perhaps—perhaps he did it to protect me! Or in self-defense!"

"Who!" yelped Greenough. "Who did what in self-defense?"

"Why, Fred—killed Jerry Manning, of course. Fred knew Jerry was the murderer—"

"Holy cats!" Abigail had never heard even violent profanity used with more feeling. She reddened as Greenough whirled on her. "So you've fed Mrs. Demarest your crazy yarn! And now, even with Manning murdered you're still trying to make out he was the killer! 'Murdered!' What am I saying?"

He turned to the men who crowded in the doorway behind him.

"Brown, get on that phone and telephone Werner! Where, Mrs. Potter? Okay, get me St. Alban's. As soon as Werner gets there I want him to call me! Dr. Friggam," he went on, giving a name to the medical examiner, "get back to Dayton and see this Manning for yourself. Phone me a complete report. And you other guys—go over the house! Check everything—especially the murder—er—the room where the attack took place.

"Now, Mrs. Potter, what happened? First you call in and say he's dead—now you say he's not. What do you know about all this and what were you doing here in the first place?"

Abigail twisted the chain of her glasses nervously, but her voice was steady. Her story sounded peculiar, she had to admit, and Eloise gave her no assistance as she told of the telephone call that had brought her out. She reviewed her cautious exploration of the grounds outside the two houses, and her discovery of Jerry Manning's unconscious and blood-stained body.

"You say Mrs. Demarest sent for you?" Greenough barked. "Then why, if she was expecting you, did you wander around in the dark outside? Why didn't you go on in?"

"I was afraid," Abigail stated simply. "I wanted to make sure it wasn't a trap."

"Suspicious, aren't you? And so you came pussying around the Manning house, even though you thought Manning was the killer and had tried to poison you! Must have given you quite a turn when you found he was a victim himself and your whole story blew up in your face!"

"But I *didn't* think he was the killer—" Abigail began weakly.

"Perhaps you'll believe me now when we say we know who the murderer is—and this time, so help me, we'll prove it! Hey! Did you say blood? Then Manning wasn't poisoned like the others?"

"Oh, no!" Eloise babbled. "He was shot. I heard it! I mean—"

"You heard the shot?" Greenough whipped out a notebook. "Now we're getting somewhere. What time?"

Eloise consulted Abigail.

"About an hour ago?" she ventured. "It was nearly ten, I think, because Maida left a little after nine thirty and it was a while after that before I called."

Abigail nodded.

"Mrs. Weston's clock struck ten just after you hung up," she confirmed.

Greenough scribbled and then held his pencil poised.

"And what time did Snyder get home?"

"Fred? Oh, he came right back after he and Jerry took Mrs. Potter—"

"Not Fred, Arthur! When did Arthur Snyder get home? And where is he now?"

"Why, Arthur's with you! I mean, isn't he in jail or something? Maida went over to Dayton to see him."

"In jail? Hell, no! Kept him as long as we could, but we couldn't hold him. That lawyer of his—great guns, lady—if you thought Arthur Snyder was locked up, who in hell did you think shot Manning?"

"What time did you release him?" Abigail asked.

"Couple of hours ago. He had plenty of time to get here."

"Then where is he?"

"That's what I'm asking you!" Greenough snapped. He reached for the telephone and dialed. "Brown!" he directed the officer at his side. "Get over to Snyder's house and watch for him! Bring him over the minute he comes in."

Then, as his call was put through, he turned his attention to the phone.

"Walton? Greenough here! Listen, Snyder's missing! That's right, Arthur Snyder. Now get this! There's been another murder try. I want Snyder picked up for questioning. You've got the description. Probably wearing the same clothes he had on when he left headquarters. Driving a—nope, he didn't have his car. Hold on a minute—"

Without covering the mouthpiece he barked at Eloise.

"You say his wife went to meet him? What time?"

"I told you. She left around nine thirty."

"Driving?"

"I think so."

"Did she say she was meeting him at police headquarters?"

"Yes—no—I mean, she just said Dayton and I thought of course he was still in jail. She said Arthur had called and he wanted to talk to her right away and I thought— You mean, you don't know where Maida is?"

Greenough ignored Eloise's questions.

"He may be with his wife," he added into the phone. "He got in touch with her after we let him go and she's gone, too. Better send out a description of them both. She's twenty-three, blond, green eyes, about five-four and weighs somewhere around a hundred and fifteen."

Sheriff Greenough, Abigail thought, had noticed a great deal about Maida Snyder. She moved closer to Eloise, who now looked really ill.

"Maida didn't say anything about their letting Arthur go!" she whispered. "What does it mean? Where is she?"

"Don't worry!" Abigail said, although she, too, wondered. For that matter, where was Fred? It seemed odd that all three of the Snyders should have vanished in the middle of the night. Or perhaps, by now, they were all at home worrying about Eloise's absence and unaware of the drama next door.

One of the policeman emerged from the back of the house. He carried something carefully wrapped about with a not too clean handkerchief.

"Here's the weapon, Sam!" he announced. "Found it under the bed in the study!"

"Okay, get on it!" Greenough finished into the phone. He slammed down the receiver. "Let's see it!" He held out his hand for the object and laid back the corners of the handkerchief to expose a small, mother-of-pearl-inlaid revolver.

"Twelve caliber!" he ejaculated. "Why, that's nothing but a popgun!"

"Men have been killed with popguns like that!" the trooper commented.

Greenough sniffed at it gingerly.

"Been fired all right. Nasty little job!"

Eloise, one hand clutching her robe together at the throat, leaned closer to look and drew in her breath sharply.

"Recognize it?" Greenough asked quickly.

"It's—it's Charlotte's—Mrs. Manning's. Jerry got it for her himself! Oh, dear!" Eloise swayed and Abigail slipped a steadying arm about her waist.

"When did he give it to her? Where'd she keep it?"

"Oh, I don't know!" Eloise wailed. "A few years ago—he gave it to her, I mean—when he was home on furlough and she was alone in the house. That was before Nelson—Jerry's father—died, but he was in the hospital, of course, and Jerry didn't like her to be alone. Charlotte thought he was silly but she let him get her this. I remember Jerry said it wasn't much better than a toy, but Charlotte said it was enough to scare anyone—and she wouldn't want to kill anybody anyway."

"Know where she kept it?" Greenough asked again.

"It was always in the drawer of her secretary—in the parlor—with her stationery. She never used it—I don't think she ever even loaded it."

"Somebody did," the trooper who had found it observed.

"Who knew about it? Arthur Snyder?"

"Oh, no, not Arthur. Everyone else, probably, but not Arthur. You see, he was never in this house after—I mean, Charlotte hated him. They didn't speak at all."

"But it wasn't hidden? Anyone could have found it, even without knowing where to look?"

"Jerry would have known where it was," Eloise suggested. "Maybe he got it out. Maybe he meant to shoot Fred only Fred took it away from him and shot him first. It could have been that way."

"What's all this about Fred? Where is he anyhow? And why would Jerome Manning be trying to shoot Fred?"

"Because Jerry was the murderer, of course, and Fred found out about it and—"

Greenough ran a distracted hand through his hair.

"Are you still harping on that? Get this, you two! Jerome Manning had nothing to do with these killings—nothing! You're crazy if you let Mrs. Potter sell you that bill of goods! It makes a swell plot, sure, but this is no book. This is real and we got to go on facts! The facts are, Arthur Snyder wanted Hawkes dead so he killed him. And then, trying to cover up, he had to kill Tom Weston and now, for some reason, Manning. Only this time he's gone too far. This time we'll get him!"

"I'll admit I was wrong about Jerry Manning," Abigail said quietly, "but I don't believe you'll solve this case until you realize the part he played in it. He didn't kill Tom Weston, but he did plant the poison that killed Hawkes and started the chain."

"Look!" Greenough roared. "I got enough on my mind! I got things to do! Why don't you and Mrs. Demarest run along? Go next door and wait! Make a pot of coffee. Anything! But leave me alone for a few minutes to find out what's what!"

"All right," Abigail said, injured. "Come along, Mrs. Demarest."

"And let me know the minute any of them Snyders turn up!" Greenough bellowed after them.

Eloise stumbled and leaned heavily on Abigail as they walked back across the lawn.

"You're very tired," Abigail said. "Why don't you go along to bed?"

"Oh, I couldn't sleep—after all this! I'm too upset!"

That makes four of us, Abigail reflected. Mrs. Demarest and I, Dora Weston and Charlotte Manning. She had been in Glen Falls a little over forty-eight hours and two staggering blows had been struck at people she had come to know and respect.

"I suppose Mrs. Weston would have gone over to the hospital with Mrs. Manning?" she ventured, hoping that Charlotte would not be alone in her tragic vigil. Or would Jerry's mother arrive too late? "She'd better come fast!" Dr. Werner had said.

Eloise, absorbed in her own anxiety, did not respond.

"I can't understand why Maida didn't tell me where she was going. I won't sleep a wink until I know she's safe!"

"They're probably at home by now," Abigail reassured her, but when no one responded to her timid yoo-hoo as they entered the big house she was not surprised. For Eloise's sake she tried to hide her concern.

"Why don't I fix a pot of coffee?" she suggested. "I think Mr. Greenough would like some when he comes over, and I know I would. If we're going to sit up—"

Eloise sank upon the couch in the living room and stretched out. "That would be nice," she said, listlessly.

Abigail waited for directions, but apparently Eloise had forgotten that her guest was not familiar with the house. When she turned her head away and shut her eyes, Abigail set out to explore for herself.

She found the kitchen at the end of the lower hall. It was a big room, basically large and old-fashioned but brightened with gay curtains and linoleum and well equipped with modern appliances.

It must be a pleasant place to eat in the mornings, Abigail thought, noticing the cherry drop-leaf table beneath the wide east windows.

The coffeepot and two used cups stood beside the sink. Abigail poured out stale coffee and disposed of the grounds and while a fresh pot was brewing she washed and dried the cups. The fragrance of coffee, released by the boiling water, teased her nostrils and she began to feel more cheerful. By the time she had found sugar and cream and teaspoons and arranged them on a lacquered tray, she felt ready for anything, but most immediately and especially for the steaming fragrant coffee.

In the living room Eloise, in spite of her protestations, had fallen asleep. Abigail did not wake her. She drank her coffee alone, finding her hostess more agreeable company in slumber. For herself, she felt no tendency to doze. Her mind was far too busy.

Jerry's story of the letter, corroborated by the crowning proof of his innocence, the attack upon himself, opened up unlimited vistas.

Her heart had never been identified with her efforts to convict Jerry but Abigail, having looked on his helpless bloody face, knew she would not vacillate in her determination to track down his assailant.

Anyone who would deliberately try to murder such a nice boy deserves to be hanged, she told herself fiercely. Or would it be the electric chair, in Ohio? At any rate, no punishment could be too drastic for such a man—or woman.

In the meantime, Abigail Potter was a long way from sending anyone to the death cell. Reviewing the facts, she knew only that the possible suspects were limited to four, all of them members of the Snyder household. Only the Snyders and Eloise Demarest would have had access to Jerry's letter or reason to open it; only the Snyders and Eloise could have poisoned her brandy. Only—

Suddenly she was brought up in mid-thought. No one but Jerry Manning would have had reason to try to kill her, for her investigations had threatened no one but Jerry! And he was not the murderer!

For the first time Abigail considered the possibility that Tom Weston's death had not been a mistake. Instead of wondering, "Who had reason to kill me?" she should have been asking, "Who wanted Tom Weston to die—and why?"

Did Tom find out something he didn't tell me, Abigail wondered. She tried to remember every word of their brief conversation. Or had he known something he didn't know he knew?

And if the poison had really been meant for Tom, why had it been in her glass? The murderer couldn't have known that Tom would reach for the wrong drink! Screwing her eyes up, Abigail leaned her head back and tried to reconstruct the scene in the living room before and during the confusion of Eloise's attack, for, Abigail assured herself, it must have been during that time that the glasses were tampered with—unless Arthur or Fred had poisoned Tom's drink at the bar—and in that case, I would have been the one to die! Oh, dear! It's all so very confusing!

She tried to picture the two glasses as she and Tom had set them down, both on the small table between their chairs. Tom had fidgeted nervously with his and, when Charlotte and Jerry came in, had left it on the table.

Suddenly Abigail sat up very straight. The scene came back to her as though a moving picture had been frozen on a single frame. Jerry and his mother had come through the French doors behind Abigail; Maida and Arthur, followed by Tom, had gone over to greet them; Fred had been standing in the doorway, staring directly at Abigail, his arms full of pink pillows. Eloise, pouring herself a drink at the bar, had ingenuously referred to Abigail's detective activities and Abigail, in confusion, had looked down, noticed Tom's glass perilously near the edge, and had reached to move it back.

Abigail could recall the feel of the slender stem between her fingers and realized that she had still been holding it when Eloise staggered and leaned against the little table. For those few moments her hand had been resting on the base of Tom's glass as though it had been her own. Subconsciously, perhaps, Tom must have noticed it and so had taken the other glass when he reached for his drink. Almost certainly the murderer had noticed!

And that, Abigail decided with mounting excitement, fixes the time of the crime. The poison must have been dropped into my brandy during the next few minutes while I was still holding Tom's glass and all of us were watching Eloise!

Then the murderer isn't after me at all! she told herself. She had felt almost secure from the moment she had chosen to believe Jerry's story of the intercepted letter, yet she had been unable to get around the fact that Tom had drained the brandy in her glass—and had died.

Now, if she could only run the movie on a few more scenes and then stop it once more she might remember something, some movement too close to her chair, some cautious gesture overlooked at the time, that would tell her who had taken advantage of the confusion. But the movie would not go on, the film had broken. It seemed ridiculous to suppose that anyone, in a roomful of people, would have dared to drop poison into a glass and even more unreasonable to believe that no one would have seen him do it. Yet it must have happened that way. The maddening thing about it was that any one of them *could* have done it, any of the six people in the room had passed close enough.

Eloise turned restlessly in her sleep. Her mouth dropped open as she rolled onto her back. On the mantel the clock ticked steadily and somewhere in the back of the house a board relaxed with a startling creak. I never did ask Mrs. Demarest what it was she heard that frightened her so, Abigail remembered. It wasn't the shot, for she was already talking to me when she heard that.

She eyed the sleeping woman with a speculative eye. Or did she really hear that shot at all? The revolver Greenough's man had found was certainly very small to have produced a report loud enough to carry from one house to the next—especially with the windows shut. Abigail made a mental note to suggest to Greenough that he investigate.

She was beginning to feel drowsy. She had no wish to fall asleep, so she forced herself to get up and carry the coffeepot back to the kitchen to reheat. It was only eleven twenty by the kitchen clock. Abigail figured that, although it seemed as though it must be nearly dawn, she and Eloise had been in the Snyder house less than half an hour.

She was still in the kitchen when she heard the front door open and slam shut. The Snyders! she thought, and hurried into the hall, as self-conscious as though she had been caught in wrongdoing.

It was only Greenough. His expression was no longer belligerent and he looked tired. Abigail noticed a subtle difference in the way he faced her, even before he spoke.

"I got to hand it to you, Mrs. Potter," he began, magnanimously. "If I'd just listened to you this afternoon—"

"Why? What is it!" He looked so dejected that Abigail felt instinctively sorry for him.

"Manning was the murderer, all right—just like you said. And I was too dumb—"

"But he wasn't!" Abigail protested, shocked. "Jerry was attacked himself!"

"All the doors and windows were locked. Dr. Werner had to break the window of the study to get in to him. Manning tried to kill himself. It's the only answer. Besides, they found a suicide note in his coat pocket at the hospital."

A suicide note! Oh, no, instinct cried out. It has to be a fake!

"I haven't seen it," Greenough went on as though he had read her mind. "But I talked to Dr. Werner on the phone and he says it's the McCoy. Manning's mother is over there and she's had to admit it's in his writing. In it, Manning claims full responsibility for these killings—told just how it was done—the poison in the medicine and so on, just like you said. He's guilty as hell! I only hope we can pull him through and save him for the chair!"

XI

Greenough rubbed a tired hand across his forehead and back into his hair.

"Is that coffee I smell, Mrs. Potter? I could sure use some."

"Coffee?" Abigail repeated, as though it were a strange new word. "Oh—yes!" She motioned toward Eloise, still asleep, and laid a finger on her lips. "Come back to the kitchen and I'll get you some."

"Who found the note?" she ventured, after she had poured Greenough a cup of warmed-over coffee and started a new pot.

"Dr. Werner." Greenough helped himself to six lumps of sugar and stirred them around and around in the cup with a hyp-notic persistence. At last, sighing deeply, he crooked his thumb over the handle of the spoon to hold it in place and drank.

"I still think the whole thing's screwy," he said finally. "It don't make sense. If this Manning guy really did plant that poi-son three years back, how come Snyder didn't get it long ago? And why the hell—beg pardon—why should Manning bump himself off? The way the thing was set up our case against Sny-der was a cinch. We'd have got him into court and he wouldn't 'a' stood a chance. The state would have done Manning's dirty work for him. He wanted Snyder dead, didn't he? Then why would he kill himself and leave a confession to save the guy from a murder rap? I don't get it!"

But Jerry hadn't wanted Arthur Snyder to die!

Abigail didn't get it either, but she was working on it, slow-ly and tenaciously. She knew that Jerry had intended to give

himself up rather than allow him to be charged with Hawkes'
murder, but why should he have tried to commit suicide? Only
that evening he had seemed willing to wait until they had exhausted every effort to find the person who had connived in the
attempt to kill Arthur. He had not lost hope of clearing himself in Hawkes' death—and in any event, he had not killed Tom
Weston. Then why?

Her first instinct, that the confession had been faked, was
apparently wrong, but what if Jerry had written it to protect
someone else? Abigail examined that possibility with increasing
excitement. Jerry Manning would not have killed himself to save
Arthur Snyder—but what if he knew that Maida was involved?
What if he had reason to suspect that she *had* received his letter
and had ignored his instructions?

"Any more java?" Greenough asked, extending his cup.

Silently Abigail refilled it, wondering if she ought to tell
Greenough that Jerry's confession of guilt was probably false.
Reluctantly she decided against disturbing his new amiability.
He had his confession and Abigail suspected that he was not the
man to consider two possibilities at once. After she had seen
Charlotte Manning and learned whether she had delivered the
letter into Maida's hands it would be time enough to suggest that
Jerry might be trying to shield someone.

"It's strange the Snyders aren't home yet," she observed.

"Damn—doggone strange!" Greenough agreed. His unwont-
ed consideration of her finer feelings touched Abigail. He consulted his watch. "After midnight. You got to admit, he don't act
like an innocent man—hasn't all along. And where are the other
two? Mighty queer they're all out at this hour. Reckon Manning's
confession'll be quite a load off the old man's mind, all right.
I'd 'a' staked my bottom dollar we had him to rights for these
jobs, too."

He shook his head regretfully and poured the remainder of
the coffee down his throat.

"Think Mrs. Demarest knows anything about them, where
they are?" he suggested then.

"By the way!" Abigail remembered, "doesn't it seem queer she would have heard such a small revolver at that distance? With the windows closed?"

Greenough shrugged.

"Guess we'd better wake her up and get her story—though it don't much matter *how* she heard the shot. There was one, so we know she didn't make it up. I got an idea she could tell us where her daughter is, though, if she'd a mind to and if she knows Snyder's in the clear she may speak up. Then I can go home and get to bed."

Eloise was sleeping very soundly for an individual who had not expected to shut her eyes all night. Abigail touched her shoulder gently at first and then shook her vigorously.

"Wake up, Mrs. Demarest!" she repeated until Eloise finally stirred irritably and opened her eyes.

"What is it?" she cried, clutching her robe about her and staring from Abigail to Greenough. "Something's happened to Maida!"

"No, Mrs. Demarest," Abigail soothed her. "Mr. and Mrs. Snyder haven't come in yet, but I'm sure they're quite all right. Mr. Greenough simply wants to ask you a few questions. See if you can tell us where they might be. You see, Mr. Snyder is no longer in danger of arrest. We know who did the murders."

"You do!" Eloise quavered. Her lips formed the next word several times before she seemed able to get it out. "Who?"

"Jerry Manning tried to kill himself," Greenough informed her. "He has confessed to the murders."

Eloise's whole body seemed to relax.

"He killed himself!" she said triumphantly. "I kept telling you he was the murderer only you wouldn't believe me. You see, I heard them—and I was terrified. Fred was a fool to speak up to him like that. I'd never dare tell a murderer to his face that I knew all about him! I was dreadfully afraid he'd find out I heard and try to kill me, too. The minute I heard him go out I called you, Mrs. Potter, and—"

"Hold on a minute!" Greenough broke in. "What did you hear, Mrs. Demarest? Who were talking?"

"Why, Fred and Jerry—after Maida left. I was just going along the hall and I heard Fred say, 'You didn't intend to kill Hawkes, did you, Manning? You meant that poisoned capsule for my dad!'"

"What else did you hear?" Greenough demanded, scribbling furiously.

"Jerry said, 'So you know!' and Fred said something about, 'Well, what do you intend to do about it?' I couldn't hear what Jerry answered, but I heard them coming toward the hall so I—I went back to my room."

Abigail smiled as she imagined the flurry of pink rushing down the hall to safety.

How did Fred know that Hawkes' death was an accident, she thought, suspiciously. Only one person besides Maida, Jerry, and herself could have known that! Then she remembered her missing notebook. Had Fred been the one to find it? Abigail suspected that Fred would not have been convinced as easily as she had been by Jerry's explanation of the intercepted letter.

"Where the devil *is* Fred!" Greenough burst out violently. "We've got to find him!"

Eloise clasped her hands to her breast, twisting them agitatedly. "Jerry *did* kill him!" she cried. "I knew it! He's dead!"

Perhaps Greenough had come to the same conclusion. At least, he made a dive for the telephone.

Even as the dial whirred, however, the front door was flung open. Abigail turned to see Maida and Arthur Snyder. Without completing his call, Greenough replaced the receiver on its base.

"Well!" he said with caustic emphasis. "Out pretty late, aren't you? It's after midnight."

"Why are you here?" Maida flared. "You released Arthur! You can't question him again, not at this hour!"

Arthur's shoulders drooped as he walked toward the hall closet, taking off his overcoat as he went.

"Your husband's in the clear, Mrs. Snyder," Greenough stated.

"We just want to know where you've been all evening—and whether either of you knows anything about Fred Snyder."

"Fred! What about Fred?" Arthur demanded.

"'In the clear,'" Maida repeated simultaneously. "You mean—you don't suspect Arthur anymore?"

"That's right," Greenough answered Maida's question first. "Jerry Manning has confessed."

"Arthur—do you hear? Everything's all right!"

She turned to Abigail anxiously. "Jerry *will* be all right, won't he? Did he tell them everything? They can't hold him, can they? They understand it wasn't his fault?"

Abigail shook her head, unable to speak. She was waiting for Greenough to explain the circumstances of Jerry's confession.

Arthur showed neither surprise nor relief. He was fumbling with the handle of the closet door, his attention directed to the turning knob.

"This door's locked," he observed mildly.

"Don't be silly," Maida replied. "It's just stuck."

She jerked at the door herself. An expression of surprise and annoyance crossed her face.

"Why, it is locked!" she said. "But that's not right! There's never been a key!"

"What!" Greenough reached the door in two strides and tried the knob. His urgency seemed to carry even to Maida and Arthur who, unlike Abigail, did not know what was in his mind.

"Got to get this door open," he panted, wrenching at it.

"Perhaps some other key?" Abigail suggested. She had noticed that the keyhole was of an ordinary type. I'd like to try a hairpin, she thought wistfully, but maybe it's not the right kind of lock. Or maybe they'll break the door down!

"All the rooms have keys like that," Maida volunteered. "Most of them have been lost, but I'll see what I can find."

Even Eloise sensed the atmosphere.

"The key to my room is under the corner of my rug," she offered, "but if I'd known that just any key—I really must have my lock changed, left all alone in the house as I am night after night—"

"Looks to me like a simple skeleton key would do the job," Greenough muttered, producing a pair from his pocket. "Have a couple here I picked up for my kid! Let's see—"

The first key he tried slid in easily and the lock clicked back. "There!" he said, flinging the door wide.

Abigail, peering under his arm, saw a heap on the floor that was not a fallen coat. Even before Arthur cried his name, she knew that Fred had been found.

"Is he—dead?" whimpered Eloise, backing away.

No one answered. Arthur dropped to the floor beside his son, but it was Greenough who eased the inert form out and turned it over, groping with one hand for the wrist.

"Call Dr. Werner!" he rapped out. "Try him at his house! This man's not dead, just unconscious!"

As though under hypnosis, Abigail moved to the phone. To her great relief, Dr. Werner himself answered and promised to come over at once.

"Looks to me like he's been drugged," Greenough was saying as she rejoined the anxious group. "Think you could make some more coffee, Mrs. Potter? I got a hunch we'll need it—for him and all of us.

"I'll make some," Maida said.

There seemed to be nothing Abigail could do for Fred, so she followed Maida to the kitchen and tried to make herself useful. Maida seemed to welcome her presence. After she had measured out coffee and the water was perking, she sank into a chair opposite Abigail at the kitchen table and brushed a tired hand over her eyes.

"What else can happen! It's like a nightmare. Who would have locked Fred in that closet—and why?"

Abigail shook her head. She knew that as far as Greenough was concerned, the attack on Fred was only further evidence of Jerry's guilt. Instead of wondering why a man who is about to kill himself from remorse would try to add another murder to his list, Greenough would probably argue that Jerry had drugged Fred and locked him in the closet to delay his going to the police, to give himself time to escape the Law.

"Where were you and your husband while all this was happening?" she asked.

Maida did not answer at once. Abigail found herself automatically counting the contented burps of the percolating coffee and waiting for the sound of the front-door bell.

"We were just—talking," Maida said at last.

"Was Jerry here when you left to meet your husband?"

"Yes." Again that discouraged pause. "He had supper with us after he and Fred drove you home. Fred had left when Arthur called, so I asked Jerry to stay here till we got back so Mother wouldn't be alone."

"You say Fred had left? But your mother said she heard him talking to Jerry just after you'd gone."

Maida shrugged.

"I didn't mean he'd gone out. He left us right after supper, perhaps to go to his room—I don't know. He and Mother don't get along very well," she added frankly, "and as long as Jerry was here anyway—"

She stood up abruptly and turned off the fire under the coffee. "This ought to be strong enough! Personally, I need a stiff drink more than I do coffee."

Abigail tried to remind herself of the unpleasant taste that had seared her throat under the name of brandy, of the liquid fire she had gulped at the house across the street, but all she could make real was the remembered warmth and strength that had flowed through her veins in its wake. She felt, with Maida, that under some circumstances liquor was to be preferred to coffee.

Oh dear! she thought with sudden misgivings. I must be very careful or I might become an alcoholic! This must be the way a confirmed drunkard starts!

"No, thank you," she practiced under her breath in case anyone should ask her. "No, thank you very much."

Fred had been moved to the couch in the living room and Eloise, supplanted, now sulked in a chair. Arthur was holding Fred's wrist awkwardly between finger and thumb.

"I can't tell," he told Maida miserably. "Is his pulse weak—or is it just that I don't know what to look for? How many beats should there be? What's *keeping* Werner!"

"It's been barely twenty minutes since we called," Eloise pointed out, "and he probably had to dress. I'll have a glass of brandy, too, Maida."

No one gave Abigail an opportunity to say no, thank you. Feeling a trifle hurt she retired to a chair in the corner. Greenough paced the floor, consulting his watch each time he made a turn at the end of the room.

At last Dr. Werner arrived, brisk and unemotional. Even Arthur's face relaxed as he moved over to let the doctor take charge. No one spoke as they all watched the expert manner in which he turned back Fred's eyelids, felt his pulse, laid a hand on his forehead.

"Overdose of chloral hydrate!" he said, after what Abigail considered a dangerously superficial examination. "Get plenty of coffee ready. We've got to get him awake—keep him walking."

"Will he—will he be all right?" Arthur asked.

"Should be. His heart's okay—but we'll have to watch out for complications."

Werner moved a lamp closer and began to draw liquid into a hypodermic syringe from a vial in his bag. Abigail seized the opportunity to ask, in a lowered tone, about Jerry.

"He's got a fighting chance!" Dr. Werner replied absently. Obviously he had dismissed all other patients from his mind to deal with the immediate need. "This young fellow ought to have a nurse tonight, but I don't know who—"

"I'll be glad to stay with him, Dr. Werner," Abigail offered. "I'm not trained, but I have common sense and I can follow directions. I nursed my aunt through her last illness," she added modestly, "and her physician said few professionals could have done better."

Dr. Werner looked relieved.

"Fine! Fine! I'll give you full instructions before I go. It may be another hour before I can leave. You'd better get some rest if you're going to be up all night."

"Rest!" Eloise moaned histrionically from her corner. "As if anyone in this house could be expected—"

"Yes, Eloise, rest! You most especially!" Dr. Werner's tone was sharp, but at once he soothed into a note of professional sympathy. "You've had a bad day and for one in your condition sleep is paramount. Mrs. Potter, perhaps you would take her upstairs, see that she is comfortable, and give her—this." He shook a pale pink pill into his hand from a half-full bottle and although he thrust it at her as though he wished it were poison, Abigail noted that Eloise seemed flattered at the attention. Probably, too, she was pleased because the medicine was her favorite color.

"It seems terrible, walking out on you like this," she protested feebly, "but I suppose—my heart— Oh, dear, Maida, I'm nothing but an extra worry and burden to you in your hour of need!"

"Nonsense, Mother! I shan't worry about you in the least," Maida denied. "You do as Dr. Werner says and go to bed."

Abigail laid a firm hand on the slippery sleeve of Eloise's dressing gown and guided her toward the stairs.

On the bottom step Eloise paused to deliver her valedictory.

"Poor, dear Fred!" she mourned, but no one glanced her way. They were all bending over Fred. With a sigh, Eloise allowed Abigail to lead her upstairs and tuck her into bed.

Abigail was positive that the sedative was superfluous, for Eloise's eyelids were drooping before her head touched the pillow.

Probably nothing but a bread pellet anyway! Abigail thought, but she fetched a glass of water from the pink bathroom. Dr. Werner had just been trying to get rid of Eloise, she was sure, but Abigail did not blame him.

She roused Eloise and conscientiously administered the pill.

"I hope dear Charlotte got my message about Jerry," Eloise murmured drowsily. Then her head fell back and she slept.

Abigail was tiptoeing toward the door but as Eloise's words registered she turned and spoke sharply.

"What message?"

Eloise was fast asleep. Abigail was about to shake her again before she remembered that it did not really matter. Even if Eloise had been referring to her telephone call to Jerry's mother after his accident it was needless to waken her now. If Eloise had

not spoken to Charlotte directly at least Charlotte had gotten
the message, for she had been at the hospital to identify Jerry's
handwriting on the note.

Outside the room, Abigail hesitated, torn between anxiety to
know how the treatment was progressing and a very real weari-
ness.

I'd be far more sensible to get some rest while I can, she
decided at last. Dr. Werner will wake me before he leaves—and
then I'll know.

Know what? she wondered. Not whether Fred was going to
live, for oddly enough she had not once believed that he would
die. And that's strange, too, she thought, for if this is another
in the series of criminal attacks he should have been dead when
found. The murderer—and in spite of Greenough, Abigail would
not believe it was Jerry—the murderer had not hesitated to use a
swift poison before.

The old saw ran through her tired brain, "A thing that's
worth doing is worth doing well." Assuming that murder had
been worth doing, the murderer had done nothing well. He had,
in fact, done incredibly badly.

She turned from the stairs and sought the nearest door, unaware until she had pushed it open on the masculine clutter that
she was again in Fred's room.

The bed was still unmade.

I should think, she reflected disapprovingly, that even on a
nominal salary the Snyders could afford a maid for such a big
house. Not but what Fred isn't quite old enough to tidy his own
room and spread up his bed!

She jerked the rumpled sheets smooth, mitered the corners.
As she tucked them beneath the mattress with vicious jabs, her
hand came into contact with something unyielding. Abigail in-
vestigated. Resting on the springs, beneath the end of the mattress, lay her missing black notebook!

Fred had been the one to find it after all! The alternate possibility, that Fred's knowledge of Jerry's original guilt presupposed
his own complicity, would have to be discarded. Abigail guessed
that Fred had found the notebook that afternoon when Eloise

was downstairs and he had gone up to fetch her pillows. Probably he had glanced through it then, realized its significance, and hidden it away in his own room to peruse at leisure—a leisure he had not found until after supper when he'd left Maida and Jerry alone.

Abigail, thinking of the night-long vigil for which she had volunteered, found the softness of the bed so tempting that she could not resist it. She would have time for a short nap before Dr. Werner needed her.

Her whole body was achingly tired, but though she longed to sleep her mind refused to co-operate. It kept going over and over the events of the day. That morning she had been frantically scurrying about looking for evidence of Jerome Manning's guilt. Tonight, and with the police convinced that Jerry was a murderer, she was fighting with equal desperation to prove that he was innocent.

Can it be that I'm wrong? she asked herself. She was uncomfortably aware that, like Greenough, she had shown a lamentable tendency to jump to conclusions. Her blunder in the case of Philip Koestler's pills, her fallacious assumption that the poison that killed Tom Weston had been meant for her, were enough to make her question her own judgment.

Determined to be objective, she set herself to examine the case against Jerry. If he had, as Greenough believed, been responsible not only for Hawkes' death but for the murder of Tom Weston and the attack on Fred, then his activities had been a fantastic series of blunders from first to last. Abigail reviewed them dispassionately.

First attempt: the wrong man was killed. Second attempt: again the wrong victim—for surely, if Jerry is the murderer, she reminded herself, I was right in believing that the poisoned brandy was intended for me and not for Tom. Third attempt: the attack on Fred has failed. Finally, he has even failed in his efforts to escape the consequences by taking his own life!

No one, Abigail thought disgustedly, could be so completely inept. Certainly not the brain whose original scheme had offered such a brilliant challenge! To assume that Jerry was guilty was to admit that the only thing he had done successfully had been to lie! Yet he had not lied at all skillfully in the beginning.

On the train his story didn't deceive me for a minute! she assured herself with literary license, yet today—and right after I believed he had attempted my life—he was able to convince me of his innocence!

And why should he have lied at all? Such a tale could only have been to allay my doubts, to keep me from going to the police, to give himself time. But time for what? Surely not to kill himself!

Abigail found that objectively as well as instinctively, she could not believe in Jerry's confession. His guilt, if any, lay in having lighted a long fuse which he had honestly tried to stamp out before it reached the explosive he had set.

The only tenable theory seemed to be that Jerry had confessed to the murders and then tried to take his own life in an effort to protect someone else. She could think of no one Jerry would be likely to shield unless he were still in love with Maida and had reason to believe that she had received his letter in spite of her denial.

Yet neither could Abigail believe that Maida would have failed to carry out Jerry's instructions. To be sure, Arthur kept his medicine locked in a safe. But Abigail was certain that in this instance at least, love would have laughed at locksmiths. If she had been unable to destroy the pills herself, Maida would surely have warned Arthur of his danger.

Perplexed and deeply disturbed, Abigail gave up her futile attempts to get to sleep.

She had no idea how long she had stayed upstairs, but it had been long enough for Dr. Werner's ministrations to take effect. Fred's eyes were glassy and his whole weight seemed to droop between his father and Dr. Werner as they propelled him up and down the hall, but he was on his feet.

In the chair where Tom Weston had died, Greenough slumbered loudly and unfeelingly. As Abigail reached the foot of the stairs Maida, heavy eyed, came from the kitchen with a pot of steaming coffee.

"I've brewed enough coffee tonight to keep all of Glen Falls awake," she greeted Abigail.

She set the pot on the hall table and spoke anxiously to Arthur. "Poor Arthur! It has been a night, but it's all right now. By tomorrow it will seem like a bad dream."

Arthur did not take his eyes from Fred's face, nor did he respond to Maida's reassurance.

"Pour another cup of coffee!" he directed, his words slurring with fatigue.

"Really, Arthur!" Dr. Werner protested as Arthur accepted a cup from Maida and raised it to his own lips. "Don't drink any more of that stuff yourself! You've got to get some sleep, man! How's your head?"

Arthur regarded the doctor vaguely for a moment. He touched a hand almost inquiringly to the base of his skull.

"Splitting!" he admitted. "But I'll be all right. Got to take care of Fred—"

"We'll get some more coffee down him," Dr. Werner stated firmly, "and then I'm going to put you to bed. Between Mrs. Potter, here, and Maida and myself, we'll make out all right. Greenough will give us a hand."

Arthur did not answer. Abigail noticed that he moved sluggishly as though he himself were drugged. His whole mind seemed to be focused, with an effort, upon Fred and the need to support him, to force him to drink the black coffee that Maida held to his lips. Abigail was not even sure he knew that Dr. Werner had spoken.

The doctor caught Maida's eye and shook his head warningly. "He's all in," he said. "I'm going to give him a sedative. If he doesn't get some sleep we'll have another patient on our hands."

"My own—medicine," Arthur mumbled. "Get my pills, Maida."

"But I can't—" Maida protested. "They're in the safe!"

"Never mind," Dr. Werner said. "I've got something here—"

But Arthur, one hand pressed against the back of his head, spoke fumblingly.

"Get them, Maida! The safe—two right, seven left, fourteen right. They'll stop this damn pain!"

His face was white and drawn with anxiety, sleeplessness, and pain. If that's nothing but migraine, Abigail thought, I'm an albatross! Maida herself looked pale and startled. For a moment she stared at Arthur blankly and made no move.

"I'll get them," Abigail offered.

"Oh, no, Arthur wouldn't—"

But Arthur reached for Maida's hand and gripped it with knuckles that showed white.

"It's all right," he said. "Let Mrs. Potter go. You stay here with me."

"Where is the safe?" Abigail asked.

"In the baseboard—behind the desk in the study."

Abigail hurried up the stairs, repeating beneath her breath, "Two right, seven left, fourteen right."

The oblong metal box, half full of gelatine capsules, stood alone in the foot-square space uncovered as a hinged door set in the baseboard swung open. Abigail seized upon it with satisfaction. This innocent metal box for three years had hoarded death before it had yielded it up to let loose a train of violence! Abigail, shuddering, wondered how Arthur could ever again feel safe in taking those capsules. She herself had a strong impulse to empty the remainder, harmless though they now were. She carried her burden gingerly as though at any moment it might go off.

She delivered the box to Maida and watched Arthur take two of the capsules that Maida tipped out into her palm and swallow them as a starving man might bolt peas.

"Lie down, now!" Maida said, leading him to the couch. "We'll wake you if there's any need."

"Keep him walking!" Arthur muttered thickly. "I ought to—"

"We'll stay on the job, Arthur," Dr. Werner promised him. "You'll only make matters worse if you fold up on us."

Arthur nodded heavily. Under the persuasive pressure of Maida's hand on his shoulder he lay back, the lines of pain already easing from his face.

Dr. Werner shook Greenough who sputtered violently and erupted.

"Whatsamatter?" Then he relaxed. "Oh—must've dropped off!" he apologized foolishly. "Howsa boy?"

"He'll be all right," Dr. Werner explained, "but he's got to keep moving. Snyder's worn out. We need your help."

Abigail knew it would be some time before she could take over her nursing duties. Although it was almost two o'clock she was wide awake and she had no desire to go off alone again. Instead, she sat on a straight chair near the door where she could watch as Maida, Greenough, and the doctor between them talked to Fred, forced him to drink coffee and more coffee, and dragged him up and down the hall against his gradually more aware and vocal protests.

At last he shook his head almost animatedly and stared at them with recognition driving away the fog of sleep. Dr. Werner stopped the endless pacing.

"Fred! Wake up, Fred!" he spoke urgently.

"Sleep!" Fred responded thickly. "Want to sleep."

"Not now, Fred. Here, Maida, give him more coffee. Fred, you've got to stay awake!"

"Can you tell me what happened?" Greenough asked eagerly, delving in his hip pocket for his notebook. Fred shook his head.

"Damn tired," he said vaguely. "Want to sleep."

Another half hour passed, during which Fred grew more and more recalcitrant and more highly vocal in his protests against being compelled to walk and against the coffee which Maida pressed upon him. Abruptly, his head seemed to clear.

"Jerry!" he cried out suddenly. "Where's Jerry? He tried to kill—"

"It's okay, son, we got him," Greenough stated. "Or rather— he got himself. Tried to bump himself off a while back!"

"Oh, *no!*"

At the cry, Abigail, whose absorbed gaze had been fastened on Fred in his struggling return to memory, turned and saw Maida sway in the kitchen doorway, coffee slopping from the pot she carried. She seemed unaware of the scalding splash on her ankle.

"You say Jerry—tried to kill himself?"

Greenough eyed her suspiciously.

"Sure! You knew that! I told you—"

"But suicide! You only said he'd confessed! Where is he? Why did he do it?"

"He did it," Greenough pointed out bluntly, "because he's the damn murderer that's been bumping off people around here— Hawkes, and Weston, and now Fred here who'd be dead as a mackerel right now if we hadn't found him."

Maida's eyes and mouth were holes of horror in a blank mask. "He didn't! It was an accident, not murder! Jerry didn't—" Suddenly she seemed to realize the discrepancy in her defense. "But then—who? I'd forgotten about Tom. Even if Hawkes' death was an accident, someone deliberately—"

"You're damn right someone deliberately! Jerome Manning deliberately and with malice aforethought— Hey, Doc, you bring that confession?"

Dr. Werner felt in his breast pocket and drew forth a small sheet of paper, folded once. Even Fred was alert now. All eyes held on Greenough as he took the paper, studied it interminably, and let out his breath on a long sigh.

"That does it!" he said, slapping the open page with the back of his hand. He passed the paper to Maida with an air of personal pride.

"Is he—is Jerry going to—live?" Maida asked, taking the note as though she could not bear to touch it. Her eyes did not leave Greenough's face.

Dr. Werner answered.

"Yes, Maida," he said gently. "He has a bad scalp wound and concussion. He's lost a lot of blood. But he'll live. You see, when Jerry was patched up during the war someone did a fine job of surgery—substituting a metal plate for a section of skull bone that he didn't have. When he shot himself he used a gun of very small caliber and the bullet, ironically enough, hit that metal plate and was deflected. And so, he's going to pull through."

"To be tried for the murder of Weston and Hawkes!" Greenough summed up with satisfaction.

Her impatience would no longer allow Abigail to stand on ceremony. Moving over to Maida, she adjusted her glasses and, taking the hand that held Jerry's note, she raised it so they both could see.

As she read the scrawled words that filled the page, Abigail knew an overpowering elation. That clears him! she thought triumphantly.

"I replaced the medicine in one of Arthur's capsules with cyanide," she read. "I thought I could go through with it, but I realize now that nothing justifies cold-blooded murder. I must have been mad. I'm going to die and I can't face whatever comes after until I have made this confession. I know that you will never forgive me."

Abigail was astonished when Maida spoke in a voice that was bewildered, but beaten.

"But it doesn't mention Mr. Hawkes, or Tom—"

"It don't need to," Greenough gloated, retrieving the note and refolding it tenderly. "It tells *how* he killed Hawkes and that's all we need to know—"

Abigail interrupted impatiently, startled at the intensity of her own contradiction. Her very nerve ends tingled; she wanted to shout for joy.

"Proof!" she snorted. "You certainly have proof, Mr. Greenough, but it doesn't prove what you seem to think! That note in your hand is going to clear Jerome Manning absolutely and completely! It proves not only that someone else killed Mr. Hawkes and Tom Weston, but that the same person tried to kill Jerry and make it look like suicide! Why, Jerry's no more guilty than—than I am!" she finished triumphantly.

XII

Stunned silence followed Abigail's pronouncement; then everyone began to talk at once. Sheriff Greenough's roar of protest
rose above the rest.

"What the hell!" he began, too shaken to temper the profanity with a parenthetical apology. "Mrs. Potter, you been plunk-
ing for this guy Manning all along. You pop up out of nowhere
and mess up a perfectly good investigation with your crazy accusations. I got to admit I had you figured for a loony—until
tonight. But I ate crow, didn't I? I apologized real pretty and
admitted you were right and I was wrong. But now!" His voice
trembled with indignation, "*Now*—we got a confession, signed
and delivered, from the very guy you picked—and you stand
there with your bare face hanging out and tell me he ain't guilty!
Mrs. Potter, now I know you're nuts!"

Excitedly, Maida sprang to Abigail's defense.

"Mrs. Potter is right! I should have seen it myself. This note
isn't a confession at all, but a part of that letter Jerry wrote to me.
Why, it isn't even complete! It proves everything he told us this
afternoon about the letter and the telegram and—"

"Hold on! What letter? What telegram! How about giving the
police a break?" Greenough ran a hand distractedly through his
shaggy gray thatch. "You folks been withholding evidence?"

"Not really." Abigail outlined Jerry's defense. "He only told
us this afternoon and he intended to go to you with the whole
story as soon as we could find the proof. And then, when you

said it was suicide I thought he must have signed a false confession. Heaven forgive me, if we'd gone to you at once perhaps the poor boy wouldn't be dying now."

"He's not dead yet," Dr. Werner assured her gravely. "I think you had better make a clean breast of everything you know, Mrs. Potter. If someone tried, as you suggest, to murder Jerry, then Mr. Greenough's case is far from closed and you yourself aren't safe."

"How about Jerry?" Maida paused in the act of taking the empty coffeepot to the kitchen. "Mightn't whoever tried to kill him tonight try again?"

"Manning's safe enough," Greenough promised. "He's under arrest for murder; I've got two men on guard."

"Guarding a murderer and guarding a potential victim of murder might be two different things," Maida suggested cryptically.

Fred waited until Maida stalked out of the room to refill the coffeepot before he spoke in a lowered voice.

"I should think, Greenough, that your best bet would be to let the murderer believe she got away with it!" (She! He can't mean Maida! Abigail protested silently). "As long as she thinks you've been taken in by the suicide story, she'll rest her case. And, speaking of rest, do you mind if I sit down?" He looked longingly toward the couch. "I feel as though I'd been on my feet all the way from Berlin to Moscow."

"Of course sit down!" Dr. Werner agreed, his fingers reaching professionally for Fred's wrist. "Have another cup of coffee?"

Fred made a grimace.

"Lord, no! I've got liquid caffeine instead of blood in my veins now. By the way," he added, "there was something damn queer about that coffee tonight! It tasted foul and it was right after I drank that— Say! What did happen to me, anyhow?"

"Suppose you tell us, if you feel up to it," Dr. Werner suggested. "You were found drugged and locked in the hall closet. By morning you couldn't have been waked up to tell the tale. Do you have any memory of how you got there?"

Fred rubbed the back of his hand across his eyes.

"Drugged!" he repeated. "So that's what it was. I'll bet you anything you like it was the coffee—"

"What coffee?" Greenough produced his notebook and expectantly licked the stub of a pencil. "Who made it?"

"Maida, I guess."

"Maida what?" Maida inquired, coming into the room.

"You made the coffee Jerry and I drank this evening—just before you left to meet Dad."

Maida nodded. "What about it?"

Fred continued, speaking slowly as though each fragment of memory came with an effort.

"Jerry came back with me from Mrs. Weston's and he and Maida and I rustled up some grub. After supper I went up to my room. I was worried about Dad, wondering if you'd try to hold him all night, and what I could do about it.

"Around nine thirty Maida came upstairs to see her mother. She called in to me that Dad had been released but that he'd missed the bus and she was going after him.

"After she left I went downstairs. There were some things I wanted to ask Jerry—" He paused, glancing sheepishly at the notebook in Abigail's lap. "I see you found it," he mentioned with apparent irrelevance, "so I guess you know what I wanted to talk to him about."

"You accused him of being the murderer?"

"That's right. You see, the whole thing read so crazy it was hard to swallow, and yet Hawkes did die and I knew Dad hadn't killed him. Somehow, your theories seemed to add up. I was ready to try anything that might clear Dad so I asked Jerry, right out. And I'm damned if he didn't—"

"Were you upstairs when you asked him?" Abigail interrupted.

"Why, no. We were right here in the living room. Why?"

"Then Mrs. Demarest wasn't upstairs when she heard you."

Fred grinned. "Do you mean the old girl was up to her tricks? I'll bet she got an earful!"

"She heard you accuse Jerry of being the murderer. She was sure we'd find you dead!"

"Damn near did!" Greenough reminded them. "I suppose Manning denied it?"

"No," Fred said. "That's what really struck me. I don't know what I expected—that he'd deny it, laugh it off, try to alibi out— All he said was, 'So you know,' almost as if he were relieved. Didn't try to explain or anything. I asked him, 'What do you intend to do about it?' and he said, 'Call the police and give myself up. I should have done it right away.' It made me feel queer!"

"But he didn't call the police!" Greenough argued.

"He tried," Fred said. "He honestly did. He went out in the hall and dialed the number. I stood right over him—but the line was busy. Just then I smelled coffee boiling in the kitchen —Maida'd put it on before she left—and I went out to turn it off. Jerry followed. He asked, sort of apologetically, 'Mind if I have some, as long as it's here?' I poured him a cup and had one myself.

"We just sat there, drinking coffee and then all at once Jerry started to unload. He told me the whole screwy story—I guess you know it by now?"

Fred looked at Greenough and the sheriff nodded.

"Well, it struck me as crazy, but true—if you know what I mean. He and Maida had been running around together since they were kids and she did play him a dirty trick. I couldn't blame him if he went off his rockers for a bit, brooding about it out there in the Pacific. And after all, Dad wasn't killed so no harm was done."

"But Tom Weston was," Dr. Werner interposed gravely.

"I know—but Jerry swore up and down he had nothing to do with that. He told me he'd sent a letter to Maida and thought she'd gotten rid of that damn pill. When he found out that she hadn't"—Hadn't what? Abigail asked herself—"he'd wanted to give himself up, but Maida wouldn't let him—"

"It was I who asked him to wait," Abigail corrected.

"Anyway, I told him he ought to take what was coming to him. I was willing to string along, but not to the extent of letting the police push Dad around while Jerry looked for an out.

"I think it was about then Jerry went outside and was sick. I was beginning to feel pretty rocky myself and I told him to go on home. There'd be time enough to call the police in the morning, as long as they weren't holding Dad. I don't even know when Jerry left. Last thing I remember was sitting at the kitchen table, wondering if it was worthwhile to get up and go to bed. If I was drugged I suppose that explains it, but how the devil did I get in that closet? And who—"

"I guess 'who' is plain enough," Greenough retorted. "He must have hung around until you passed out and then dragged you there."

"You mean Manning?" Fred asked dubiously. "But I thought someone attacked him, too!"

"That's what *you* decided!" Greenough corrected. "*I* still think he shot himself!"

Fred shook his head as though to dispel a fog.

"I don't get it," he said.

Abigail, also groping through a dense uncomprehension, felt sympathy for his bewilderment.

"Anyway," Fred finished, "I'm sure it was that lousy coffee. It was bitter as all get-out, but we figured it was just because we'd let it perk so long."

"Where's the pot?" Greenough demanded, starting for the kitchen.

"There's only one coffeepot," Maida answered, pointing to the aluminum percolator on the hall table. "It's been emptied and refilled a dozen times tonight."

"Hell and damnation! There goes the evidence! Wait—what did you do with the grounds? The stuff might have been dumped in the coffee while it was cooking."

"I'm afraid I just dumped them out in the sink and rinsed them down the drain each time."

Greenough looked bitter.

"And the cup Fred drank out of—I suppose that's been washed and put away?" he asked without hope.

Abigail recalled something.

"When I first came over here from the Mannings'," she volunteered, "the coffeepot was on the kitchen table with two used cups. I'm afraid I threw out the coffee and rinsed the cups—"

"Oh, God!" Greenough lamented.

"—but I didn't throw the grounds down the sink," Abigail continued defensively. "I found a paper sack and emptied them into that. I should imagine the sack is still in the garbage container where I put it."

Greenough raced for the kitchen.

While they waited for him to report, Abigail surveyed the faces of those about her. Maida and Fred showed only suspense and concern; Dr. Werner, as might have been expected, seemed to wait with detached interest. In a few minutes Greenough was back, triumphant, bearing a soggy paper sack carefully on a china plate.

"Mrs. Potter!" he said fervently, "you're a honey! I'll send these over to the lab right away and have an analysis made, but I'll lay dollars to doughnuts Fred's right about that coffee. If he is, well, I'm willing to admit Manning's been damn clever, but I'll still put my money on him. Look at it this way! Who else would have had a motive for doping Fred? No one! But Manning had to keep Fred from phoning me. I'll bet he didn't drink any of that lousy coffee himself!"

"I'm afraid you're wrong there," Dr. Werner corrected. "Manning was drugged, too. We got him a lot earlier, however, and if he'd gotten rid of some of it as Fred says— But I think you can assume that he and Fred were drugged with the same stuff, chloral hydrate."

"Then that proves that Jerry couldn't have shot himself, doesn't it?" Maida asked.

Greenough seemed to be laboring to fit Dr. Werner's new evidence into his preconceived picture.

"Wait a minute! Yup! It all fits in. Look at it this way! You say that note proves it's murder faked to look like a suicide. Well, I got a hunch it's just the other way around. Manning writes that note, trying to make it sound like a part of the letter he claims he sent and knowing damn well Mrs. Potter, here, and Mrs. Snyder will take it for evidence of foul play.

"And here's what cinches it!" Greenough continued, bellowing exultantly and punching his forefinger at them. "Jerome Manning had no more idea of bumping himself off than I have this minute! He staged the whole job to look like a fake suicide—but what does he do? He takes a gun he knows is nothing but a toy and then he aims for the one place where a small caliber bullet would not be fatal! He picks the spot where he's got a silver plate instead of the bony skull the good Lord gave him, that's what he does!" Greenough warmed to his subject. "And why does he take a drug? First, to make it look like he and Fred have both been attacked, and second because he's not shooting to kill—and he knows it will hurt like hell!"

"One can argue equally," Dr. Werner suggested mildly, "that the very fact that the bullet entered where it did indicates attempted murder. I give you my word that a man who's been through the mill with a head injury like Manning's isn't willingly going to inflict the same punishment on himself again. As a matter of fact, he couldn't be certain that such an experiment wouldn't be instantly fatal!"

"Awl" Greenough scoffed. "Nobody that really wanted to kill a man would use a lady's pop gun like that."

"It looked deadly enough to me," Abigail objected.

"That's because you don't know guns!"

"At any rate," Abigail persisted, "I think your theory should be easy enough to prove or disprove. Isn't it possible to test that note—to see whether it was written last night or several years ago?"

Greenough scratched his head.

"Reckon it might be, if we sent it to the state lab. I don't want you folks to think I'm going off half-cocked. If Manning's innocent, that's okay with me but I'm only saying I got to have a lot better proof than a phony suicide attempt before I let him go. The easiest way for a murderer to draw attention away from himself is to make it look like he's been attacked, too. In the meantime, let's sleep on it."

Abigail sensed a sudden release of tension in the room. Fred yawned and Dr. Werner moved toward the door. A swift annoyance took hold of her, blotting out the momentary though unwilling admiration she had felt for the sheriff's unexpected imaginative powers.

"Just a minute yourself," she said. "I know all of this is really none of my business. Murder, rightly enough, is the province of the police. But I can't help feeling, Sheriff Greenough, that you are not fulfilling your duty."

"Huh?" Greenough challenged, irritated. "You trying to tell me how to run my job?"

"No, indeed! I merely want to call it to your attention that Jerry Manning's guilt is far from established. Until it is, every person connected with the case should be held suspect. If I were you, Mr. Greenough, I should want to know the movements of every member of the household during the past evening."

Greenough had the grace to look uncomfortable, although he blustered, "Well, now, Mrs. Potter, it's after three in the morning and reckon we can go into all that tomorrow." He forced a snicker. "Anybody who figures on cooking up an alibi would have done so already. Besides, we ain't got a quorum!"

He beamed at his own choice of words and waited for a vote of approval.

"I agree with Mrs. Potter," Dr. Werner put in unexpectedly. "This case calls for an open mind and proper police procedure. I am sure that none of us has the slightest objection to accounting for our movements tonight."

"Oh, now," Greenough protested, "no one's suspecting you, Doc."

"I'm afraid my own mind's pretty much of a blank after ten o'clock or so," Fred contributed. "As for the time before that, I just covered that pretty thoroughly."

"How about you, Maida?" Dr. Werner persisted. "Where were you all evening?"

Greenough, yielding to pressure, reluctantly produced his notebook once more.

"Okay, Mrs. Snyder, just for the record—where were you between the time your husband called and the time you two walked in? It was after midnight, you know."

Maida began to recite as though by rote.

"I was with Jerry, as Fred told you, until after nine thirty. Then Arthur called and asked me to meet him at the Alabaster Cow. It's a sort of roadhouse a few miles this side of Dayton."

"How'd he get there from headquarters?" Greenough asked. "Isn't it sort of out of the way?"

"I don't know. Perhaps he taxied. Does it matter? As for being out of the way, it is off the main highway but it's a place we go to often and it's quiet—" Her tone became defensive. "Arthur had missed the last bus and besides, he wanted a chance to talk to me alone, without policemen drooling over our shoulders."

"Then you met Arthur at the Alabaster Cow? Were you there all evening?" Dr. Werner prodded gently.

"Until about eleven thirty," Maida answered. "Then we came home."

"I reckon you can produce witnesses," Greenough said. It was a statement rather than a question. He was already closing his notebook.

Maida nodded.

"What time did you meet your husband at the—the Alabaster Cow?" Abigail asked.

For the first time, Maida looked uncomfortable.

"Sometime after eleven," she admitted in a low voice.

"But you left here at a quarter to ten!" Fred exclaimed. "It's only nine miles by the shortcut!"

"I know, but I ran out of gas."

Greenough's look of boredom vanished. He quivered like a cat that readies itself to spring.

"Ran out of gas!" he repeated.

"I thought there was enough," Maida explained, "but our gauge doesn't register. I should have stopped for some before I got out of town, but—well, Arthur is usually very careful to keep the tank full and I was in a hurry. I know it sounds silly," she acknowledged, "but that's what happened. There's a shortcut Arthur and I always take, but it's a back road and there are very few farms—and hardly any traffic at night—so there I was. I had to wait until someone came along to give me a lift."

"How long did you wait?"

"I don't know. Maybe three quarters of an hour, maybe more. It seemed like years."

"And you just sat there all that time?"

Maida shrugged.

"There was no point walking—there aren't any gas stations on that road. Besides, I kept thinking someone was sure to come along."

"So what happened?"

"A nice couple finally did stop. They drove me several miles to a filling station and then took me back with the gas and helped me get the car started. I'm afraid it doesn't sound very convincing."

Greenough was scribbling furiously.

"How about this couple? Anyone you knew?"

"I'm afraid not."

"Get their license number?"

"No." Maida looked as though she were about to cry. "Why would I?"

"Now, now, my dear!" Dr. Werner reassured her hastily. "No one is suspecting you. We all know that such accidents do happen, and after all—"

"What time did you say you finally met your husband?" Greenough demanded. "We can check it, of course."

"I don't know exactly." Maida's voice was barely above a whisper. "After eleven, I think."

"Well!" Greenough shrugged. "I'll have to check your story, of course, but don't worry. It's just routine, you know, just routine."

He spoke now, Abigail noticed, as though he had always leaned heavily on police procedure.

"How about you, Mrs. Potter?" The sheriff turned on Abigail and she knew he took great pleasure in thus intimating that she, too, was not above suspicion.

"I've already told you everything that happened before I found Jerry," she reminded him. "Mrs. Demarest can vouch for it that I was at Mrs. Weston's when she called me there, shortly before ten—and both Mrs. Weston and Mrs. Manning can tell you when I came in and that I was in my room the entire evening until Mrs. Demarest called. For the rest, I'm afraid you'll have to take my word."

"Not forgetting the fact that you were the first to discover Manning!" Greenough pointed out to the company at large, shutting his notebook with finality and reaching for his hat.

"But I wasn't!" Abigail cried. "Dr. Werner, who called you and told you about Jerry?"

"Why, I understood that *you*—"

Abigail shook her head firmly. "When I called, your wife said you'd already left. So someone else found Jerry first!"

"I'll ask Hilda, but I'm sure she'd have told me if she'd recognized the voice. I was resting and she simply told me that there'd been some accident at Mannings'—that I was to go right over."

"It's plain enough!" Greenough observed. "Manning was taking no chances on not being found at once. He was the one who phoned—probably disguised his voice—and then he went into the study and pulled the trigger!" He jammed his hat on his head. "Well, folks, I think I'll talk to Arthur and Mrs. Demarest in the morning. It's almost four and I'm dead. The rest of you can sit up and solve the crime if you want. Coming, Doc?"

"Presently. Good night, Greenough."

Dr. Werner's tone was curt, and his comment as the door closed behind the sheriff showed little sympathy with Greenough's methods.

"Bumbling fool!" he said. "I was beginning to think he'd start building a case against you, Maida, and end by waking Arthur to check your story. He may be a good man, but he certainly has a tendency to make up his mind first and find evidence to support his conclusions afterward. I'm afraid he must have given Arthur a time of it. I've never seen him in such bad shape. Does he have these headaches often?"

"It was mostly due to fatigue—and shock. His head bothers him a good deal when he's overtired or excited, but his medicine always helps. He should have taken it earlier, but of course with Fred—"

"You've got to get him to take it easy," Dr. Werner said soberly. "Perhaps you can persuade him to come around for a thorough physical. He's not a young man and he looks far from well."

Dr. Werner turned to Abigail. "And now," he went on, "if you're still willing to sit up with Fred, I'll give you a few instructions. I don't think it will hurt him to sleep now, but I want you to keep an eye on him, see that he doesn't get uncovered. The main thing to avoid is exposure—"

With a pot of coffee to stay her, Abigail settled herself once more in the big wing chair in Fred's room. The coffee she had already consumed was churning miserably inside her. She felt sorry for Fred, who had been forced to take so much more.

To keep from dozing, she willed herself to pick at the tangled threads of mystery, mentally worrying first one "granny" and then another. With her black notebook closed upon her lap she regretfully faced the fact that it was of no further use to her.

Like Sheriff Greenough, she thought sadly, I was so sure I knew all the answers that I closed my mind to any evidence that didn't fit my preconceived pattern. Now I must simply do it all over!

The problem now, she realized, was to discover who had intercepted the letter that Jerry had sent Maida; who, having opened and read it, would deliberately have allowed the deadly capsule to remain among Arthur Snyder's medicinal pills.

A strange murder case, she reflected, where a murderer may be convicted because he had a motive for the death of a man who is still very much alive!

One by one, Abigail considered each member of the Snyder household, trying to decide which of them might have tampered with Maida's private correspondence, straining to remember any scrap of conversation that might give her a clue to their true relationship with Arthur Snyder.

Once, on the pretext of making fresh coffee, she went downstairs and, while the coffee was brewing, searched the front-hall closet—for exactly what she did not know. Two or three hairpins, picked up on the closet floor; a length of twine from a sweater pocket; a safety pin that held up the torn lining of a woman's coat; an ordinary doorkey from among a jumble of fishing line, lead sinkers, and corks in the pocket of an old leather jacket—these Abigail took with her as being of possible further interest.

Her body ached with fatigue. She dared not sleep lest she fail Fred, but her brain, jumpy with caffeine, was weary of the squirrel cage in which it scrambled a ceaseless round. A pile of Dayton papers on the pantry shelf suggested possible relief from her fruitless thoughts. Abigail realized that since she came to Glen Falls she had been too busy, and too sure of herself, even to read the newspaper accounts of the events with which she was concerned. Selecting those issues that covered the period immediately following Hawkes' death, she carried them back with her to Fred's room.

The initial story in the *Dayton News* had rated the front page. Several columns were devoted to it. Abigail skimmed them, finding nothing she had not already heard discussed, until she turned to the inside page where the story was continued.

A name she had not expected to see leaped at her from the fine lines of type. Abigail stared at the words incredulously.

"Mrs. Charlotte Manning was a guest at dinner, but both Mr. and Mrs. Snyder are agreed that she left shortly after the meal and was not present at the time of Hawkes' collapse and death."

Charlotte Manning had been in the Snyder house on the day of Hawkes' death! She had eaten that last dinner with him! Yet she had made no mention of the fact at Sunday dinner when the murder had been under discussion.

An elusive doubt worried Abigail, something that had puzzled her briefly during the evening, something in connection with Charlotte Manning. At last she pinned it down.

Where had Charlotte been when Eloise Demarest had phoned to tell her of Jerry's accident? Since she had not been at Dora Weston's to speak with Eloise, when and where had she received the message?

Bearing only a tangential relationship to that problem, a second question raised its troublesome head: Abigail did not for a moment believe that it had been Jerry who had telephoned to Dr. Werner. But if not Jerry, who? And why?

Dawn was beginning to break outside, if not in Abigail's mind. She pushed back the curtains and looked across at the Manning house, lonely and empty in the gray half-light. Greenough had been too sure of his case against Jerry to leave a guard on either house, and Abigail was suddenly seized with a desire to go through the rooms next door. She tried to justify the impulse as a wish to examine once more the scene of the crime, but deep in her heart she knew that she had become strangely curious about Jerry's reticent mother and hoped that, in Charlotte's absence, her house might reveal more than she herself would tell.

Abigail stepped softly as she slipped out the unlocked back door into the early-morning chill. The lawn stretched before her, bright green with new grass and powdered with an untimely frost. Only one patch, near the edge of the driveway, was still sere and brown. Along the walk the thin shoots of crocuses and daffodils were well along.

Abigail picked her way carefully, feeling herself the only soul awake in a sleeping world. The doors of the Manning house, as she had anticipated, were locked but it was an easy, if embarrassingly compromising job, to push open and climb through the window Dr. Werner had so conveniently broken.

Abigail began her search with the secretary in the living room. She herself habitually made voluminous notes on her correspondence and never threw anything away, and she was hoping that in Charlotte's desk she might come across the very note that Jerry had sent his mother three years before, endorsed by Charlotte as to when and how she had carried out his instructions. Her search was doomed to disappointment, however. The pigeonholes, the drawers, held nothing but unused stationery, canceled checks, leaflets on crochet, and letters of recent date in a bundle marked "To Be Answered." Apparently Charlotte Manning kept no diary and saved no letters from the past. Her possessions were orderly and impersonal.

Discouraged, Abigail made her search more general, but with no more success. She knew she was violating every rule, both legal and ethical, by thus taking advantage of Charlotte's absence, but the promptings of conscience were not strong enough to cause her to overlook any drawer or cupboard that might contain a clue.

And conscience was forgotten altogether when she found, on the top shelf of the medicine cabinet in the bathroom, a small bottle labeled "Chloral Hydrate."

A few drops remained in the bottom of the vial.

XIII

Dawn had ripened into daylight and the morning sounds of occasional cars in the street drifted in to Abigail. With a trapped feeling she tried to estimate her chances of climbing out of the study window as she had climbed in, without being seen. No matter how she looked at it they seemed remote until, foolishly, she recognized her own stupidity.

You *must* be tired, Abigail Potter, she derided herself. House doors lock on the inside; there'll be no trick to getting out!

She waited until a milkman had made his deliveries across the street and driven on before she slipped out the front door and heard the Yale lock click into place as she pulled it to behind her. No one was in sight, but for the benefit of any neighbors who might chance to be looking out of their windows, Abigail walked sedately down the steps and along the sidewalk and so up to the Snyder house. She met no one as she let herself in the back door and stole up to Fred's room. Fred was asleep, still firmly tucked in as she had left him.

What do I do now? Abigail asked herself. Throughout my entire investigation I have been alternating between a mad chase after wild geese and a patient waiting for some snipe to walk into my sack.

Despondently she faced the fact that all her deductions had been based on one premise, that Hawkes' death had been an accident, the miscarriage of Jerome Manning's plot. Now, no longer sure of anything, Abigail asked herself, was Harrison Hawkes killed deliberately? She was becoming increasingly aware that almost anyone in the Snyder household would have had a motive for desiring his death.

Resolutely she tried to free herself of the entangling preconceptions in which she had become enmeshed and to set her course anew, but her mind refused to function. Before she could do anything further she knew she must sleep. And sleep she could not until someone else came to take over the supervision of Fred.

Arthur was the first of the household to awake. He tapped on Fred's door and peered in.

"How is he?" he inquired, with muted concern.

Abigail gave him her reassuring report and gratefully allowed him to relieve her of her duties.

"Call on me if there's anything else I can do," she told him. "I'm going back to Mrs. Weston's for a little nap."

The short walk in the cool air was refreshing. Abigail let herself into Dora Weston's house softly and was startled when an angular young girl with short brown hair popped out of the living room. The girl's eyes were red and puffy, her face blotched from crying. Abigail, overcome with embarrassment, hastily explained her presence.

"Mom Weston's sleeping," the girl said. "She was up all night. I'm Tom's wife."

"Oh! I'm so sorry! I mean—"

"Thank you."

There was an awkward pause. The girl looked so forlorn that Abigail hated to leave her.

"You've been out of town, haven't you?" she asked. "When did you get home?"

"I flew back to Dayton last night, after I got Mom's telegram—and came in on the last bus. Mom told me about you. You were—there, weren't you, when—when it happened? Do the police know yet who—"

Abigail saw an opportunity to find answers to some of the questions that had been troubling her.

"The police are holding Jerome Manning," she said. "He signed a confession."

"A confession!" Young Mrs. Weston looked incredulous. "You mean Charlotte Manning's son? But I thought the murderer shot him, too!"

"The police believe he shot himself. Were you here last night when Mrs. Demarest called to tell Jerry's mother?"

The girl nodded. "She'd left and Mom took the message. We just couldn't believe it—and we didn't know how to reach Mrs. Manning. Was it really suicide? How terrible!"

Abigail was too intent on obtaining information to answer. "How long was it before Mrs. Manning came back? How soon did she get the news about Jerry?"

"Oh, she didn't come back here at all. Mom called all over town and couldn't find her and then finally Hilda Werner, the doctor's wife, called from the hospital to say that she and Mrs. Manning were already over there—"

"And you don't know where she'd been?" Abigail persisted.

"No. After I came there was no need for her to stay with Mom. She tried to call Jerry to take her home but no one answered, so she said she'd walk."

"What time was that?"

"Some time after nine thirty. I got here at nine thirty on the last bus from Dayton."

Abigail had lost her desire to go to bed.

"How soon can I get a bus to Dayton?" she asked abruptly.

Mrs. Tom Weston's eyes questioned her, but she gave a verbal timetable. There would be a bus in half an hour, she said. She seemed to hope that Abigail would stay until then and talk, but Abigail was too restless to wait. She would walk down to the Elite Café, she decided, and get some rolls and coffee. No, not coffee, she amended, shuddering—but at least some fruit juice and a glass of milk.

She had to see Charlotte Manning right away, to find out where Mrs. Manning had been the night before when her son was attacked, and how she had gotten word of his accident. Above all, she wanted to settle the question, of paramount importance, of the letter Jerry had sent to Maida. Abigail had not given up

hope that Charlotte would be able to verify Jerry's story and that
she might even be able to name the person who had intercepted
her son's letter.

At St. Albans, Abigail was able to elicit only the barest details
from a reluctant desk clerk. No, Jerome Manning had not yet
recovered consciousness. Yes, the doctor thought his chances
were good. Yes, Mrs. Manning was with him. No, Abigail could
not see him; no visitors were allowed.

Abigail was able to learn that Jerry was on the sixth floor.
Up there, a sympathetic nurse agreed to carry a note to Jerry's
mother. She led Abigail to a sunny waiting room at the end of
the broad corridor and Abigail scribbled a few lines to Charlotte
Manning, emphasizing her belief in Jerry's innocence and her own
immediate need for assistance that only Charlotte could give.

The waiting room was a light, cheerful place, a welcome an-
tidote to the depressingly disinfected hospital atmosphere of the
corridors. Windows stretched the length of two walls and a third
was of glass brick. All four walls were lined with green wicker
stands of potted plants, many of them blooming, and at one end
of the room bright orange fish swam soporifically in an enormous tank.

Abigail felt the tension of overtiredness leaving her as she relaxed in a comfortable basket chair and watched a student nurse
siphoning water from the aquarium. She felt sure that Charlotte Manning would respond to her appeal for help, but she
was deeply touched when she saw Charlotte hurrying toward her
with both hands outstretched in welcome.

"I'm so *glad* to see you!" she said, with characteristic directness. "Tell me how I can help."

Abigail was startled to learn that Charlotte knew nothing of
the circumstances of Jerry's involvement. Throughout the night,
as she had sat in stunned helplessness outside his room, Jerry's
mother had known nothing beyond the existence of the suicide
note that Dr. Werner had shown her for her identification.

"If you can tell me what this is all about," she said with quiet
dignity, "I'll be most grateful. Of course I know Jerry had nothing to do with these deaths—but that note! I can't understand it!"

Abigail longed to reassure her, but she prudently resisted the temptation to tell Jerry's mother the whole story at once.

"First I must ask you something," she said. "It may be vitally important."

Charlotte nodded. Her stern countenance showed no flicker of emotion, but Abigail knew she was tense and expectant.

"A few years ago Jerry was in the hospital," Abigail began. "He was seriously wounded."

"I've only just learned how seriously," Charlotte agreed soberly. "Dr. Werner says it must have been a miracle that he lived."

"The doctors didn't write you of his condition?"

Charlotte shook her head. "My husband was very ill. I suppose Jerry refused to allow them to add that anxiety to what I was already going through with Nelson. Jerry's own letters were always cheerful and matter of fact, though they were short and infrequent." Her lips tightened for a moment. Then she asked, levelly, "Why have you referred to that?"

"I want you to think back. During the time your son was in the hospital, did he ever write to you, enclosing a letter for someone else, which you were to deliver?"

Abigail held her breath. A great deal might depend on Charlotte Manning's answer.

"Why, yes!" Charlotte replied slowly. "I had forgotten it completely." She sat silent for a moment, as though trying to recall the circumstances. "The letter came the morning of the day my husband died. Jerry enclosed a letter addressed to Maida Snyder, marked 'Confidential' and 'Urgent.' He asked me to give it to her."

"And   did you?"

After an interminable pause, Charlotte shook her head. She looked perturbed.

"No," she said. "No, I didn't."

"What did you do with it?"

"I put it in the Snyders' letter box. I know that must seem strange when Jerry had asked me so particularly— There was no justification, but it was while I was reading Jerry's letter that they phoned from the hospital and told me to come at once. My husband had been sinking for days. I did call the Snyders, to tell Maida about the letter, but she was out and I couldn't wait. Jerry had said it was urgent, and so—well, before I left for the hospital, I put the letter in her box. After all, he had already marked it confidential. Why, what has that to do with—with all this? I meant to mention it to Maida when I next saw her—but Nelson died that evening and afterward I quarreled with Arthur. It slipped my mind completely."

With tangible proof at last, proof that did not rest on Jerry's word alone, Abigail felt a tremendous elation. Jerry's mother had confirmed his story!

Nothing can stop me now, she exulted. Jerry's going to live, and together we'll make Greenough believe in his innocence!

Abigail poured out the whole story to Charlotte, glad that for once it was not necessary to convince her listener of his innocence or to explain away his initial guilt. Charlotte did not interrupt; her features betrayed neither incredulity nor disbelief.

When Abigail had finished she said, simply, "Now we know where we stand. What can I do?"

Uncomfortably, Abigail realized that although she had a staunch ally in her battle to clear Jerry she did not know how freely she could confide. Charlotte Manning herself was not yet above suspicion.

"There are a number of puzzling aspects," she began apologetically. "I suppose you know that Jerry and Fred Snyder were both drugged last night before Jerry was shot, with chloral hydrate!"

"Chloral hydrate!" For the first time Charlotte showed a flash of fear.

"I'm positive," Abigail told her frankly, "that it was your own medicine that was used. The police will want to know where you were last night when Jerry was shot and Fred was attacked."

"But—surely no one could suppose that I would give my own son an overdose—"

"I don't think so," Abigail admitted. "And I know you'd have more sense than to put the empty bottle back in your own medicine chest after carrying it clear over to the Snyders. But Sheriff

Greenough gets harebrained ideas. He might argue that you yourself had intercepted and read Jerry's letter to Maida, that you wanted Arthur dead and did not tell him to destroy the pills, that you knew your own son was about to give himself up to the police and confess his part in Hawkes' murder. He might even suggest that you deliberately wounded Jerry, with no desire to kill him, in order to prove that he could not be the murderer the police were after. He has already suggested that Jerry might have doped himself to deaden the pain of the bullet wound!"

"If he could think that, he must be crazy!" Charlotte Manning said dispassionately. Her face might haves been carved out of stone.

"He's likely to be particularly suspicious when he figures out that Dr. Werner received a call from someone who reported Jerry's accident a few minutes after Jerry was shot. By the time I called, Werner was already on his way. Greenough will begin to wonder why the murderer should have wanted to secure such prompt assistance for his victim!"

"Greenough must be a fool. Or is all this your own idea?"

"Where *did* you go after you left Dora Weston's last night?" Abigail insisted.

"Walking." Charlotte did not elaborate.

"Walking!" Greenough's scornful voice interrupted from the doorway. He bore down upon them. "You're just the one I want to see, Mrs. Manning. We're checking up on everybody—don't want to leave you out. You were about to tell Mrs. Potter where you were between nine thirty last night when you left Mrs. Weston's and ten forty-five when you turned up over here."

"I was walking," Charlotte repeated calmly.

"Do you mind if we have a play by play description—just for the records?"

"Certainly not. After Dora's daughter-in-law arrived, I tried to call Jerry to come after me, but he wasn't home. I walked over to the house, found the car parked out in front, and decided I'd go for a drive. It had been a very disturbing day and driving relaxes me."

"Thought you said you walked!"

"I did," Charlotte continued without emphasis. "I found the car was locked and I'd given Jerry my keys. So I walked."

"Why didn't you get the keys from him? He was right next door, wasn't he?"

"I didn't know that. Our house was dark. I didn't feel like staying alone, nor did I feel like paying calls at that hour. If I'd stopped at the Snyders' and Jerry hadn't been there I'd have had a time of it getting away. So, as I said, I walked."

"Where did you go?"

"To no particular place. Out toward the south end of town and around by the cemetery. It was a beautiful night."

"See anyone you know?"

"No."

"How'd you find out about your son?"

"On the way back I passed the Werners' home. Hilda was on the front porch and she called to me—and told me. She offered to drive me over here. I accepted."

Charlotte folded her lips together and regarded Sheriff Greenough levelly.

With a sudden grin the sheriff stood up.

"Okay!" he said. "I won't prosecute—this time! Gave her a bad time, there, for a minute!" he remarked to Abigail with immense good humor.

Abigail was furious.

"Murder seems to be just a game to you!" she snapped. "Instead of checking up on the people you ought to suspect you spend your time posting guard over the innocent victim of a brutal assault and badgering his mother! You ought to be ashamed!"

Greenough looked abashed.

"Well, now," he said. "I didn't mean no harm. Couldn't help overhearing her call me a fool and it made me a little sore. And I have been checking, don't you worry. Just came from Snyders'. I talked to Mrs. Demarest again, and got Arthur's version of his doings last night. Checked with his wife's okay, but we're not leaving it at that. The police are thorough! We've had men checking with filling stations in the vicinity of that shortcut."

"Was Maida telling the truth?" Abigail asked, interest over-coming indignation.

"Well, can't say, yet. A fellow at a Sohio station remembers a car that drove up about eleven last night. A man climbed out and bought a gallon of gas and then turned around and drove back the way he'd come. The attendant couldn't describe him and says he don't remember any ladies in the car. But it was dark and he was tired—he might not have noticed. It was the same man returned the empty can later."

"How about that roadhouse, the Alabaster Cow?"

"Matter of fact," Greenough told her genially, "I'm going there now. If you want to see how the police work, why don't you ride along?"

This was what she had wanted, Abigail remembered, conjuring up her vision of glory from the past. She pressed Charlotte's hand in farewell and hurried after Greenough. "To work hand in glove with officers of the Law—" What a fool I was, she thought.

The Alabaster Cow was a long, low building of weathered pine with a veneer of quiet elegance. A bar extended the length of the dim, pine-paneled room, deserted at this hour. A fat little man in a not-too-clean white apron was dusting bottles behind it.

Abigail listened without comment as Greenough, flashing his badge, began to display his technique.

"Know a guy named Snyder?" he began. "Arthur Snyder? Says he comes in here a lot, with his wife."

"Sure, sure! Nice fellow. He was in last night."

"What time?"

"From nine ten to somewhere after eleven. Why, he in trouble?"

"Just checking. You seem mighty definite about when he came! You sure it wasn't later?"

"It was nine ten—by that clock up there!" The bartender gestured to the wall behind him. "I know, because a couple was sitting here at the bar when he come in. They was on their way to Cincy and got off their road—only kind of tourists we get in here!" he interpolated.

"What's that got to do with Snyder?"

"Well, he come in and this couple, they was arguing about how much time they'd lost. The man blamed the woman for missing the road sign, see, and says she's made them lose a whole hour. She says, 'Nonsense, it's only ten after nine, we'll make Cincinnati in plenty of time.' And then he says, 'Yeah, but I figured on getting some sleep—'"

"Okay, okay!" Greenough interrupted tolerantly. "So it was ten after nine when Snyder came in. How long'd he stay?"

"All evening, like I said. He was waiting for his wife. Right after he got here he called her and then he asked if they could use one of the rooms in back as he wanted to talk to her private. It was his wife, see!" he added belligerently. "We don't let just anyone use them rooms!"

"And what time did she show up?"

"Must have been over an hour and a half! Snyder was chewing his nails off by the time she come. About quarter to eleven he comes out and tries to call her again." He gestured to the phone booth at the end of the bar. "Stayed in there about ten minutes, but he couldn't get no answer—she's already left, see. 'Maybe she's had an accident!' he says, and he's white as a sheet. Just then she walks in. Ran out of gas, she tells him! I looked at the time good, then—almost an hour and a half it's taken her to come nine miles!"

"Okay," said Greenough. "*That* checks. How long'd they stay after that?"

Abigail considered that the subject had been adequately covered. While Greenough delayed for a drink "on the house," she wandered through the cubicles at the rear of the main room which the bartender had designated as "private." Each, she noticed, was furnished with a table, two chairs, and a day bed.

Not a very nice place, she thought distastefully, rejoining Greenough.

"One thing people don't realize," Greenough proclaimed after he had herded Abigail back to the police car and headed toward Dayton, "is what a lot of routine we have to go through just to eliminate possibilities. Lot of useless running around, checking up on people's statements. It's a headache."

Abigail was not listening.

"I wonder who would get Arthur Snyder's money if he died," she mused.

"Huh? What's that got to do with anything?"

"I was just wondering," Abigail explained, "who might have wanted him to die."

"Give him a few years and he'll have something worth leaving. Right now I gather he's downright poor—been paying out about every cent he got to Hawkes for blackmail. Whoever killed Hawkes sure done Arthur Snyder a favor!"

"You mean—but of course!" Abigail had not considered before that Hawkes' death, aside from relieving Arthur of a blackmail threat, would make a substantial difference in the financial prospects of the entire Snyder menage. She wondered how much the Mannings had agreed to pay to regain control of the foundry.

"Anyway," Greenough pursued, "why don't you quit worrying? All the Snyders are in the clear as far as last night goes, and you've got to admit the attack on Jerry must be tied up with the rest. Whoever did that—and doped Fred—is your murderer. Personally, I'll settle for Manning."

"But that note is part of the letter he wrote—"

"Look at it this way," Greenough said patiently. "If it was like you said and someone got hold of a letter to Mrs. Snyder saying there was poison in her husband's medicine and telling her to throw it away, what would they do? They might sit tight and wait for Snyder to die, sure—if they hated him enough—but would they keep the letter? No! So, there wasn't any letter, except in Jerry Manning's mind!"

Abigail had not thought of that. She considered it now. Greenough guided the car through scattered traffic on the outskirts of the city.

"Where to, milady?" he asked with heavy facetiousness.

"I think," Abigail replied soberly, coming to a sudden decision, "you had better drive me back to Glen Falls. But first I think we ought to pick up Mrs. Manning and take her with us. You see, I've just realized who killed Harrison Hawkes and Tom Weston."

XIV

Abigail surveyed the little group that had gathered, at Greenough's official invitation, in the Snyder living room.

This is it, she thought. This is what I've wanted. Then why are my legs shaking?

The curtain was about to go up on the last act, but the audience showed no curiosity, only apathy and dread. But they're not the audience, they're the principals, Abigail corrected herself. They all know that the murderer is one of them!

Eloise Demarest alone appeared untroubled. She's probably the only one that got a decent night's sleep, Abigail guessed resentfully.

Maida, obviously, had not. Rouge and lipstick could not conceal the deep shadows under her eyes, the drawn lines in her face. She sat in a corner of the couch and looked only at her lap where her fingers alternately smoothed out and pleated the sash of her dress.

Beside Maida, Arthur rested his head against the back of the couch, his glance straying frequently toward his son, who stood by the fireplace as usual, with one arm resting along the mantel. Apparently Arthur was still uneasy about him, although Abigail could not see that Fred's experience of the night before had left any ill effects. His attitude, bored and withdrawn, suggested that he was there of necessity but that he defied Greenough or anyone else to claim his attention. Abigail, who thought she understood him better now than when they had first met, was sure that his cynicism was a pose that would soon be shattered.

In the chair where Tom had died, Charlotte Manning waited quietly, her lips compressed, her face inscrutable, her hands relaxed on the arms of her chair.

After that first quick survey, Abigail avoided all their eyes. In her hour of triumph she found she had no taste for what she was about to do.

"Mrs. Potter, here," Greenough began, speaking his lines in character, "says she knows who murdered Hawkes and Weston. I thought—"

"Murdered Hawkes!" Eloise repeated shrilly. "But you said Jerry Manning—"

"Mrs. Potter thinks different. This is a free country and I figure she's got a right to speak her piece. How about it, Mrs. Potter?"

There was a tense silence as Abigail began, addressing herself exclusively to the sheriff.

"Before I can explain why Jerry Manning is not guilty of these deaths," Abigail began, "I think you should all know why Sheriff Greenough—and I myself—thought that he might be."

Mrs. Demarest and Arthur admitted ignorance, so, for the last time Abigail reviewed the circumstances of Jerry's original plan, his story of the letter he had written to Maida, and her own belief that someone had intercepted and, for reasons of his own, ignored Jerry's plea that the deadly capsule be destroyed.

"I asked myself who might have had a reason to open a letter addressed to Maida Snyder, a letter marked confidential. A jealous husband might, if he doubted his wife's love, but certainly if Arthur had been the one to read Jerry's letter he would immediately have destroyed the pills that threatened his own life.

"But there was someone else who might have been jealous of Maida. Mrs. Demarest told me that Fred, too, was in love with her. He—"

"Eloise lied," Fred contradicted without heat. "I despise them both!"

"That may be true—now," Abigail argued, still speaking to Greenough as though Fred were not there. "Fred resents Maida not only because she refused him but because, by marrying his father, she took the place of the mother he had loved devotedly.

Maida's youth must have made his position doubly humiliating—"

"Of all the idiotic—" Arthur interrupted furiously, but Fred silenced him.

"Let's hear what she's got to say, Dad. I'm fascinated!"

"In addition to which, Arthur's marriage undoubtedly changed Fred's status as his father's sole heir," Abigail continued, heedless of interruptions.

"Then Jerry wrote that letter and Fred got hold of it. Perhaps he hoped to find evidence to turn his father against Maida, or perhaps he was curious to know what private correspondence his stepmother was having with a former sweetheart. But when he read Jerry's confession he learned of the poisoned capsule that had been put among his father's pills.

"To Fred, jealous of his father and resentful of Maida, that knowledge must have offered a fearful solution. If Fred could simply forget he had ever seen the letter—if his father were to die through no overt act of his—he might marry Maida and share equally with her in his father's estate."

"But even if he didn't get rid of the pill that killed Hawkes," Greenough pointed out, "why would he have killed Tom?"

"Tom was in Fred's room that afternoon. Perhaps he found the letter from Jerry and realized how Hawkes had died. To protect his secret, Fred would have had to kill Tom before he could talk."

"Wait a minute! Why would I have been so stupid as to keep that letter?" Fred suggested.

"Fred! Don't talk as though—as though—" Arthur could not finish the thought.

"That's right!" Greenough interposed. "Why would he have kept the letter, Mrs. Potter?"

"Because it would have given him a hold over Maida. I imagine that if, after Arthur's death, Maida had refused to marry him, Fred would have seen to it that the letter was 'discovered' among her things. She would have been charged with complicity in Arthur's murder—and the Law would not have allowed her to inherit."

"For God's sake, Greenough—" Arthur's voice shook with anger. "Are you going to let—"

"Dad!" Fred spoke warningly. "Take it easy. Anyone would think you took this seriously! Let Mrs. Potter prove her story, if she can!"

"I don't understand what this is all about!" Eloise complained. "After all, someone tried to kill Fred—"

Greenough seemed to have forgotten last night's attack.

"Yes!" he said. "How do you explain that, Mrs. Potter?"

"Don't you remember what you yourself said last night? That the easiest way for any murderer to divert suspicion is to fake an attack on himself?"

"Sure, but—"

"I think that's exactly what Fred did. He drugged Jerry after Maida left last night. Either Jerry went home of his own accord when he began to feel sleepy, or Fred dragged or carried him there after he was unconscious, and shot him. He knew that Charlotte Manning kept a gun in her desk drawer, but he likely doesn't know a great deal about firearms. Certainly he didn't know of the metal plate in Jerry's skull. That gun must have seemed ideal for his purpose.

"After he had shot Jerry and pressed his fingerprints on the gun, Fred dropped it beside the bed and slipped the 'suicide' note into Jerry's pocket. Then he came back here, drank a quantity of the drugged coffee, and locked himself in the hall closet—from the inside."

"Have you any proof?" Greenough asked promptly.

"Yes." Abigail pulled a doorkey from her pocket and handed it to the sheriff. "Last night, after you left, I found this. It was in the pocket of an old leather jacket, among a clutter of odds and ends where Fred supposed it would never be found."

Greenough eyed the key respectfully, turning it in his fingers. Without a word he walked across to Fred and laid a heavy hand on his shoulder.

"Looks like she's got a case," he began.

"You're both insane!" Arthur cried, leaping to his feet. "If you'd take the trouble to try that key you'll find that it's the key to the back door and that it won't lock the closet. It's been in the pocket of that jacket—"

"Thank you, Mr. Snyder," Abigail said unhappily. "Maida told us last night that the hall closet has never had a key, has never even been locked. Then how does Arthur Snyder know that the key to the back door will not lock the closet?"

Abigail heard Maida's sob, Fred's startled exclamation. Arthur's mouth opened and closed.

"Because—because I—" he stammered.

"Obviously," Abigail summed up relentlessly, "it is because Arthur himself tried to lock that closet with the key of the back door in an effort to find a key that *would* work!"

"You're insane!" Arthur repeated. With an effort, Abigail forced herself to look at him. His eyes wavered as they met hers.

I wasn't wrong, she thought, but she felt no elation.

"You gave yourself away when you went straight to the closet last night, to hang up your coat. Ordinarily you fling it on the chair by the door, but last night you had to make sure Fred was discovered at the earliest possible moment."

The sharp summons of the telephone jangled every nerve. Greenough picked it up.

Fred, for once, had nothing flippant to say. He was staring at his father with horror and pleading. He knows, Abigail thought pityingly. She crossed over to him and laid a hand on his arm.

"He didn't really intend to hurt you, you see," she said compassionately.

Fred turned away and buried his face in the crook of his arm.

"Fred!" Arthur made a last attempt. "You can't believe her! Why, you've stuck by me—" He appealed desperately to Greenough, who had finished his telephone conversation. "*You* know where I was all evening. You must have checked my alibi at the Alabaster Cow!"

"Yes," Greenough answered grimly. "I checked it—and it sounded okay to me. But not," he added, as Arthur's face showed a gleam of hope, "to Mrs. Potter. Tell him how you figured it out," he prodded, patting Abigail forward as though she were his own precocious child.

"Of course I can't be sure of all the details," Abigail apologized, "but Sheriff Greenough agrees with me that it could be done. You were released by the police last night at nine o'clock. You arrived at the Alabaster Cow at nine ten—that seems to be established, and the police have located the taxi that drove you out there. At the Alabaster Cow you heard a man and his wife talking about driving on to Cincinnati. Immediately, you made a telephone call, which the bartender overheard, asking your wife to meet you there. You only pretended to call, however, as you did not actually talk to Maida until after nine thirty!

"On the pretext of wanting a room so you could talk to your wife in private, you slipped out the back door of the roadhouse in time to get a ride with the couple who were going on to Cincinnati—right through Glen Falls. By nine thirty you must have been outside your own home."

Abigail caught Maida's eye and glanced hastily away. She could not bear the look of resigned horror she saw there.

"You reconnoitered and found the Manning house dark, and Maida and Jerry together over here. You had to get Maida out of the way, but you couldn't let her get to the Alabaster Cow before you could get back there yourself. This morning, at the hospital, I watched a nurse siphoning water from a fish tank with a length of rubber hose. Later, I remembered and realized what you could have done.

"The car was standing in the driveway. With a piece of shower hose, perhaps taken from the Manning house, you siphoned most of the gas out of the tank, letting it drain onto the ground. Early last night I stumbled over the tube—and this morning I saw the patch of brown grass that had been killed over the area where the gasoline had soaked in.

"Then, from the Manning house next door, you telephoned to your wife and asked her to meet you immediately at the Alabaster Cow."

"But I did meet him!" Maida reminded her. "How could he have gotten there—without a car?"

"But he did have a car! A little before ten o'clock, Charlotte Manning wanted to take a drive in her car. At that time it was parked in front of her house, locked. Jerry had the only keys. At ten twenty, when I ran across the street after finding Jerry, the car was not there. Only Jerry, or the murderer who attacked him and took the car keys, could have driven it away."

"You can't prove—"

"I'm afraid we can, Snyder!" Greenough interrupted. "This morning, before we drove over here, Mrs. Potter suggested that we send out a search alarm for Mrs. Manning's green sedan. One of my men just reported that it's been found—in the water at the bottom of an abandoned quarry, half a mile from the Alabaster Cow!"

XV

Abigail stood at the window, watching the Sheriff's car drive off, and a deep depression settled upon her. Greenough had played his part well. After failing to find Arthur's fingerprints on the Manning telephone or medicine chest as Abigail had hoped, he had agreed to her plan to trap Arthur through accusing his son. The ruse had worked. Arthur Snyder was again on his way to Dayton "for questioning," but this time Abigail knew he would not return.

All of them knew—Maida, huddled in a corner of the couch; Fred, phoning without hope to his father's lawyer; Eloise, sagging in her chair and moaning, unheeded, "Oh, my God! What will become of me?"

It was Charlotte who, with a look of disgust for Eloise, went to Maida and held her close. Clinging to her, Maida wept, not as one who has lost something dear but like a hurt, frightened child.

No one noticed when Abigail, sick at heart, let herself out of the house and started slowly back to Dora Weston's.

You have made a miserable mess of everything, Abigail Potter, she told herself. The police knew before you came who the murderer was. The only thing you accomplished was to cloud the issue and postpone his arrest so that he was free to kill again. Because of your interference, Tom Weston is dead and Jerry wounded, perhaps dying, in the hospital.

I'm so terribly tired, she thought, but she knew that her exhaustion was more than physical.

Arthur Snyder was arrested Tuesday afternoon. Wednesday morning, after sleeping for sixteen hours, Abigail woke up, but she was not refreshed.

Perhaps I can go away quietly without seeing anyone, she planned miserably. I wonder how soon the next train leaves?

But Dora Weston and Charlotte Manning were lying in wait for her downstairs.

"I'm so glad you're all right!" Dora exclaimed. "I must have peeked in on you a hundred times, but Charlotte wouldn't let anyone disturb you."

"I was about to wake you up myself," Charlotte confessed. "You slept so long we were all worried. Jerry made me promise to bring you over to the hospital the moment you awoke."

Then Jerry was conscious! A sliver of light pierced Abigail's gloom.

"Is he going to be all right?" she asked.

"All right—and free! We're both deeply grateful to you." Grateful! Abigail stared at Charlotte in amazement. Grateful to her? Didn't Jerry and his mother realize—

In the Snyders' car, borrowed from Maida, she tried to express her sense of guilt, but Charlotte would have none of it.

"Jerry *did* do a terrible thing," she pointed out. "You mustn't blame yourself for having implicated him."

"But if I hadn't interfered, Sheriff Greenough would have arrested Arthur in the first place. Tom Weston would still be alive, and Jerry—"

"They wouldn't have arrested Arthur in time to save Tom. You forget he was already dead before Greenough arrived with the warrant."

"But if it hadn't been for me Arthur wouldn't have killed Tom at all! You see, I'd told Tom just enough so that he knew Hawkes had been poisoned by one of Arthur's migraine capsules. I suggested that he find out whether Arthur had given one of his pills to Hawkes, and I imagine Tom put it up to him at once in such a way that Arthur was afraid he'd stumbled on the truth. I've brought nothing but grief to everyone—to Dora Weston, to Tom's wife—"

"You needn't worry about Tom's wife," Charlotte told Abigail crisply. "She'd left him. That's why she was out of town. She was suing for divorce and Tom was heartbroken. Perhaps he's better off—"

"But Maida," Abigail persisted. "I can't bear to know I was the one—"

"Maida's young; she'll get over it. She was loyal, but her faith in Arthur was destroyed the night my husband died. Until then she had respected and admired him, as a young girl will an older man, but after she realized what he'd done to Jerry's father she never really forgave him."

"But when she spoke to us—to Jerry and me—she was so very proud of him, for the courage he'd shown in standing up to Hawkes."

Charlotte snorted.

"For a while she believed in him again, because she wanted to. But even before yesterday she knew that he was the murderer."

"But how—"

"When Jerry first came home, Arthur said something to him that made her wonder, something about Jerry having been close to death a few years before."

"I remember. It was just after you and Jerry came in, that afternoon."

"Yes. It puzzled Maida. I'd always told her everything I heard from Jerry; we used to read his letters together. As far as we knew his condition had never been serious. After you suggested that the suicide note intimating that he was going to die was a part of the letter Jerry had written to her, Maida realized that only the person who had intercepted that letter could have known what Jerry never let me guess, that when he was first sent to the hospital the doctors did not hold much hope for his recovery. So you see, Mrs. Potter, Maida doesn't blame you for being the one to trap Arthur. And you mustn't blame yourself."

"But that isn't all," Abigail protested.

Charlotte swung the car into the hospital parking lot.

"Let's wait till we see Jerry," she advised. "He'll want to hear all about it. In fact, we both have a lot of questions."

Jerry was sitting up in bed. His head was bandaged, but he looked, Abigail thought, remarkably healthy.

"Hello!" he cried. "Mother tells me that if it weren't for you I'd be in jail this minute, a self-confessed murderer! Pull up a chair and tell me all!"

Indeed I will! Abigail resolved, determined to clarify her position. "What do you want to know?" she asked.

"First of all, why did Snyder pick on me? Mother told me how you proved he was the one who shot me, but why?"

"Because that's what he intended all along!" Abigail was astonished that she had failed to make the motivation clear. "From the moment he decided to murder Harrison Hawkes—"

"To murder Hawkes! But Hawkes' death was an accident!"

"No, indeed it wasn't. The poisoned capsule you left among Arthur's pills wasn't the one that killed Hawkes, for Arthur destroyed those capsules long ago."

"He did! How do you know?"

"It just came to me," Abigail admitted humbly. "Yesterday, when Greenough was trying to convince me that you were the murderer, Jerry, and that your whole story of the letter was false, he said, 'If someone had got hold of a letter saying there was poison in Arthur's pills they might have sat tight and waited for him to die—but they wouldn't have kept the letter!' That's when I knew it had to be Arthur!"

"I don't get it!" Jerry confessed.

"Don't you see? Anyone who would have left the poison in Arthur's medicine would have destroyed the letter, which would have been incriminating as soon as Arthur died. The very fact that the letter wasn't destroyed meant that the poisoned capsule was! Maybe Arthur kept it because he planned to try a little blackmail on his own if you ever came back, or perhaps he suspected that Maida had never really stopped loving you and he intended to show it to her—and threaten to use it against you—if she ever tried to leave him.

"At any rate, he was the one who read Maida's letter. And he destroyed the pills that very afternoon!"

"But how can you possibly be sure?" Charlotte pressed.

"The other day," Abigail explained patiently, "Maida told us about the night Jerry's father died, how Arthur had quarreled with Mrs. Manning and was so upset that he walked the floor all night in agony. But, if his medicine could have helped, why hadn't he taken it? Obviously, because he had disposed of it that very afternoon after reading Maida's letter and he had not had time to get the prescription refilled. The very next day," she added, "he did. Sheriff Greenough checked with the pharmacist yesterday."

"Then the poison I planted had nothing to do with Hawkes' death!" Jerry repeated incredulously.

"No. Arthur merely borrowed from your plot to gain his own ends. He wanted to kill Hawkes, for he couldn't see any other way of removing Hawkes' threat to himself. I think," she interrupted herself, "that Arthur probably did murder his wife, too, because she was writing to the police to tell of his guilt in that hit-and-run accident. The statement, in her note, that she 'couldn't live with this knowledge' would simply have meant that she could not keep his secret. Perhaps it was Hawkes, and not Arthur, who found her dead from an overdose of Arthur's sedative, before Arthur had found the letter to destroy it—or perhaps Arthur realized that it was worded so that it could be used to suggest suicide. Of course," Abigail added modestly, "that's only my guess. I haven't seen the actual note.

"Aside from removing the blackmail threat," she went on, "by eliminating Hawkes Arthur could in one stroke advance himself from a mere hireling to the owner of the Midwest Foundry, since all the papers of ownership were drawn up in his name."

"But he really did turn it back to us," Charlotte protested, "the very afternoon Jerry came home!"

"And was he paid?"

"In full," Jerry admitted. "Five hundred thousand dollars—the very securities he gave my father when he bought it and that Dad would never let us touch."

"Exactly! With that amount secure, Arthur could have disappeared and gotten a fresh start in a new place before any investigation of Hawkes' undercover activities had disclosed the facts of Hawkes' true ownership."

"But then why would Arthur have told Maida all about it, and confessed to the blackmail? That was what made him the obvious person to suspect when Hawkes died."

"He couldn't have hoped to keep that secret for long in any case. Perhaps he knew about the photostat in Hawkes' safe, but his main purpose was to justify himself to Maida for his treatment of you. If he pleaded coercion in all that he had done she might think he had been weak, but he knew she would forgive him and respect his courage in taking a stand at last against Hawkes' pressure. She had to believe completely in his remorse and his desire to make atonement in order to understand his anxiety for Jerry's return and so she would be willing to connive in giving Hawkes the sleeping pill.

"The next night, when Hawkes arrived, Arthur told her that Hawkes had brought the letter with him. He suggested to Maida, apparently in jest, that if they could only be sure Hawkes was a sound sleeper they might recover and destroy it and Maida, ashamed of her condemnation of her husband, acted on the suggestion as Arthur had been sure she would. Supposing he would never consent, she sent him from the room and helped herself to two of the pills he had purposely left unguarded. After she had put them in Hawkes' room it was a simple matter for Arthur to slip in and substitute capsules containing cyanide for the harmless ones Maida had left."

"But you still haven't explained why Arthur planned to kill Jerry!"

"That was an integral part of his plan from the beginning. He realized that a portion of Jerry's letter would serve admirably as a suicide note and confession to murder and that, as such, it could be used to cover up his own scheme to kill Hawkes. To succeed, however, he had to bring Hawkes to Glen Falls and persuade Jerry to come home. He managed both by his announcement that he intended to sell the Midwest Foundry back to the Mannings. On Thursday evening, when he poisoned Hawkes, Arthur believed that Jerry would be home in the morning. He must have been frantic when he learned that Jerry's arrival had been postponed—and that Eloise had overheard his quarrel with Hawkes!

He knew it was only a matter of time before the police would arrest him, and his whole scheme depended on Jerry's returning before that happened!"

"Do you mean that Arthur really intended to kill Jerry—from the very beginning?" Charlotte demanded.

"Looks like it, Mother. I was the fall guy! Snyder got you to wire me to come home just so he could bump me off with a signed confession at my side, and neatly close the Hawkes case!"

"It's my fault he so nearly succeeded," Abigail said bitterly. "If I hadn't persuaded Sheriff Greenough that there was a doubt of Arthur's innocence, he would have been in jail Monday night! If only I hadn't interfered."

"If you hadn't interfered, as you call it, I'd be dead now, instead of poor old Tom!"

"Oh, no, it was because I—"

"Jerry's right!" Charlotte said suddenly. "Arthur must have planned to kill Jerry the very day he came home! That's why he had the poison with him that afternoon. And then, when Tom looked like the more immediate threat, he poisoned Tom instead!"

"In a way," Jerry said soberly, "Tom died—to save me!"

All three were silent for a moment.

Tom's death was my fault, Abigail reflected, but if it had to be Tom Weston or Jerry, I think Tom would have chosen that himself, she justified her relief. He was intensely loyal. I'm glad he never knew how wrong he was about Arthur!

"But I still don't understand why Tom was a threat," Jerry puzzled.

"Mrs. Potter explained that to me," Charlotte said. "It was because she'd told him about the poisoned capsule and Tom must have told Arthur."

"Tom was eager to get hold of Arthur's medicine," Abigail dab- orated. "I imagine he suggested that Arthur open the safe right then, but Arthur probably put him off, intending to get to the safe first and remove Jerry's letter. Then after I warned Tom to keep an eye on Arthur—I thought then that you might try again to kill him, Jerry," she added parenthetically, "Tom watched him so closely that he had no chance to slip upstairs. He probably convinced himself then that Tom had discovered the truth and so, in the confusion of Eloise's collapse, he slipped the poison into what he thought was Tom's glass."

"Why do you say he had Jerry's letter in his safe?"

"Because, on the fact of it, only a man with something to conceal or protect has a safe installed. Even Maida didn't know the combination, yet Arthur gave it to me, a stranger, and allowed me to go for his medicine the night Fred was drugged. Whatever it had been necessary to lock away from prying eyes was gone by then. The safe contained no papers or valuables to explain its existence—only the box of capsules."

"What about Fred?" Jerry asked. "Why would Arthur have taken such a risk of killing his own son?"

"That was an accident he didn't foresee. When he looked in the kitchen window that night he saw only you and Maida and he saw the coffee on the stove. He'd grasped at the opportunity to get back to Glen Falls without anyone knowing he was there in the hopes of getting Jerry alone and staging the fake suicide, and all he could think of was getting Maida out of the house. He phoned from next door, supposedly while at the Alabaster Cow, and asked Maida to meet him there. Probably he suggested that she ask you to stay with her mother until she came back. As soon as she had left, and while Jerry and Fred were in the front of the house, he slipped in and poured nearly all of your mother's bottle of chloral hydrate into the coffeepot. Then I should imagine he went back to your house to wait, hoping you'd pass out soon and he could finish the job. You made it easy for him by going home when you felt ill. After he shot you, with the gun he'd found in your mother's secretary while he was telephoning, he went back to dispose of the drugged coffee—and found Fred, unconscious, at the kitchen table!"

"How horrible!"

"It must have been a shock! Probably he would have tried to help him, even at the risk of destroying his own alibi, but just then I telephoned to Mrs. Demarest. Arthur picked up the downstairs extension and heard me say I was coming right over. He had no time to lose, so he shoved Fred into the hall closet, found a key to one of the rooms that would lock it, and hoped it would look as though Jerry had drugged Fred and locked him up before shooting himself."

"Then the call to John Werner was to save Fred?"

"Indirectly. He couldn't tell Dr. Werner about Fred, obviously, but he could make sure that Jerry would be discovered promptly and the police would be able to fix the exact time of his death—as Arthur supposed. Then, as soon as he had met Maida at the Alabaster Cow and established his alibi, he intended to come straight home and 'find' Fred. He could only hope it wouldn't be too late!"

"No wonder he looked so white and shaken!" Charlotte observed. "It's a wonder he didn't use cyanide instead of my sedative. How terrible it would have been if he had killed not only Jerry, but his own son!"

"That's one thing I can't understand," Abigail admitted. "He'd used a swift poison twice before."

"I can guess!" Jerry broke in. "He couldn't take a chance on going to the foundry for a fresh supply. The police had held him so long in Dayton that he had to grab the first chance and use whatever weapon came to hand. He found Mother's chloral hydrate and then, when I staggered home, shot me with her gun to make doubly sure."

"You're probably right. The shooting seemed out of character and I'm sure it wasn't a method he'd have chosen if circumstances hadn't forced his hand. The one thing everyone was agreed on from the beginning was that Arthur wouldn't 'hurt a fly.' Eloise even said he couldn't bear to set a trap for mice—but many people who won't commit an overt act of violence will resort to some passive means, like poison."

"I should think he'd have realized, though, that it was too late anyway to pull his suicide-and-confession job. He must have known I'd ask Maida about the letter as soon as I learned of Hawkes' death—say, that's why he was so careful never to mention it all that first afternoon when we were together!"

"He had to take the chance," Charlotte said grimly. "And he very nearly got away with it. If Mrs. Potter hadn't seen through that suicide note—"

"That was the afternoon," Abigail remembered suddenly, "that you were following me about and scared me half to death!"

"I—followed you!" Jerry looked blank.

Abigail explained, describing her increasing uneasiness as she had seen, everywhere she went, Charlotte Manning's green sedan trailing her with Jerry at the wheel.

To her indignation, Jerry laughed uproariously.

"That's what happens when you have a guilty conscience, Mrs. Potter! Maida and I picked up Mrs. Weston on her way home from paying some calls and dropped her at her house. After that we drove with Arthur to his lawyer's office—which happens to be above the Elite Café!"

"I'm afraid I've been very silly about the whole thing," Abigail said, sheepishly. "I've made the most idiotic mistakes, and—"

Jerry's face crinkled delightedly.

"When an idea for detecting takes hold of you," he advised her solemnly, "I strongly advise you to write it all down on paper and get it out of your system! Mrs. Potter, I really think you ought to write a book!"

Abigail laughed.

"Do you know," she said, "I think you're absolutely right. From now on that's exactly what I'll do!"

Barbara Leonard Reynolds

ABOUT THE AUTHOR

Barbara Leonard Reynolds (1915-1990) was born in Milwaukee, Wisconsin, into a family of educators and writers. She married Earle L. Reynolds in 1935, and they had three children. *Alias for Death* (1950) was her first book, and only mystery. She continued to write children's books and non-fiction. In 1951, the Reynolds family moved to Japan for three years as Dr. Earle Reynolds studied the effects of radiation on children who had survived the atomic bomb blast of Hiroshima. Following this study, the Reynolds began to protest atomic weapons and nuclear testing. After divorcing in the early 1960s, Barbara went on to found the World Friendship Center in Hiroshima, continuing her peace activism for the rest of her life (later incorporating Cambodian refugee relief into her efforts). Much of her peace-related reference materials are now archived in the Peace Resource Center at the Quaker-founded Wilmington College in Ohio.

COACHWHIP PUBLICATIONS
CoachwhipBooks.com

PATTERN
IN BLACK
AND RED

FARADAY KEENE

A JUDGE MASSIE MYSTERY

THE CORPSE IS INDIGNANT

DOUGLAS STAPLETON
and HELEN A. CAREY

COACHWHIP PUBLICATIONS
COACHWHIPBOOKS.COM

The Serpentine Club Investigates
Murder in Washington, D.C.

THE CAPITAL
MURDER

JAMES Z. ALNER

COACHWHIP PUBLICATIONS
CoachwhipBooks.com

COACHWHIP PUBLICATIONS
CoachwhipBooks.com

COACHWHIP PUBLICATIONS
CoachwhipBooks.com

THE JINX
THEATRE
MURDER

ALEXANDER WILLIAMS

COACHWHIP PUBLICATIONS

CoachwhipBooks.com

www.ingramcontent.com/pod-product-compliance
Lightning Source LLC
Chambersburg PA
CBHW020641260626
47157CB00008B/2860